The Bridge
at DOLCEACQUA

Also by Merryn Cocoran

The Silent Village
The Paris Inheritance
The Peacock Room
Behind The Butterfly Gate

The Bridge
at DOLCEACQUA

MERRYN CORCORAN

CORK PUBLISHING

Published by Cork Publishing

2023 Merryn Corcoran

The right of Merryn Corcoran to be identified as author of this work has been asserted by her in accordance with the sections 77 and 78 of the Copyright, Designs and Patents 1988.

Soft Cover ISBN 9798867223595

All rights reserved. No part of this publication may be reproduced, stored in a Retrieval system, copied in any form or by any means electronic, mechanical, photocopying, recording, or otherwise without written permission from the author

A CIP catalogue record for this book is available at the British Library

Cover design by Patrick Knowles.wwwpatricknowles.co.uk

This Book is Dedicated to my granddaughter.

Poppy Merryn Françoise Ashton Bengué

Who brings me outstanding joy.

ACKNOWLEDGMENTS

I offer my sincere thanks to those who have supported me, tolerated me and shown an interest in my writing journey.

Especially to Jennifer Sutcliffe for her insights, her talented Public Relations, editing, marketing skills and her unfaltering support.

Andrea Eremita the bee keeper from Dolceacqua, who pointed me in the right direction.

To all my girlfriends who are always there for me, you know who you are.

My daughter Emily who always listens to my 'angst'.

And to Tim my constant friend, companion, lover, cook and husband for his patience, spelling, and calming influence.

INTRODUCTION

This story is fictitious, but I am of the belief we write a better story when we write about what we know, where we have been, and where our interest lies.

During my life I have regularly experienced déjà vu and repetitive dreams. So, the fact now that science is proving we can store memory, especially through the matriline within our DNA intrigues me.

As humans we only use twenty percent of our brains, so over the past few years, I have been exploring different ways of viewing the world, dealing with health issues, and generally attempting to stretch my thinking process to make better use of the complex, amazing brain that we are born with.

I have enjoyed travelling through this story with my leading lady Aggie who is a middle aged and slightly overweight. As always when I write, my characters seem to take off on their own, I am but the scribe, the wordsmith, typing where they take me into my laptop. I never quite know where we will end the tale. I hope you enjoy reading this as much as I have enjoyed writing it.

ONE

BAYSWATER, LONDON

Aggie needed to get out of her apartment and walk. It seemed the only way to combat the aftermath of that same dream. The one that made her doubt her own sanity. It was irrational, and she couldn't have a mind that was cluttered with a fear of her unconsciousness when she was under pressure to complete her new book within the week.

Aggie followed her favourite, picturesque route, just five minutes from her apartment building. Through the Italian gardens in Hyde Park, past the Peter Pan statue - a loving tribute to her favourite childhood author JM Barrie, then arriving at the initial expanse of water that languidly coiled itself through the lower reaches of the park to form the famous Serpentine Lake. Here she paused to watch the early morning cleaning ritual of magnificent Royal swans, and reflected on what a ⸏cial place this was. It was 7.30am in the morning and ⸏ter, as the day stretched its limbs so would the yummy mummies', swathed in designer Lycra, feigning exercise as they chatted over coffee and changing the dynamics of the park dramatically. Nearby, out of earshot, their children threw stale bread at the ducks with foreign nannies who knew more about them than their mothers did. Even more annoying would be the droves of tourists. They clogged up the paths and Aggie's overactive imagination saw them as characters in a new brand of pirate sci-fi movie and flexing their intrusive selfie sticks like gleaming, futuristic swords.

Aggie arrived in front of the Pavilion Café and selected a seat close to the tranquil water she'd come to rely on. She collected her coffee and croissant, and as she removed the pastry from its paper bag, felt a pang of something uncanny about its perfect crescent. The shape had triggered a fleeting thought so momentary she struggled to place it, something from recurring dream, she thought, possibly. It drew her thoughts to the history she'd once half-read about the croissant, while waiting for a coffee somewhere else. While some said the pastry was invented by an Austrian officer in the French military who opened a Viennese bakery in Paris in 1838, there were earlier references to it being derived from a Turkish pastry called Kipteri which explained its shape, the crescent borrowed from the Turkish flag.

Aggie sipped her coffee, and, in an effort to rid the confusing tangle of thought now occupying her, took a large bite of the buttery croissant. It's crescent now ruined, she quickly ate the rest.

Yet the dream-memory was harder to shake and she remembered being in a room that had the appearance of a mediaeval building, possibly French, but she couldn't pinpoint anything specific. The dream amused her the first couple of times, but then its continual nightly recurrence began to disturb her. She couldn't shake it off. It had become an imposition. In the absence of a husband or lover, her son Jackson was her obvious 'go-to' person to offer a sympathetic ear. But she was reluctant to burden him with this obscure infliction – it was only a dream she tried to persuade herself each morning.

The brisk walk home eventually shifted the earlier anxiety, but Aggie felt a soreness in her legs that was harder to shake and couldn't imagine where that had come from. As her thighs rubbed together, she blamed her weight gain on the menopause. It would have been okay if she had been blessed with the bonus of height. Yet later in life it had become clear that the very small number of compliments she did receive were more about her cinnamon-coloured, shoulder length and naturally wavy hair. This was most likely a kind deflection from the reality of her short, 5 feet 2 inch stature, chubby thighs, and loosening body. In her heyday, she would have described herself as cute and Rubenesque. One suitor had called her his "pocket rocket" when referring to her energy between the sheets. However, her full breasts had headed south immediately after Jackson was born and within a year his attractive but flakey father – her then husband – had headed permanently north, out the door.

At home, Aggie peeled off her walking gear, stepped into the shower and as the hot water cascaded over her wobbly bits, deflected her thoughts from her fattening body by focusing on the plan for the final three chapters of her latest novel. She always loathed the days leading up to her deadline, when Penelope, her agent, would be hustling her for the completed manuscript.

TWO

"Hello, Mama. You smell delicious! Is that the new Fragonard fragrance I gave you?" Aggie's son, Jackson, said as he walked straight through the front door and into a hug.

"Yes, I love it. And as you are always telling me, the French do it best. Wine, fashion, food and perfume!"

Aggie's son was her happy place (albeit a constantly moving one) and she walked arm in arm with him along the hall to their usual places, facing each other across the scrubbed wooden table in her roomy kitchen.

Jackson had lived the first twenty-five years of his life in this large Victorian apartment and his memories were all like this, just the two of them. He held no early memories of his parents together and whilst his father had made occasional contact while he was growing up, Jackson had announced he was gay at the age of 15 and after that his macho father had no longer bothered with him. Instead of feeling that as pain, Jackson was wise enough to see his life with his mama as wholly fulfilling. She had given him everything and he had never once missed having a father.

Their family home was welcoming - fragrant being the key word. Aggie enjoyed a habit of spraying herself with her current favourite perfume when expecting visitors. She loved to continually burn scented candles, which created a constant, pleasant aroma. A vintage crystal vase full of fresh flowers on the kitchen table, completed the aromatic ambience.

Jackson's friends teased him about being the ultimate gay cliché, dominated by a single mum: a mummy's boy. But it wasn't true. Aggie, as all his friends called her, was many things, but not at all dominant. She had always shown him unconditional love. Aggie took an interest in all his pursuits, even though some only lasted for a few weeks. Most importantly she had been stalwart as he manoeuvred through puberty and accepted his place in the world.

Under new and extreme pressure to generate enough income as a single parent, whilst being there constantly for her son, Aggie wrote what she termed "formulaic but romantic, sexually-erotic novels". She left the last couple of words out depending on the age of those she was talking to but sex sold and Aggie had done very well. Her pushy agent didn't want to know about any of her other manuscripts, the ones that perhaps required more intellect. Penelope was all about the specifically successful genre of historic, bodice-ripping romances that made money. In the trade they were known as 'bonk-busters'.

Growing up, Aggie had encouraged Jackson to read, plying him with all genres except her own yet of course these were the ones Jackson wanted to read the most. His mother's unpublished manuscripts – being the first reader – had become Jackson's passion, and as an adult he savoured the clever pliability of his mama's writing.

Looking at him, Aggie had now decided he should be the first reader of her dream.

"I don't really want to burden you with this rather obscure problem I am having, but, my darling boy, there is just no-one else I can speak to frankly, without them worrying about my sanity," Aggie said, taking a sip of her coffee.

"Go ahead, Mama," Jackson said, leaning toward her with a concerned look.

"I have been having this recurring dream for about four months now. It is not the same each time but every time it seems to be set in mediaeval France or maybe Italy or somewhere in Europe, as the room I am in during the dream has heavy stone walls and an old fire burning. Things in the room alter in different versions of the dream but every time I force myself to walk out the door so I can see where I am, the door won't open. I manage to push the wooden shutters open but when I go to look outside, I wake up. Then, once awake I am left with this strange sensation of being drawn to things that are crescent shaped. I bought a new shirt with half-moons printed on it in a colour I don't even like and look, I even cut out a picture from The Times Magazine of a perfect shaped rainbow and stuck it on the fridge," she said, pointing to it. "Other than recipes, I have never clipped out anything from a magazine in my life. You know I hate the M-word but obviously strange things can happen when the menopause kicks in, but I found no reference to upsetting dreams when I Googled it."

"What about your writing? Have you been writing about anything like that? About French mediaeval villages?" he laughed, knowing it would be unlike her. "The conscious can leave such a dent on our subconscious mind," Jackson replied.

"I wondered about that but I can't see how - my new one's set in Russia before the revolution. A married Duke fancies a wench, seduces her, wench gets pregnant, wench kills the Duchess, and you don't want to hear the rest," Aggie let out a big sigh.

"You know what, Mama? I think you need a break from your work. It's been twelve months since you suffered that nasty bump to your head when you fell. The hospital told you to rest from the screen for a bit. Which you haven't taken any notice of. A break from 'pushy Penelope' and the bonkbusters would do you the world of good. It's not like you need to make money anymore," Jackson reached over and squeezed his mama's hand.

"And what would I do instead? "Aggie placed her free hand on top of his.

"Get away. With me," he said. "And Lyall," he added quickly – Lyall, Jackson's boyfriend, went everywhere with him. "To France," he said – they'd had the plan for a while, Aggie knew. "We both love all things French, so take an apartment for six months somewhere wonderful and research and write the manuscript you've always wanted to write, not one just to satisfy 'pushy Penelope's' pocket. Lyall and I will visit frequently, the rest of the time you can do whatever you please. French men are quite charming, I hear."

Aggie snorted and offered her son a prolonged Mona Lisa smile.

"I will have to think about it. You know I'm not great with change. Especially now that I'm over fifty. And I would be worried about leaving this place empty. But the idea of you two coming to hang out with me appeals. Anyway, what has taking an apartment got to do with these dreams?"

Jackson knew his mama; she regularly diverted from the subject when she didn't wish to say no, she hated being negative and he had triggered another line of thought. Self-doubt. She would dwell on it for a couple of days, then get back to him.

"I think you should discount the dreams being connected to menopause and perhaps research what mild head traumas can do to dreams. Many cultures have more belief in dreams than we do – people that can remember them are held in huge respect." Then he added: "Besides I always thought menopause meant you were just having a 'pause' from men!" He laughed at his own joke.

"I'm always having a break from men," she said. "Tell me about your life – it's far more interesting."

Thirty-year-old Jackson worked in the City managing a corporate catering company and his boyfriend Lyall was a librarian. Lyall was of Caribbean descent and Aggie was often asked to join the boys for Sunday lunch at Lyall's wonderful family home for traditional dishes so much more exciting than the British Sunday equivalents. Jackson and Lyall were renting a small flat together and trying to save to buy one of their own, but the cost of property in central London was so high. Aggie had offered to put her property up as collateral, but Jackson refused to even discuss that option.

Once Jackson had hugged her goodbye, Aggie experienced that momentary sense of loneliness a mother always does when her only child closes the door. He was a fully grown man and had lived with her a lot longer than other people's children did, so she knew how blessed she was but nothing would ever better the companionship and the love a mother had for her son. Without him she didn't know if there'd be any point to her life.

THREE

Aggie felt frightened. There was a man in the room. He was looking out the open window through the faded blue shutters. It must have been summer, as there was no fire burning this time and a shard of sunlight cast a warm halo around the man's head. She could only see his back and he wore what looked like an 18th century jacket of a tweed-like fabric and loose trousers from what appeared to be rough cotton. He was very short for a man, about her height and his hair, which flicked around the back of his collar, was jet black. Aggie walked towards him, but as he began to turn and reveal his face, she woke up.

Aggie sat bolt upright in bed; her forehead glowing with sweat. She struggled out of bed, splashed her face, made a coffee then typed into Google 'How do I know what my dream means? But after scanning the answers, she didn't read anything that offered a clear answer. She was interrupted by her phone buzzing with the name Pushy Penny.

"Now Aggie, the publishers are loving 'The Russian Duke' and we really need a sequel pronto," Penny bellowed down the line.

Aggie was not in a frame of mind to be bossed about, and Jackson's comment about her being financially secure enough not to worry had stuck.

"Penelope I am not sure who the 'we' are, you speak of? I am the only one doing any writing and I am not interested in doing a sequel or any other randy Russian novel just now," she snapped.

There was a rare silence on the other end of the phone. Aggie heard Penelope swallow. Then she responded with a more restrained voice.

"Now Aggie, this is not like you, are you tired? You know how much advance I could secure you for a sequel. Don't be a diva!"

That did it. Aggie hung up and turned off her phone.

She threw her trainers on and walked off to the haven of the park. It was still early, and after moving along at her old pocket rocket pace she took a seat at the Pavilion Café and turned her phone back on. Immediately a missed call message popped up from Jackson. She called him back.

"Hi Mama, where were you? Your phone was off." Aggie gave him the short version of her Pushy Penny encounter and expanded on the latest version of her dream.

"Let's talk about it tonight," he said. "Do you fancy meeting us at The Groucho Club for a bite around seven? I have some news."

*

Aggie loved being a member of The Groucho. It gave her the comforting feeling of belonging to a tribe of like-minded people. Interesting, accomplished, a bit badly behaved and not given to 'entitlement' like the types she met at the clubs Penelope paraded her around.

Putting on her best pull-up, squash-in bra, she slipped on her Izzy Miyake pleated, long navy dress, which easily skirted over her ample hips and full-bodied breasts. She threw a plum-coloured velvet fringed jacket over the top, then flinched as she squeezed her feet into the highest heels she could manage. 'Car-to-bar' shoes, knowing the secondary reason was that she needed the height to look even half decent these days. At least her hair was still impressive, she thought, cheering herself up by imagining how shocked Penelope would have been to be hung up on and deciding to take an Uber into Soho. These were not tube train shoes.

The boys (she still thought of them as that) were waiting at reception. "Oh, Aggie you look and smell divine," Lyall said as he hugged her.

He was tall, slim, with a shaved head and wonderful, shimmering bronze skin. He wore circular tortoise-shell glasses that enhanced his natural bookish look. Jackson was around the same height, his hair cut military-style, short back and sides, with the lop on the top, and inky black in colour. They were both dressed in a similar style, narrow jeans, trendy sweatshirts, and designer trainers.

It was such a joy having two handsome young men escort her up to the first-floor restaurant. They snuggled into their favourite banquette, one on either side of Aggie. Once the chilled Cloudy Bay sauvignon Blanc had been poured, Jackson opened the conversation.

"We have had a big discussion about this, and Mama, please first hear us out before commenting, and secondly don't feel in any way obliged to agree to anything just because I am your only child. We are adaptable and young. This is your time to flourish and that should be your priority."

He paused, Aggie squeezed his hand, and nodded for him to continue.

"I work with a chap in the city called Nick. We have become quite good mates. I was telling him about getting you to somewhere like France for a sabbatical when he said his mum was just about to rent her apartment out there. She apparently married the next-door neighbour and has moved in with him. It's in a town called Menton on the French Riviera and very close to the Italian border as well as Monaco. Doesn't it sound perfect?'

"It sounds expensive," she said. "And I can't just leave my place that easily?"

Jackson raised his eyebrows at Lyall who took up the conversation. "If you were to consider it, we were wondering how you would feel renting your place to us. It would be much bigger than our place and much less expensive without our commutes cut that much shorter. Who knows, if there was a family discount, we might even have a chance to save more and buy sooner. Plus you'd be getting the money and not our awful landlord."

Then Jackson chipped in. "Nick told me how much his mum is asking and it's not a lot. Plus she is adamant she only wants a single occupant, and someone who comes recommended, so I thought you would fit the bill totally."

He offered his mum a warm smile and the boys sat patiently while Aggie Googled Menton on her phone. It did appear to be the perfect location. Jackson said he would ask if Nick could forward him some photos. He knew not to push his mother in any way; she always took stock for a day or two before agreeing to anything, but he noticed that she wasn't declining it outright.

"I'm certainly sick of Penny's constant demands about what I write," she said. "Suddenly the path I imagined when I was a naive University student, writing books without compromise, based on facts that required real research and some intellect, seems even more appealing. A book I would be proud to put my *own* name to, rather than Tabatha Heart's." That was Aggie's long-time pseudonym.

"That sounds wonderful! To embrace some of your incredible talent Mama, in something that interests you.

It's totally the right way forward. I always loved reading your unpublished work. Growing up it gave me the best education ever," Jackson stated as he reached over and squeezed Lyall's hand, then added "and is probably the reason I fell in love with this handsome librarian."

Before the boys left the table Lyall cleared his throat. "Aggie, Jackson told me about the dreams that keep bothering you. I was reading a new book that came into the library last week. Well, I didn't actually read it, I skimmed it. But apparently our DNA has memories, and it has been proven that when we experience déjà vu or repeated dreams, they could be memories of situations that our ancestors experienced. They're stored in our DNA. So you should investigate the current thinking in the science community - it might be helpful. They might stop after that," he said, patting her hand reassuringly.

"Have you spoken to your father about your dreams? Maybe your mum went through something similar?" Jackson asked.

"I haven't even considered that," she said. "But you know I don't talk to Dad about anything to do with Mum. I've only just worked through her leaving us so I'm not sure that's a good idea, resurrecting all that grief. Best keep this to ourselves," Aggie said, then abruptly stood up, making it clear the subject of her parents was not up for discussion - she'd leave with them.

With all the conversation that had been examined at dinner, Aggie's thoughts, doubts, and angst were jostling inside her head as she gazed out the cab window on her way home. Lying in the dark, in the sanctuary of her bed, Aggie allowed memories of her mother to gently wander through her head. It was a proven, soothing mechanism for her. She grasped at her imagination, wondering what a mother's love would feel like now. She pictured all the fantasy stories her mum would read to her at bedtime, so many stories she'd never got to hear. She imagined her mother would still draw. She remembered her as such a good artist. She remembered such happy days in the ones her mother let Aggie help her bake scones and their laughter from the tickle sessions. Most of this was probably a false memory, and the love had a time limit. The happy mother slowly morphed into an angry, often confused woman and one day when she was around thirteen, Aggie came home from school and her mother was gone.

She never really understood why she had walked out. Her parents argued, but in retrospect, no more than other couples.

It was a 'no go' area of discussion with her father for years. He had struggled to bring up a teenage girl on his own. But time had mellowed him. Now that he had a regular companion in his life, he was a lot happier. In one of their rare talks about her mother, he had stated that he now realised she had never gotten over her own mother's death and her fathers' remarriage. This seemed to trigger all sorts of psychological issues when she parented her own child. On reconsideration he believed she had been suffering from an undiagnosed mental illness and suffered psychotic episodes.

As an adult, Aggie didn't wish to dwell on her mother's desertion; it had taken too much happiness from her as a teenager. She had stored it away in a compartment in her mind so deep it may as well have been at the bottom of an ocean most of the time. Only in her private, most desperate moments did she swim down to it in memory.

FOUR

The back of the man's head had a familiarity about it, something in the shape and the way his hair brushed across his collar. Aggie softly called out "excuse me?" He shifted a bit as if he heard her but didn't turn around. He was looking out the small open window from which the sun streamed into the dreary stone-walled room; the illumination allowing her to observe her surroundings with clarity. She took stock of the wrought iron utensils that hung beside the fireplace. Next to her was a large, scrubbed wooden table, with a potted plant of basil and another clay-brown bowl of extra-large lemons sitting in the centre, the fresh fruit releasing a strong enticing citrus fragrance. Then a knock at the door startled her and the man began to turn as before in response, but before Aggie could see his face she woke up.

This time the fragrance of the lemons was still so strong after waking that the dream felt very real. Aggie knew, there were no lemons in the apartment.

Aggie felt dazed and pulled herself out of bed to make a strong cup of coffee. She sniffed the citrus air and opened her laptop.

Are there really traces of our ancestor's memories in our DNA? She typed it into Google.

If you are talking about phobias such as fear of spiders, snakes or heights, then maybe. Scientists at Emory University applied electric shocks to mice as they exposed them to the smell of cherry blossoms. The mice then bred, and both the children and grandchildren of the affected rodents demonstrated a fear of the odour of cherry blossoms the first time they smelt it. Dr Brian Dias of Emory University said: "Such a phenomenon may contribute to the intergenerational transmission of risk for neuropsychiatric disorders such as phobias, anxiety and post-traumatic stress disorder."

Epigenetics shows how you may inherit a tendency to put on weight and often inherit diabetes from grandparents that survived a famine. Grandfathers were somehow passing down brief but important childhood experiences to their grandsons. You would have to have the memories before you have children, and these memories would have to have impacted your genetic makeup in a way that would be manifested in the genetic inheritance of your child. If that has not happened, then there's nothing to unlock the memories. Instinct could be considered a form of ancestral memory as it is carried in the genes and shapes the brain.

This was interesting. Next, she read about a psychologist called Carl Jung who she had heard of. He theorised that we are born with memories of our ancestors imprinted in our DNA.

Aggie was fascinated just how much there was about this phenomenon online, so many theories and versions as well as personal testimonies.

The phone buzzed somewhere in the apartment, so she tore herself away and ran to answer it.

"Hi Mama, I've just emailed you some photos of Nick's mum's apartment in Menton. Her name is Sarah, and she is only asking for a thousand euros a month, which is a great price and if we pay you the same amount in pounds, we'd still be saving at least four hundred a month."

Aggie's disturbed mind felt in stark contrast to Jackson's excitement, and she decided to keep the conversation to a minimum. "Sounds interesting, thanks love, let me go and look. I'll let you know later what I think."

Aggie didn't go directly to her laptop but instead ran a hot bath. Adding lavender drops to the bath water to rid the cloying smell of lemons from all around her, she then put on the new French jazz CD that Lyall had given her and lit a Jo Malone jasmine candle, avoiding any notes of citrus. As she immersed herself in the deep, claw-footed iron Victorian bath, she watched her loose breasts slide sideways, almost nestling in her armpits. Oh, for the resurrection of gravity and the bounce of youth, she thought, wondering if she ever appreciated it enough when she'd had it.

Soaking in the aromatic hot water calmed Aggie and she began to have a more relaxed handle on everything.

There was something mystifying about her dream experience, and she should try to be more open minded and exploratory. This was what she had trained to do as a creative writer; research all possibilities and since science had moved so far forward she must approach what was happening to her without preconceptions. As her dad would often say to her when he was pushing her to think differently: "What is the worst that can happen?"

Maybe Jackson's suggestion about a temporary change of situation was worth proper consideration.

The photos of the Menton apartment were stunning; it looked about the same age as her own Victorian home. The owner was offering it fully-furnished and Aggie loved the high ceilings and the old-world charm the photos disclosed. She could also see some modern contemporary additions in the bathroom and kitchen.

The thought of not having to deal with her agent Penny for at least six months, or maybe never again, prompted a spike of positivity for the plan. Aggie noticed the address and a phone number for Sarah. Before the cautious side of her brain engaged, Aggie picked up her phone and dialled the number.

FIVE

Sarah had a warmth in her voice that inspired Aggie to agree to a weekend visit to Menton in two weeks' time, to meet and inspect the apartment with a view to taking it for a year and to meet its lovely-sounding owner in the process.

The two weeks passed quickly. Jackson and Lyall had a wedding to attend on the weekend of her excursion, so she would be travelling solo. She booked her flights and then a seat on a minibus from Nice airport to Menton, where she'd stay for three nights at the Napoleon Hotel. According to the map, it was within walking distance of Maison Manera, where Sarah's apartment was located.

Aggie requested a window seat on the flight and was lucky enough not to have anyone sitting beside her. The plane coasted up gently through the clear, ice-blue sky, settling above the fantasy-like puffs of white cloud. Aggie pressed her nose up against the window, gazing at the magnetism of the white softness as it moved constantly into an array of silhouettes and surfaces. Then, all the foamy structures began to morph into uniform crescent-like shapes. It took a minute or two for Aggie to realise this wasn't quite real, but she couldn't pull her eyes away from the sea of croissant-shaped clouds that now surrounded the plane. She stayed glued to the window, determined to immerse herself in the strangeness of it.

The air hostess tapped Aggie's shoulder and the dream-like sequence of crescents shattered. "Tea or coffee?" she asked.

On arrival in Nice, it was easy to find the minibus to Menton. The driver was standing in the arrival hall with three names on an iPad, including hers. He was talking to the other passengers in French and Aggie was able to catch a few sentences. She realised if this French sojourn was going to happen, she would have to take some serious French lessons.

Hotel Napoleon was slick and functional but lacking in any historic charm. The bonus was a small balcony with a brilliant sea view. If she looked to the left, she could see the Italian border, and to the right, across the bay was the magnificent, mediaeval village of Menton. At its heart the central Basilica tower stood tall and regal, overseeing a mish-mash of five-hundred-year-old houses dusted in various shades of terracotta and pale lemon. As if predestined, the Basilica bells pealed out on cue.

Aggie glanced at her watch, five o'clock, time to begin her adventure.

She had arranged to meet Sarah the next day, as she wanted this first evening to look around and gain a feel for the surroundings by herself.

Aggie debated which of the two dresses bought specifically for the trip to wear on this solo night out. It was a perfect, balmy spring evening, so she settled on the pale blue shift dress and her new navy sandals. The shop girl had assured her it was more flattering for a dress to slide over fuller hips with less fabric, than the waisted, gathered style that Aggie had first selected. Looking in the mirror, Aggie agreed. The knee-length dress seemed to flatter her now-chubby body in a way the gathered ones never did.

As she walked along the promenade towards the town, Aggie spotted the Italian restaurant that Sarah had given as a landmark to find Maison Manera, so she crossed the road to Square Victoria to take a closer look. She had promised Jackson she would take lots of photos.

Directly beside the road sat a large monument surrounded by fountains that was dedicated to Queen Victoria. Apparently, the widowed Queen adored visiting Menton and stayed in a villa just up the road. Behind the monument stood a row of old, struggling trees, their bark appearing mottled with some sort of mould. The Leone Restaurant, Sarah had mentioned, had outdoor seating under canvas canopies and directly beside the restaurant stood a double door with "Maison Manera" written above it. The door looked as if it had not been upgraded since Queen Victoria's time there. The deep green paint was peeling and there were dents in the wood, however the battered entry point proudly displayed an ornate, elegant iron door knocker in the shape of a woman's hand. Aggie took this as a sign that other treasures may be hidden behind the ramshackle entrance.

She stepped back from the door and looked up to the third floor where her proposed apartment was located. At the tall window framed with blue traditional shutters, she caught a glimpse of a woman silhouetted in the light, then in the window directly next door she could see the silhouette of another woman, or was it a mirror? The silhouettes were identical. Fascinated, Aggie quickly reached for her phone to take a photo but as she looked up again the second silhouette had disappeared.

She walked back to the promenade, then down the steps to the boardwalk which had been conveniently built alongside the beach. On the other side of the boardwalk an array of interesting eateries offered various menus. Their colourful, enticing lights began to shimmer as dusk settled and the setting sun tinged everything with a soft pink glow. It illuminated a pathway across the water to where Aggie stood on the breakwater at the mouth of the bay taking in the sounds and scents of the sea. The evening was perfectly still, not a breath of wind.

As she returned across the beach Aggie took her sandals off and felt the sand cool and shifting between her toes. She absent-mindedly drew a crescent shape with her toe, then stood back and gazed down at it. She had made three more before the sharp sound of a car horn in the distance flicked her out of her daydream. "Damn, what is wrong with me?" she said out loud as she brushed the grains of the beach off her feet and put her sandals back on.

Aggie perused a few of the menus as she passed the restaurants; most featured pizzas and pasta, and, given the proximity to Italy, that made sense. She finally settled on one offering fish dishes and salads. She ordered grilled Loup accompanied by baby potatoes, cherry tomatoes, black olives and slices of fennel. The vegetables had been cooked to perfection; the aniseed from the fennel enhanced the flavour of the fish like salt. Aggie agreed to the waiter's suggestion of a small carafe of rosé from nearby Provence. With the soft sounds of the sea mingled with Jazz floating from a nearby street-musician she texted Jackson.

"Arrived in Heaven - the perfect Riviera evening! Thanks for the push. Love Mama x"

The moon formed a perfect crescent shape above her as she walked back to the hotel along the beachfront. The recurrence of the shape seemed less aggravating in this new environment and Aggie made the decision there and then to enthusiastically embrace this unsolicited obsession and follow it to the end.

SIX

A charge of anticipation engulfed Aggie as she pressed the doorbell at Maison Manera.

"Hi! Push the door. There's no lift. Come up two flights to the second floor," Sarah called out as she buzzed Aggie in.

Aggie pushed the tall, heavy door open and stepped onto the black and white-tiled hall slightly underwhelmed. The foyer lacked windows and an ugly bank of modern letterboxes was mounted on one wall. She located the light switch, then proceeded up the marble staircase, holding firmly to its wooden handrail atop the ornate iron bannister. As she moved upwards her surroundings became more attractive. At the first floor landing a tall double window, with a distinctive leadlight pattern, offered a glow of natural light to the area. An impressive fresco of cherubs smiled down at her from the ceiling above. The ancient painting had a distinct Italian feel to it and included several women in sensual poses surrounded by flowers and fruit in various shades of yellow and blue.

Aggie walked up the next set of stairs and past peeling paint walls with faded frescoes peering through, until she arrived at Apartment Three on the second floor.

Sarah was waiting at the door and offered a firm handshake coupled with a smile that revealed a perfect line of whitened teeth.

"Come in, I have the coffee ready," she said.

Aggie followed the elegant, slim woman down the long hall; three large chandeliers, evenly spaced overhead, gave a hint of past grandeur in contrast to the simple terracotta tiled floor below. The window at the end of the hall, carefully framed in a crimson taffeta curtain with oversized tassels hanging down on one side, offered a peak outside to the enchanting courtyard.

The main salon was roomy with two big comfy chesterfield sofas strategically positioned and an elegant gilt armchair. The remainder of the furniture was antique, probably French, and best of all not entirely flawless. Aggie preferred a room to feel inhabited. She was enchanted. The salon featured double floor-to-ceiling doors opening onto the courtyard at the rear, and two more sets of windows in the front with a view to the sea lapping at the beach directly opposite.

The two women sat on facing sofas, subtly taking stock of each other. Sarah was only a few inches taller than Aggie and wore fitted black trousers and what looked to

Aggie like a silk Hermes blouse. Her shoulder-length hair was impeccably highlighted with a wonderful shade of golden blonde.

Sarah gave her a brief history of her own circumstances, and like Aggie, told her she had initially come to the Riviera to review her life. Her husband had died, she was middle-aged with two, grown children and had nothing to keep her in London. Then she met Jean Pierre, her neighbour as well as the local doctor, who lived across the hall. They had recently married, and he had won the battle as to which of their apartments they would live in. Aggie sensed there was more to Sarah's story but didn't question it any further. She responded with an abridged version of her own reasons for leaving London, referring to her wish to write a more credible novel than the ones she had been doing for the past twenty years.

They chatted comfortably about the similarities between their respective sons, Aggie stepped carefully not knowing if Nick was gay or not. Then Sarah referred to her son's girlfriend whom he had brought recently to visit, and Aggie added that Jackson had a partner called Lyall.

Sarah had written out a list of what she termed "things to see" and handed it to Aggie as she got up to leave.

"Would you like to join us for lunch tomorrow, next door at our apartment?" Sarah asked as they reached the door.

"That would be wonderful! Thank you." Aggie smiled.

Following Sarah's instructions, she exited via the stairs on the floor above the apartment which took her directly onto the upper street that led into the mediaeval village, which Sarah had referred to as "the old town".

Aggie was floating on air; she had immediately fallen in love with the chic apartment. It was such a contradiction inside to the shabby exterior of the building. She could clearly see Jackson and Lyall coming to stay, eating out in the courtyard and spending time on the beach. The walk through the old town gave her more cause for joy. The narrow, cobbled street was snugly overlooked by tall narrow buildings on either side. A true sense of a close community was confirmed by an array of various sizes of knickers and other undergarments unashamedly hanging from washing lines strung from some of the shutters overhead.

Shadowy, arched side exits veered upwards at intervals. These zigzagged up the steep, terraced hill to the top where the best view in Menton was reserved for the cemetery with its many gold-domed crypts. Aggie had spotted the shiny, opulent structures from her hotel balcony that morning.

Once out on the other side of the old town Aggie found herself in a busy pedestrian street with an assortment of colourful tourist shops positioned between various cafes offering pastries, panini, coffee and beer.

In what appeared to be the central square, a vibrant vintage-style carousel set the scene. Young mums sat alongside proud grandmothers chatting and supervising their small children on the wooden horses. Locals sat on an ancient, low stone wall, alongside an old water well, which would have once been the only source of water in the village, Aggie guessed. Sets of outdoor chairs sat in anticipation for a hungry lunch crowd outside brasseries everywhere.

To Aggie, it was the epitome of a picturesque Riviera scene. Her assumption so far was that Menton was a genuine town for families and everyday life, in contrast to the pretentious coastal equivalents of St Tropez or Cannes.

*

The following day as Aggie dressed for lunch, she thought about how welcoming and easy Sarah had been. Her standard of grooming was impressive, verging on intimidating; she clearly put a big effort into maintaining her great shape. Sarah was probably older than her but looked much younger. Aggie needed to up her game.

She pulled on her "fat" pants which managed to flatten her tummy. She would wear the second new dress she had purchased for this trip; it was a knee length white shift dress with a V-neck that offered a hint of cleavage, and a tiny floral pattern in pale lemon. It seemed the colour had followed Aggie out of her dream and into her waking life and she now saw it everywhere. Aggie felt confident about her hair, but she took extra time ensuring her makeup was immaculate.

Sarah's French husband, Jean Pierre, or "JP" as Aggie was instructed to call him, was a few inches taller than

Sarah. He spoke English with a delicious French accent, dropping the "H" in most words which Aggie found endearing. He poured her a glass of cold Chablis. Then, to Aggie's astonishment, Sarah's doppelganger walked into the room. She was slightly heavier than Sarah, her hair was less blonde with a few natural streaks of grey, but their faces were identical and both had the same rich brown eyes and warm smiles.

"Aggie, this is my twin sister, Rebecca," Sarah signed with her hands as she spoke. "Rebecca is deaf, but she lip-reads and can sign in English if you know any sign language."

Aggie knew a few basic signs so signed "hello" and apologised out-loud for her lack of fluency.

JP opened the pre-lunch chat by asking Aggie what type of books she wrote.

"Well, not ones I think would interest any of you," Aggie admitted. "I fell into the genre of what we in the business call bodice-ripping novels. I was a single parent, and it was a way to make money at the same time as parenting my son. I am hopeful the time I will spend here will allow me to write something more credible. Even if I don't get a publisher, I will enjoy the process."

Sarah speedily signed to her sister who looked a little puzzled, then responded with something that made the sisters roar with laughter.

"Don't mind them, they often exist in a world of their own. Rebecca only speaks Italian, but Sarah can sign in

Italian and English and has taught her twin to sign in English." JP said.

Aggie was fascinated. She hadn't thought of Sarah Italian.

"That sounds very odd, I know," chipped in Sarah. "But I was adopted at birth to an English family and Rebecca was brought up by our Italian father in a small hilltop village across the border in Italy. We were reunited only three years ago so we have quickly developed ways to communicate as we have a past lifetime to catch up on."

"Wow! How wonderful, so did you only learn to sign three years ago?" Aggie asked.

"No, coincidently I trained as a teacher to the deaf when I was younger; I only worked in the role for a few years before my first marriage; but it all came very naturally to me."

"It sounds like it was almost predestined," Aggie replied.

Sarah put down her glass of wine, walked to Aggie and affectionately squeezed her hand. "How right you are, and I am so happy to know you think that way. I feel sure we shall become great friends."

The lunch table was covered in a crisp, white damask cloth. Three tempting salads in glass bowls and a smaller bowl of delicate small potatoes sat on either side of a substantial, poached salmon. The fish was sprinkled with finely-chopped dill and artistically surrounded by perfectly cut pieces of lemon and tiny capers; it had been expertly laid out on a mirrored dish.

Aggie believed a well-set table set the scene for a successful meal and she was impressed with the delicately-fine wine glasses, heavy crystal water jug, the immaculate linen napkins and the pure white porcelain plates edged in gold.

The main course was followed by two strong cheeses that they ate with torn pieces of baguette. Aggie figured her diet could commence Monday, so confidently went with the flow today – she was a guest after all and wanted to make a polite impression. After the cheese, Rebecca proudly brought in the most fabulous tiramisu, served individually in old-fashioned cocktail glasses and lavishly sprinkled with freshly grated chocolate.

"This is the best tiramisu I have ever tasted!" she told the table.

Rebecca beamed as Sarah signed Aggie's comment.

Sarah accepted Aggie's offer to join her at the hotel for breakfast the next day to sign the rental agreement and finalise dates to move in. She wandered back along the promenade exhilarated by the prospect of her new Riviera life.

SEVEN

Jackson and Lyall sat at the kitchen table in London while Aggie put the finishing touches to the meal. Despite suffering another rough night in her recurring dreamworld, Aggie was energised after her French excursion and couldn't wait to tell the boys about it.

"Come on Mama tell us all, stop tantalising us with your new French Riviera grin!" Jackson said, as Maggie placed his favourite meal, homemade cottage pie, on the table.

Aggie sat down, still smiling. "Well, it was the best time I have had since you were a little lad who did exactly what I told him, "She replied, laughing.

"Come on Aggie, tell us. Was there a man involved?" Lyall asked, which caused more laughter.

"That's what was so enjoyable - it wasn't about a man, it was about me," she said.

They dished up the pie and the accompanying fresh asparagus and after a couple of mouthfuls, Aggie continued.

"Menton is everything you said it would be, and Sarah, Nick's mother, is a class act with a sexy French husband and an almost identical sister. I have signed a lease for the apartment for a year and will move there next month. I have taken you both at your word about living here, which I am very happy about." The men clapped and whooped with excitement.

"Oh, Mama, that is fantastic news! We promise we will look after the house and love it just as you love it," Jackson said.

"Good! So - I expect you to book flights to come and see me well in advance so you can get some cheap deals and keep your promise of regular visits."

Aggie told them all about the apartment. Then Lyall asked how her dream research was going.

"From what I have found out so far, studies do show that our DNA carries memory, just like it can give us hereditary diseases and eye colour. These memories are generally inherited from our mother's side, but not always. What is becoming clear to me is that my dreams may be a part of some memory of a relative from the past. So, although I have no desire to revisit the difficult parts of my childhood, I believe I need to talk to my father again and see if I can find my mother, or even her sister. They may be able to enlighten me."

She let out a small sigh.

"Phew! Mama, that is a big step. Is it worth the emotional distress?" Jackson asked as he reached over and stroked her hand.

"A month ago, I wouldn't have considered it. But I have much to look forward to now, so I want to deal with this dream business and move on with life in France," she said.

The following morning Aggie texted her dad to agree on a time for her to visit. She kept it casual. He would clam-up if he had advance warning of anything confrontational.

The next day she arrived at her childhood home in Enfield in time for morning coffee. Her father, as always, was so pleased to see her. Aggie experienced a pang of guilt knowing her visits were far too infrequent.

He listened dutifully as she explained about the dreams and the research, alluding to the hereditary factor, then gently approaching the subject of her mother.

Aggie was pleasantly surprised when he responded.

"It's okay, darling, I can deal with this all a lot better now. I have come to understand more comprehensively your mother's bipolar condition and how it led to some psychotic episodes. Listening to you just now talk about your dream, I remember some of her ramblings when she woke in the night screaming from what we said at the time were nightmares. You know, she often would prolifically sketch pictures of buildings and scenes, then the next day rip them all up. So, maybe there is a connection?"

Aggie's eyes welled up with tears. "Poor Mum! Now I have had these dreams I can see how they could unhinge you." She wiped her eyes then continued. "Dad, do you have any idea where she is; do you know where her sister lives?"

Her father sat silent for a few moments before responding.

"My darling, I don't even know if she is alive. I just believe if she was, she would have come back to check on you at some stage in the past thirty-nine years. It's been such a long time. I have an old address for her sister, but remember it is her half-sister and they weren't exactly close - you could start by trying to track her down, I suppose."

Their chat continued about what an awful woman Aggie's aunt was and how her mum didn't even invite her to their wedding.

It was the most transparent, honest conversation Aggie had ever had with her father and she hoped when she reached the age of seventy-eight, she too would have garnered enough wisdom and found the courage to confront the past. She promised him she would keep him updated.

*

The room had a new scent this time. The fire was burning, and the smoke emitted a fragrance of a damp autumn forest. There was no one in the room and it was daylight, but Aggie struggled to see as without the sun shining in, the flames from the open fire was all that offered illumination. Being alone in the room she felt more confident looking around. There were several pencils scattered over a pile of sketches on the table. She picked up one of the sketches to have a closer look just as the door opened.

Aggie froze.

In walked a man with thick, black hair. She could see that he was wearing a bowtie, but his face was blurry. He immediately put his back to her.

"Hello!" Aggie exclaimed.

He appeared not to hear her. She suspected he didn't want to talk to her. She stood very still as he walked over to the fire, took the iron poker, and gave the fire a stoke. He then sat down close to her. Maybe he couldn't see her? she thought. She could smell him and he smelt of turpentine. He turned his attention to the sketches on the table; he still didn't look at her. Aggie was engulfed with a massive sense of dread about what he might say to her. He walked over to the table and began tidying the sketches. Aggie felt desperation for him to acknowledge her, to reassure her somehow. She reached over to gently touch his shoulder. But then, wham! She woke up.

This time when Aggie woke, she wasn't as disturbed and felt she had gained more control. It was as if she had been in someone else's body. Not that any of that made logical sense. But the brain was a powerful tool and this was her brain - she wanted to understand it.

After a strong coffee, she focused the next hour online investigating how to confirm from the electoral roll if someone lived at a given address. She needed to find her mother.

Her aunt lived in Manchester and after a couple of hours she managed to chat to a man from the relevant council department. He confirmed that her aunt, Karen Black, was registered as alive and still residing on a council estate at the address Aggie had given him.

Next Aggie checked all social media, but her aunt's name didn't correspond with photos of any older looking women on Facebook, Instagram, or Twitter. That wasn't surprising as her aunt would be around seventy. In the absence of sourcing any phone number or email address, Aggie figured she might have to just go there.

Wondering if this was a great idea, or a terrible one, Aggie booked a train ticket.

EIGHT

Just in case her Manchester mission couldn't be accomplished in a day, Aggie packed a few things into a small overnight bag and arrived at Euston train station early the following day. Armed with a takeout coffee, a croissant and a copy of The Times to help her 6am start, she boarded the train. In two-and-a-half-hours she'd be stepping off the train and into Manchester's commuter hour.

Aggie figured not arriving until 10 o'clock at someone's house was civilised enough, and not too late that her aunt may have gone out on an errand. She grabbed a cab outside the station and once she had sat back and secured her seat belt, the beads of perspiration began to gather on her forehead. For Aggie, after thirty-nine years of no contact with her mother or her mother's family this was a big moment. A moment she had sworn would never happen.

The taxi pulled into what appeared to be her aunt's council estate. It looked rough, most of the houses clearly needed repair. The cabbie turned to Aggie and asked if she was ok.

"Well, I hope I will be," she replied as she paid him.

He handed her a card. "Look, you won't be able to hail a cab around here, so give us a call when you want a lift back."

Her aunt's house was one of many on a long terrace that reminded Aggie of a 1970s episode of Coronation Street. Grubby, net curtains hung in the front window obscuring any sign of life within. Two bins sat under the window spewing out unsightly rubbish, accompanied by a broken wheelie bag.

Aggie instinctively clutched her bag to her chest as she stepped from the cab to the footpath and hesitantly walked to the door and knocked. No answer. But out of the corner of her eye she was pretty sure she saw the curtain move.

Intrigue, desperation, and adrenaline can be a powerful tool. She banged hard at the door and called: "Karen Black? I am from the National Lottery commission; I have some good news for you."

There was a scurry from behind the door and the sound of two locks clicking open. The woman who appeared was a sight! Her fine hair sat like a tuft of a small bird's nest on her head. One of her front teeth was missing and the remaining teeth were badly stained. Matching stains featured on the scrawny fingers of her left hand, and she wore a soiled, grey tracksuit.

"What fucking lottery?"

Aggie mentally pulled up her big girl knickers. "Best I talk to you inside, may I come in?" she stated as she walked past the wretch of a human being standing in the door.

The door led directly into the living room. The woman shut the door and stood facing Aggie.

"Well, have I won something?" the woman asked.

"Actually, no," said Aggie, as she tried to stand as tall as she could.

"Well, who the fuck are ya? A bailiff or what? There's nothing here for ya, as you can see!"

The room housed a sagging worn sofa, a wooden table with two chairs. There were newspapers piled up in one corner and a cardboard box of beer and wine bottles under the table.

"I am Aggie Sutcliffe, your sister Maria's daughter," Aggie stated, her bravado beginning to ebb.

"Well, fuck me!" Karen said as she lit up a cigarette, then stood back and stared, flicking her eyes up and down Aggie. "Yep, you are fat like her; are ya nuts as well?" She blew smoke in Aggie's direction.

It took all Aggies' inner strength not to punch this excuse for a human being in her ugly face. But instead, she took a deep breath.

"Aunt Karen, I would be most grateful if you could help me?"

"If it's about your fucking slut of a mother, the high and mighty Maria, I have nothing to say. She was as mad as a March hare! Besides, she was only my half-sister; I'm no 'wop', I have proper blood."

Aggie had to sit down, despite fears of what she might catch from the sofa; she was feeling very faint.

Karen continued to take long sucks on her cigarette and sat down at the table, flicking her ash into a tin ashtray, which was ironic given the state of the carpet.

Aggie dug deep, mustering up courage with a fake smile, acutely aware she would have to win this woman over to achieve her goal.

"What do you mean she was mad. Has she recovered now?"

Karen took a long suck on her ciggy, flicked the ash then moved her stained tongue around her mouth into the space where her tooth had once been. Then she replied.

"Well, she's dead just now aint she!"

The room spun. If Aggie hadn't already been sitting, she would have fallen. A sharp pain pushed through her temple and down through her body.

She cried out. "My mother is dead?"

"Yeah, I would have thought you knew by now. Fuck it was probably over ten years ago - topped herself with pills didn't she. Right there in that room." Karen pointed to a door leading off the living room.

"Why didn't you let my father know?" Aggie fought for control, unasked for tears poured down her cheeks.

"Didn't know his full name or where the fuck you lived. She registered me as next of kin. I had to deal with all the death shit. Had her cremated, didin' I."

Then her aunt got up, opened the fridge, and offered Aggie a beer. Aggie had the tears under control, but the anger was building from a very deep place. She had enough presence of mind to hold her tongue. She took the beer and nodded thanks.

She waited until the woman had taken a few gulps before she asked the next question.

"Did you know anything about her mother?"

"Vera Raimondo - some greasy *wop*! That's why they called your Mum Maria, so me Dad said. She snuffed it right after Maria was born."

Aggie struggled to process what was being said, grappling to comprehend that her mother was dead and to imagine she was in any way connected, let alone related to this revolting woman in front of her. But she believed this may be her only shot at getting any details about her mother's past so she had to hold it together.

"Do you have any photos of her? Or can you tell me about my mother's life after she left us?"

Her aunt continued to suck on her cigarette, staring at Aggie.

"If ya can help me out with some cash, I may be able to help ya out with some stuff?"

Aggie's skin crawled. She inwardly repeated her mantra "I must be as cool as a cod on ice," before she answered.

"I would like to see some of this stuff before I can tell you if I have any cash."

This woman was desperate; Aggie must hold her ground. After what seemed an age, her aunt stubbed out her butt in the battered ashtray and walked over to the closed door. Aggie stood up, the room spun, she wanted to be sick, but she held on.

The bedroom was piled with old clothes, shoes, and boxes of discarded household things. Dog-eared, cheap magazines and old newspapers were piled up on the floor. Her aunt reached up to the top of a low, free-standing wardrobe and took down a small, old-fashioned leather suitcase. It had the word Maria printed in faded gold letters on the top and was secured by two straps.

She plopped it down on the bed.

"All her stuff is in here!" her aunt hissed, emitting a spray of spittle. "I want two hundred quid."

Aggie navigated her way cautiously towards the small single bed.

As she reached out to touch the case, her aunt slapped her hand on Aggie's arm. "Cash first!"

Aggie had had enough! She pushed her aunt's arm away with force, demonstrating her strength. "Listen to me Aunt Karen, you will allow me to see what is in this case before I agree to pay you anything!"

Her aunt backed off and Aggie immediately began to unbuckle the leather straps. The locks were a bit rusted but after a bit of pushing she managed to ping them open.

At a glance, she could see there was a pile of small diaries, the top one had a battered cover. There was also some sort of delicate clothing wrapped in tissue paper and a few black and white photos tied with a red ribbon.

Aggie didn't want to waste time. Her access could be curtailed by a mistimed word or phrase with this woman. She picked up the case, locked it and took it back into the living room. Scared to let it go, she managed to open her purse with her free hand, and took out a hundred pounds, thrusting it with her business card at her aunt. She grabbed the money, and after a quick examination protested "Eh, I want two hundred quid I said!"

Aggie moved fast. She was at the front door.

"That's all the cash I have in my wallet, and it's all I'm giving you. Call me if you find anything else that belongs to my mother!"

She opened the door, rushed into the street, and walked in the direction the taxi had brought her. Moving at a desperate pace, her bag slung over her shoulder, she clung to the leather case with both hands.

Aggie gradually became aware of her surroundings as she arrived at an open space. It was what constituted a park in this poor area of Manchester. A barren wasteland, with two very sad swings, a bent slide, and a lop-sided goal net at the far end. The perspiration poured from Aggie's forehead, her hands were clammy and slippery from her unreasonably tight grip on the leather case. She cautiously lowered it and held it by the handle as she walked across the scrappy dry grass towards a seat. After ensuring her aunt hadn't followed her, and checking there were no unsavoury characters nearby, she sat down and placed the case on her lap.

Aggie laid her sticky hands on the top of the case. An extreme surge of current pulsed through her body, the hairs on her arms stood straight upwards. Her first impulse was to push the case away, but then her natural curiosity kicked in. She took a deep breath, leaving her hands flat, outstretched on the case, absorbing the moment of connection.

Aggie didn't wish to liberate her mother's legacy in this environment. She wanted to take her as far away as possible from this neighbourhood, from her aunt. How wretched must she have been to seek refuge with such an evil woman. she thought. Aggie needed to talk to her father, she needed to grieve. Somehow, she managed to phone the number the cabbie had given her and explain where she was. Within ten minutes she was relieved to see the black cab pulling up at the park gate.

Feeling in no fit state to navigate her way back to London, Aggie asked the cabbie to drop her off at any reasonably-priced hotel. He was obliging and wished her well.

The hotel was a good choice – old-world style with charm. Her room was immaculate. She laid the case on the bed, went to the mini-bar, poured herself a gin and tonic, then sat down beside the case and opened the locks.

She took out the bundle of tissue first, carefully unwrapping it to reveal an aged cotton baby's gown. Aggie assumed by the ornate embroidery and handmade lace it was at least a hundred years old. As she held it up to inspect it more closely, a tatty piece of paper fluttered out onto the bedspread. In spindly faded writing it read "Mama's christening gown". She laid it back down and turned her attention to the stack of small books. They were old fashioned notebooks, with fake leather covers. As she picked the first one up her phone rang with her father's name.

"Hello darling, I have been anxious about you," he said.

"Oh Dad! I am in Manchester. I have just been told by that dreadful woman that Mum died fifteen years ago." There was no response from her father.

"Dad, are you still there?" she could hear a sniffle.

"Yes, I am."

Aggie knew he was crying; it triggered her own torrent of tears. Still holding her phone, they streamed down her face.

Eventually her father spoke. "Aggie I am so sorry you are there on your own; I should have come with you."

"It's okay Dad; it's been my journey to make. We all need closure in different ways."

She went on to tell him about the suitcase.

"I vaguely recall the christening gown. We never had you christened so you didn't get to wear it. Your mother may have worn it."

Aggie said goodbye and promised her dad she would be in touch in the next few days. They agreed they would have a farewell of some kind to remember the wife and mother she once was.

Aggie was eager to read the diaries, but she was in such an emotional state she reasoned it was best to try and calm down a bit first before taking on any more revelations.

Her tummy was telling her she was hungry so she ordered a toasted sandwich and a pot of tea from room service.

As she waited, she took a more detailed look at the gown. A neat row of crescent horseshoe-like shapes had been carefully embroidered in thick thread on the hem of the gown. Aggie compulsively ran her finger over the crescents.

Without a doubt, she knew her mother would have done the same. Whatever circumstance, whatever process was triggering her dreams she felt sure it was hereditary from her Italian grandmother. She would work through this grief; she finally sensed a glimmer of a way forward.

After she had eaten, Aggie was grateful for the large, deep marble bath that had been preserved in the refit of this old hotel. She sank down into the hot water, Cat Stevens singing out in the background from her phone as she tried to remember her mother's face. Images of a pretty young woman with black hair floated around her. Going by how ugly her aunt was, her mother must have favoured her maternal side in appearance – and no wonder Karen Black had always been so jealous of her.

Having wept her tear ducts dry, and cosily wrapped in the fluffy white hotel gown, Aggie sat propped up on the pillows with the pile of diaries beside her.

Some of the writing appeared precise and legible but some entries were just scrawls that didn't form words. However, most of the diaries were dated on the front page, so Aggie searched through and, as best she could, she put the pile in chronological order.

The first diary was dated 1968, the year her mother had met her father, and a year before Aggie had been born. She began to read, savouring every word, as if her mother was telling her one of the bedtime stories she'd missed as a child.

I now know my real Mama came from Italy to England in 1949 because of the poverty that was prevalent there after the war. Dad met her when she was cleaning hotel rooms; he said she was crazy about him; they were married by a Catholic priest. Her English wasn't great, but she learnt fast. When I arrived, Mama was totally besotted by me. She was very unwell, but the doctor didn't seem to be worried. They had me baptised at one-week old in the christening gown my grandmother had sent from Italy. The doctor was incompetent, Mama became very sick; they didn't recognise she had an infection and, before I was one month old, she died. Dad had kept the christening gown in its original postage bag; there was no note inside, and the post mark was somewhere called Liguria in Italy. He could barely cope with a new baby on his own and re-married in haste. He lost all contact with my Mama's Italian family. He told me before he died, he had regretted remarrying so soon. His second wife was a bad mother to me. I tried to convince him to help me locate my Mama's family so I could go and meet them. But he never did. When Dad died, he left everything to my stepmother and half-sister. I hate them so much. The only thing he left me was an envelope of old photos and the christening gown. One day, when I have some money, I will go and find my Mama's family. I looked up Liguria on the map. I will find them, and they will love me."

There were a few blank pages and the next entry seemed to be a few months on.

"I will have to put off my trip to Italy as I need to save some money. London is so expensive, but I love it and I have met a really nice fella. We get along well. Who knows, he may want to marry me!"

The next entry was dated six months later. Maria had written a full description of Aggie's dad. He sounded just the same as he was now - reliable, kind, and loyal. They were clearly in love.

Then, as Aggie opened the second notebook, which had been started just after she had been born, things began to take on a very different tone.

"It's so hard being on my own all day with the baby. She is sweet, but she cries a lot. I can't sleep and when I do I have

horrible dreams. Peter, my husband, helps me when he comes home, but he must work, he can't stay with me all day. I just want her to stop crying, I just want to sleep peacefully. I wish the doctor would give me something. He just says it is 'baby blues'."

Aggie was tired. She could see where this was leading. Her heart ached for her mother; a young woman who had clearly been misdiagnosed by the doctor.

She closed the diary. She would continue reading it once she was home, once she had properly processed her mother's death.

Yielding to the softness of the hotel mattress and the comfort of the crisp white sheets, she snuggled down, closed her eyes, and asked the universe to give her an undisturbed sleep.

NINE

It was a fresh and bright Sunday in London, two weeks before Aggie was to leave for France. Her father had opted not to bring his partner Barbara, so it was just Jackson, Lyall and Aggie making up the intimate foursome to say farewell to Aggie's mother.

From the early entries in Maria's diaries, Aggie could see she had been desperate to find her Italian family before mental illness had destroyed her life.

As a tribute to her Italian side, Aggie chose to serve an Italian-themed lunch. They started with a caprese salad; tomato and mozzarella with a lot of basil, followed by salmon pasta then a wonderful Italian-style cake Jackson had bought at his local deli.

Aggie's dad shared memories about the happy times he had with Maria, and how the pregnancy had seemed to go very smoothly. In the early days, there had been no signs of the anxious behaviour that eventually engulfed his young wife. It was only after Aggie was born that his wife's episodes began and that made Aggie feel slightly guilty, but sadder than anything. Her mother had clearly wanted to be pregnant.

His eyes welled up as he said, "if only I had understood the symptoms…" and Aggie placed her hand on his to reassure him it wasn't his fault either. It was all in the past and they were celebrating the good things today.

Aggie had decided at this juncture to keep the contents of the diary mainly to herself. Some of the subject matter was upbeat but most of it was the ramblings of an increasingly disturbed mind. Her instinct was to protect her father from any further guilt and not to unload onto Jackson, given she was already displaying some rather unusual behaviour herself with her repetitive dreams.

However, she brought the christening gown and the black and white photos to share around. Her father was able to identify most of the people in them and explain to others, including a stunning shot of her mother when he'd first met her. The only one that presented a mystery was an old sepia-toned photo that was of another couple and looked like it had been taken somewhere in Europe. A small girl posed between them.

"I think that girl is your Italian grandmother with her parents, Aggie," her father said.

"Let me take a copy and try to enlarge it on my laptop," Lyall offered.

They made a toast to Maria, a wife and mother who had lived and loved before her illness took over. Aggie's father made a small speech. He said without Maria, his beautiful daughter and grandson would not exist. He had worked through his anger at her desertion; he now had a better understanding of the how and why. He saw now, she'd had run away to protect her loved ones from her demons.

When the men had left, Aggie finally relaxed. She had formally said goodbye to her mother and felt grateful to her for both her father and her son. But she knew that to progress she now must deal with these dreams and how they were connected to her mother and what may still be unresolved in Maria's life.

*

She was beside a river, sitting on a low, stone seat in front of a stone wall at the side of a low-built, mediaeval house. It was a bright day with sunshine, but Aggie didn't feel warm. She was wearing a black dress and a patterned apron. Two men were seated near her at easels, painting. She couldn't see what they were focusing on, the subject of their painting, maybe it was further round and they had chosen this shady spot to keep cool. Both men wore loose shirts and baggy dark pants; one wore a beret and one a sun hat. Aggie moved towards them. They didn't seem to notice her; she was keen to see what they were painting. But as she got closer to them everything went blurry and she woke up.

The dream had taken quite a dramatic change to a different location. But Aggie sensed it was the same village. If she had seen the men's faces, she now had no memory of them, they had become just a blur. But she had a strong desire to see what they were painting.

Aggie had set aside a day to carry out some initial online research. She wanted to have direction and some contacts ready for when she commenced her research in earnest after settling into her new life in Menton.

She had identified an American research company called DENNA which specialised in memory being hereditary through DNA. They sounded suitably professional and credible and appeared to be conducting their studies using proper scientific methods. Aggie constructed an email to Dr Viner, whose name she sourced from the company website. She told him about her own experience and what she knew about her mother's dreams.

The word "epigenetics" kept coming up in her searches although there were different "takes" on its meaning.

One read: *The field of epigenetics is based on the concept of changes in gene expression and the concept of active and inactive genes. Epigenetic scientists study how cells change to adapt into skin cells, or liver cells, or even cancerous cells. They also study how genes are inherited and the changes to those genetics that we exhibit, even when those changes are not essential to our DNA. These changes can be affected by our experiences, age, environment, and health. Recent studies done by scientists and researchers even suggest that we receive loads of genetic memories from our parents, grandparents, and ancestors further back, in an instinctive effort by their DNA to better prepare ours for difficult experiences that they have faced, such as fear, disease, or trauma.*

A statement from one of the people she researched stated: *The first dream I had which made me feel that something more was going on began when I was a teenager. It was the strangest thing. I felt myself floating down a corridor which emerged into a 17th Century bedroom. There was a truckle bed to the left, and an old lady with a small child standing in front of a window. As I floated, I felt myself go into that old lady and become her in that instant. I felt what she felt and saw what she saw. I even drew a picture at the time as it was so strange. I remember looking out at a crossroads and from each direction I could see parliamentarian men and the King's men heading towards each other. I felt fear, real fear as I knew that there was going to be a fight. That dream has stayed with me all these years. Why on earth would I dream that? I do believe it's one of two things: a form of reincarnation or genetic memory. Why not just a dream? Because it was so real! Anybody who has had a 'real' dream will know just what I mean. You can feel, see, hear, smell and touch those dreams. Seems simple to me."*

A week later, Aggie received a reply from Dr Viner.

He was very formal and said that maybe she would be interested in becoming a "case study" based on her recurring dreams and mother's background. If she was interested, she could complete the attached form and send it back, which in turn he and his research team would analyse to see if she would be a suitable candidate.

Aggie opened the attachment. There were many questions that would require comprehensive answers. She could see it was designed to establish how competent Aggie would be at articulating her experiences.

She replied that she was keen to be involved but was in the process of moving homes and would come back to them with the completed form in due course.

The next week was spent clearing out her apartment and packing for France. Discouraged by what she now felt were the dowdy, dark-coloured clothes in her wardrobe, she resolved to start that moment on the changes she intended to make to her life.

Accompanied by Jackson and Lyall, they arrived first thing Saturday morning at Duke of York Square on the King's Road and hit Zara with a vengeance.

To fellow Chelsea customers they must have appeared an interesting trio - two tall, well-groomed, handsome young men accompanying a short dumpy woman with a main of lush brown hair.

The men confidently plucked various garments from the rails; Aggie tried to pluck out a few herself, but mostly the men shook their heads.

"Mama, we will only be honest with you. All that floral and gathering fabric isn't flattering on a vertically challenged, Rubenesque beauty like yourself!" Jackson said with a smile, adding she should "keep the colour solid and bright but not broken up. "

Lyall chipped in, "with some hem and shoulder alterations, we will have you looking more than sophisticated - full of Riviera chic. Just trust us!"

The men stood outside the cubicle while Aggie tried on multiple outfits. They convinced her to buy three pairs of narrow-legged jeans in three colours, with matching shirts; two shift dresses, one a floaty, long, white and transparent, peasant-style dress Jackson told her was only to be worn with cleavage showing and on a romantic date.

Then they addressed the shoes. They chose natural-coloured sandals with a high wedge heel.

Conveniently Aggie's great friend Pauline, dressmaker to the ladies of Chelsea, lived just off the King's Road. Charmed by the gorgeous men appearing at her door, Pauline was outnumbered and agreed to do alterations in time for Aggie's departure.

"That was a marathon! Come on, let me treat you both to lunch at the Asia Ivy," Aggie said as they walked back towards the heart of the glamorous street.

"Yes please! A first for us," Lyall replied.

As they walked up King's Road Aggie pointed out where Mary Quant's shop used to be. That was all before the men's time. They remembered the punk era, but other than that it was only for Aggie that this high street held special memories of youth.

The Asia Ivy was an eccentrically-decorated, visual feast, coupled with fusion taste sensations from the far east. The staff were impeccably-dressed in Chinese brocade jackets and the service was wonderful.

Once they had ordered, Lyall pulled out an envelope from his leather backpack. It was the enlargement of the photo that Aggie had found in her mother's case.

"I cleaned it up a bit, so the faces are more distinct. Also, you can now clearly see the faded writing: 'Vera, Claudio and Sophia Balbo.' So I believe we can now assume the girl is your grandmother Vera, and Balbo was her maiden name."

Aggie studied the photo; the trio were standing in front of a stone wall. "Stone walls, both within the room and outside, appear in my dream. Perhaps it is Italy rather than France in my dream!" Aggie exclaimed.

She then told them about the research company she had contacted in America.

"So, are you saying we have memories stored in our DNA and we see them in our dreams?" Jackson said, captivated.

"Well, this company is very reputable, and they have scientifically-proven that we inherit memories. Some manifest themselves in a brief glimpse - like when you arrive in a place you have never been before and seem to recognise it, or when you have *Deja Vous* déjà vu type sensations. They claim that parts of DNA are passed directly along the female line – a woman holds them in her uterus, then passes them on when she gives birth to a daughter. Their current research is focused on testing people who have repetitive dreams and endeavouring to establish that the subject matter was experienced by past family members."

"How do they test that?" Lyall asked.

"I will soon find out! They have sent me a list of questions to answer to see if I might be a suitable candidate for the study. I am going to spend time addressing it all once I am settled in my new French home. I can't wait to begin!"

Three days later, with London life temporarily behind her and sporting a refreshed haircut and whole new wardrobe, Aggie was on EasyJet soaring through the clouds once again towards France.

TEN

The minibus driver arrived at Maison Manera via the street above the apartment; this made it easier to haul her suitcases through the back entrance and down one floor to her new home.

Sarah greeted her at the door with the keys and an offer for Aggie to join her and JP for supper, but Aggie declined.

"That is very kind, thank you so much, but it's my turn to host you, once I have settled in," Aggie said before she closed the door.

She pushed her cases into the dark entrance and flicked the light switch. The crystal brilliance of the chandeliers immediately illuminated the long imposing hallway. As if gliding on air in her own fairy tale, she floated down the hallway, taking time to peruse the paintings that adorned the walls. The style was specific, very colourful with depth and detail - most likely they had all been painted by Sarah, she thought.

At the end of the hallway, just as she remembered, an impressive terracotta urn holding a large Kentia palm sat directly in front of the window. The window was framed with a swarth of deep ruby-coloured taffeta curtain, the oversized tassel hanging down on one side offered a dramatic counterbalance to the view of the well-manicured terrace beyond.

Moving into the salon, Aggie found that Sarah had placed a generously large vase of snow-white hydrangeas in the middle of the circular table beside the front window.

Since Aggies first visit, Sarah had updated the sofas with red velvet fringed cushions which complimented the antique furniture. The shutters to the front of the salon overlooking the beach were open. Aggie sat down on one of the sofas and took in the view.

She pushed open the wooden shutters at the rear of the room taking her out to the terrace. A heavy green marble table sat well positioned, surrounded by outdoor chairs. Pots of freshly manicured shrubs and flowers were placed attractively around the edge of the outdoor area. Aggie inhaled a pleasant aroma of lemongrass and lavender, strategically planted to ward off mosquitos.

In the galley-style kitchen, Aggie opened the fridge and was delighted to find a crisp salad, smoked salmon, butter, and a small bottle of prosecco. A fresh baguette sat on the chopping board on the bench. She opened the bottle, poured a glass, and toasted herself. "To the first day of the rest of my life," she said out loud.

The next couple of days were spent unpacking, filling the kitchen cupboards with food she'd hauled back from the market in a trolley bag found in the hall cupboard, and generally putting her own stamp on things.

By Friday, Aggie had made a commitment to herself to commence her research on her "dream project" as she had termed it.

*

She was by a river on a cobbled path. On the other side of her, a stone wall formed a part of what she assumed was the village which Aggie now believed was somewhere in Italy. The subtle sounds of the river dancing over the stones, and the clipping sound of horses' hooves was all she could hear.

A fragrance, slightly tinged with Jasmine, hinted it was spring. Aggie was dressed in a long, pale blue frock and a white apron; she clasped her hair, which was long and black and it all felt normal.

Across the river was a young man - he was dressed in tweed trousers, laced-up black boots and a brown shirt buttoned to the neck. He looked up and waved. Aggie waved back, then glanced down into the still river at her reflection. She could see she was quite young, short, and very slim.

Aggie figured there must be a way to cross the river, so she moved quickly along the path hoping to find a bridge. As she moved forward a spontaneous splash came from the river, startling her.

Aggie woke in a sweat, feeling more frustrated than disturbed. She was desperate to cross the river and get a closer look at the man. It was 4am and she was wide awake now, so got out of the bed and put the kettle on.

The dream sequences seemed to be leading her somewhere, but how could she know where? And how could she control them? She jotted down her immediate recollection of the dream, knowing a journal might form a map and also be necessary for a future study, if she joined one.

By 5am the darkness was receding, and the welcoming radiance of dawn was emerging across the bay, as if destined to herald Aggie's first Saturday morning in this magical French village.

As she looked across at the deserted beach, Aggie felt totally inspired by the sunrise. She pulled on her bathers, threw a large loose shirt over the top, grabbed a towel and her keys, and pulled her door shut.

As she walked through the tunnel under the road that accessed the beach a dishevelled man lay on a makeshift bed, snoring loudly. As she walked past, he let out an almighty fart, then turned over and continued snoring. Aggie burst into giggles and was still wearing her smile as she dipped her toes in the clear, clean, azure-blue sea. Aggie swiftly removed her shirt, secured her hair up in a knot, and plunged into the refreshing water.

Feeling energetic, she swam out to the middle of the bay, then turned to take in her surroundings. The Old Town was directly in front of her now, the sun kissing the buildings with a golden glow which perfectly enhanced the many shades of terracotta and soft lemon that dominated the skyline. The water was crystal clear, void of any waves or undertow, so Aggie floated carefree, enjoying an incredible sense of freedom.

Once back at the apartment and after a leisurely breakfast at the green marble table on the terrace, she sat down to study the questionnaire she had been sent by the research company. It was very detailed; the first part asked questions that Aggie would term intensely personal, probing about her sex life, her past and her family, specifically her mother's side. Had there been a recent head injury prior to the dreams commencing? This got her thinking; she had slipped and banged her head and been unconscious for what she thought was only a few seconds. Could this be related? Was this a trigger?

The second part was all about her dreams, to which she was much more comfortable responding. The questions were comprehensive. When did her dreams commence? How long did they last for? At what frequency? Did the content change? Did it develop? Were there always other people in the dream? Could she hear and/or smell things?

Ever since university when she first started writing, Aggie had been a consummate researcher; it was what she did best. She appreciated the merit in these questions and was able to articulate with clarity in her responses. She felt a great sense of satisfaction once she had completed the survey and pressed "send" on her laptop, realising only then how much she wanted to be included in the study.

ELEVEN

Aggie answered the door to Sarah's knock around 9.30am.

"I know you are starting your new book today and I don't wish to disturb you, but I just wanted to ask if you would like to go across the border to Italy with me on Friday to the Ventimiglia morning market? Then perhaps we could drive up the valley to where my father and sister live for lunch."

"Don't stand at the door," Aggie urged and ushered her neighbour in. "This is my new life, and you are my first friend, have you time for a coffee? I was just about to make one."

The two women settled across the terrace table from each other. Sarah didn't probe, but Aggie sensed she was genuinely interested to know what her book was about. She outlined her dream experience then related the death of her mother and the mystery of her Italian grandmother.

"Well, what a coincidence that I have an Italian birth father I only discovered four years ago, and you have an Italian grandmother. That's a big adventure ahead of you! My advice is to keep an open mind and expect anything," Sarah suggested as she walked into the kitchen with her cup. Then added, as she said goodbye at the door: "To be honest Aggie, I rarely believe things are a coincidence. My children laugh at me, but I believe the universe brings people and situations together at the right time for a reason. It's a part of the life cycle." She kissed both Aggie's cheeks. "See you Friday!"

Aggie spent the rest of the morning looking up various sites online where the meaning of dreams was being discussed. Many, she felt, were fantasists and nutters but there was a consistent thread being mentioned through many of them.

This thread was that memories were passed through DNA from grandparents. Also, the words 'neuroscience' and 'epigenetics' came up in many of the articles and she felt in a way that grounded it in genuine scientific study.

One article, written in association with the DENNA institute, was compelling reading. It was titled: *Why Dreams of Your Ancestors are Important to Your Soul's Health and Wellness.*

You wouldn't be here if your ancestors hadn't survived difficult life situations—famine, war, poverty, slavery, displacement. Most of us have at least one of these traumas, if not all of them, in our ancestral lineage. Due to epigenetics, the impact of your ancestors' trials and tribulations may have been passed down from generation to generation. This type of inheritance can have a deleterious impact on your soul's health and wellness, making it difficult for you to access your deepest, truest self.

Through epigenetics, memories can attach themselves to our DNA and influence how our genes express themselves. If, for instance, your family lived in Salem during the witch trials, as mine did, you might feel a fear of expressing your psychic, healing abilities due to a subconscious memory of being part of the witch burnings.

Those traumatic memories may live in your subconscious, impacting your life and preventing you from expressing or accessing the true nature of your soul. Fortunately, ancestral healing can help you connect with your ancestors and release the difficult memories from your subconscious, freeing you from the trauma that blocks your soul purpose from manifesting. Ancestral healing also heals your ancestral lineage, impacting all living and deceased family members.

Fascinated, Aggie read on. The next section urged: *It's Time to Heal Our Ancestors.*

As Westerners, we're not taught how to listen for the whispers of our ancestors, but they speak to us nonetheless.

One way to hear these messages is through our sleeping dreams. Our dreams show us how ancient events still impact our lineage hundreds (and thousands) of years later. And our dreams assist us in becoming aware of the wounds and destructive traits we inherit so we can heal them and choose new ways of being.

Aggie didn't feel she really needed healing, but she had been traumatised by her mother's desertion when she was only thirteen and so maybe she did? From the information she now had on her mother, perhaps her mental health issues had been triggered by Maria's trauma as well. She really didn't know what suffering had been caused by Aggie's grandmothers' early death. What had happened to Aggie's great grandmother? Was it something equally distressing and unresolved? Her mind buzzed with questions.

It was five o'clock when Aggie heard the peel of the church bells and realised she had been working for five hours straight. She closed her laptop, opened the music app on her phone and put on Édith Piaf, then ran a deep bath, peppering it with a wonderful mixture of essential oils.

As she lay in the soothing warm water, she ran her fingers through her hair and felt that the small bump she'd suffered several months ago was still there. It had been a whole year since her fall, and she no longer felt the pain of it. She had forgotten all about it in fact, trusting the doctor that it would eventually disappear completely.

*

Friday came around fast. Aggie was ready for 8am as Sarah had instructed as the Friday morning market in

Ventimiglia was hugely popular up and down the French and Italian Riviera, so it was essential to get there early, parking was at a premium.

Both women smiled seeing they had unintentionally dressed alike. Loose, cotton sundresses and white sneakers. They carried Panama hats and wore sunglasses. She must be settling in, if she already looked as cool as her neighbour, Aggie thought.

Aggie was most impressed as Sarah confidently piloted the car around the busy coastal road. Once they crossed the bridge into Ventimiglia, the traffic became frantic. It was like navigating a dodgem car at a funfair. Aggie closed her eyes at one point, sure they would crash into something, as cars whizzed everywhere apparently unconcerned by the chaos.

Sarah's demeanour had promptly changed from that of a controlled, middle-class English woman into a feisty Italian racing driver with an impressive array of, what Aggie could only assume, were Italian profanities that she shouted at other drivers accompanied by a rude gestures with her immaculately manicured hands. Aggie guessed Sarah hadn't always driven like this and wondered if she'd one day pick up the same skills.

They finally reached the car park and Sarah turned off the engine, let out a sigh then looked at Aggie. "Sorry about that, I should perhaps have warned you. It's my Italian side, it just bursts out from nowhere once I get behind the wheel. However, I release a lot of tension doing it and I feel marvellous afterwards!"

Aggie laughed. "I wouldn't have believed it if I hadn't seen it! Friday morning shopping has never been like this before."

First stop was coffee. They agreed to share a tomato and mozzarella panini that Sarah recommended in consideration of now being in Italy. They were surrounded by a wonderful buzz of animated Italian greetings as locals drank a quick espresso at the bar or lingered over a panini or pastry at a table.

As they entered the covered food market Aggie was in sensory overload. There was the largest, most colourful array of fruit and vegetables she had ever seen. Luscious red strawberries sat alongside ruby-red pomegranates. She counted at least three types of courgette next to four types of rich purple aubergines. There were specialty cheese stalls alongside arrays of preserved meats and elaborate pastries.

The stall holders shone with enthusiasm and charm, calling out what Aggie assumed were the prices in loud, rhythmic tones. The cheese man offered Sarah and Aggie a sample of a wonderful soft cheese called "Duo" - a combination of gorgonzola and mascarpone. The first taste and Aggie was hooked.

After putting their food purchases in the car inside cool bags Sarah had brought to keep everything chilled on the warm ride home, they walked onto the next Aladdin's cave of items - a weekly "souk" that covered at least a kilometre of stalls.

Although only 9am, the sun offered a strong sense of summer to the large, diverse, bargain-hunting crowd. Aggie immediately noticed a core group of women wearing the Riviera uniform - Panamas and large sunglasses, with woven basket bags slung over their shoulders.

There were many layers of interesting people here. Aggie was rubbing shoulders with every race and creed in this amazing potpourri of stall holders, customers, and hawkers. African men clutching armfuls of fake Louis Vuitton, Fendi and Christian Dior bags hovered in the isles between the stalls. "Lookie! Lookie!" they called as Aggie took a closer look at the impressive copies.

"Only engage with them if you intend to buy," Sarah warned. "They turn very ugly if you negotiate then don't purchase."

"Why do the police allow it?" Aggie asked.

"Well, they are mostly illegal refugees stuck here, so I guess they turn a blind eye, as well as an open-hand. There is a lot of back-handed commission that takes place in Italy. Plus, it's the only income these men have."

An hour later they arrived back in the welcomingly cool air-con of the car with several wonderful purchases (but no fake handbags!) Aggie was prepared this time for Sarah's driving as she negotiated the car out of the carpark, through the lively village and onto the main road, while offering a commentary on some of the history of the place.

On the town's outskirts, she pointed out the ruins of a small Roman amphitheatre nestled beside the road. Aggie laughed as Sarah pointed out that it had been conveniently built opposite a McDonald's.

Soon they turned off the main road and Sarah informed Aggie that this was the Nervia Valley. There were five mediaeval villages positioned within it. Her father and sister lived at the very top of the valley in a village called Castel Vittorio.

The landscape morphed into a more rural landscape as they drove along the leafy road.

"The first village coming up is called 'Dolceacqua' which means sweet water in English. It has a castle ruin and was where the Duke Doria ruled in the 14th century," Aggie heard.

Aggie could see the joint towers of the crumbling castle in the distance as they neared the village. The mediaeval village sat under the shadow of the spectacular castle ruin, with the river creating a border between the very old and the more contemporary part of the village.

Suddenly Aggie felt a rush of heat surge through her body, her universe shifting and her eyes resting on the perfectly crescent-shaped stone bridge arching over the river.

"This bridge is around 1,000 years old; it is deemed lucky for couples to cross it on their wedding day," Sarah said and glanced over at Aggie who had gone very silent and pale.

Seeing beads of perspiration on her face, Sarah quickly pulled the car to the side of the road and turned off the engine.

"Aggie, the colour has drained out of your face, are you alright?"

Aggie was speechless, she sat deathly still staring at the stone bridge. Eventually she found her voice. "I am so sorry Sarah, but something very weird has just happened, you will probably think I am mad. Maybe I am?"

"It is perfectly okay; I don't think you are mad. I will just park the car in a safer place, and we will get some water and you can tell me all about it."

Sarah reassuringly touched Aggie's clammy hand and they drove across another small bridge that ran parallel to the large crescent stone one and parked the car.

As she stepped onto this foreign yet familiar land, Aggie was sure her legs were going to give way. Sarah was immediately at her side; she slipped her arm through Aggie's and guided her along the cobbled street towards a café.

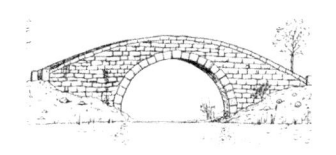

TWELVE

The friends sat at a roadside café directly beside the stone arch of the bridge, Aggie facing it. There was an extended silence which was eventually broken when their cappuccinos arrived at the table.

"I really appreciate you being understanding about my behaviour Sarah, I am so sorry, this has never happened before," Aggie sighed, snapped out of her trance. "I am not sure that you want to hear my story. It's a bit strange," Aggie sighed and raised her eyebrows simultaneously.

Sarah took a sip of her coffee before she replied. "I would very much like to hear it; I think I may have an equally strange tale to tell of my own. But we have plenty of time and the stage is yours," she said with a warm smile as she opened the palm of her hand and gestured to Aggie.

Aggie recounted her dreams, gave a brief outline of her mother's family history, and her unwanted obsession with crescent shapes as well as her research to date.

Sarah was totally focused. "Wow, that is so intriguing! So it was the shape of the bridge that triggered your reaction?"

"It seems to be more than that. I recognise the river and the stone wall of the building over there." She pointed to the wall of the mediaeval village just before the slight bend where the bridge is revealed. "I have been there in my dream, but the bridge hasn't appeared yet. So, when I first saw it, it was as if it was jumping out of the landscape at me; it has a message I need to discover."

She took a sip of her coffee then continued. "My mother, in her diary, said that her christening gown was from Liguria. This town is in Liguria, isn't it?"

"Yes, the Liguria region extends right along the coast beyond San Remo," Sarah replied.

"So, if my DNA supposedly holds memory from my mother's ancestors this may well be the village where they lived," Aggie said as she gazed up at the ruins of the ancient castle which lorded majestically over the terraced mediaeval village.

Sarah told Aggie there was an ongoing campaign to restore the castle and offered to accompany her up the steep walk. Aggie said she would do that another day.

Sarah added she couldn't make any local introductions as she didn't know anyone in Dolceacqua, but her father would be able to point her in the right direction; he was ninety and had lived in the valley all his life.

Aggie felt quite recovered and was keen to continue their journey up to Castel Vittorio. She would research Dolceacqua once she was back in Menton. For now, she was grateful for Sarah's company and keen to see the rest of the valley and meet Sarah's father.

They got back in the car and passed through the very small village of Isobalona, Sarah pointed out a turn-off to another hillside village called Apricale, adding that each village had at least two wonderful restaurants serving local cuisine.

Sarah slowed down as they drove below the mediaeval village of Pigna which sat above the road on a very steep incline. She pointed out the bullet holes that had purposefully been left in the wall of a building on the main street, so that no one ever forgot the massacre that happened in the valley at the end of World War Two.

Then just as they drove out of Pigna, Aggie was surprised to see a large, contemporary building positioned awkwardly on the bank across the river. It looked totally out of place amongst the lush greenery of the surrounding hills.

"Ugly, isn't it? My Papa says it's a carbuncle and a blight on the serenity of this beautiful place. It's a hotel that was built with cheap EU money without any proper due diligence and was never economically viable. It has closed now. Such a big effort for no result," Sarah said as she pulled in on the edge of the bridge opposite the hotel.

She opened the car door and smiled as she pointed upwards. Aggie shaded her eyes and looked up, there, as if floating in the soft clouds, was an enchanting mediaeval village. A tall tower in the centre gave it the appearance of a castle; the rooves of the dwellings were in different shades of terracotta.

"This is where my father and twin sister have lived most of their lives; my mother was English and died soon after we were born. It's a long story I will recount to you when you are ready to hear; the wonderful thing is we are all together now!" Sarah said with what Aggie would later describe as a dreamy look on her face.

Aggie usually processed situations in descriptive terms; she had spent so much time writing novels that required words which conjured romantic notions for her readers. She had automatically snapped a few shots of the fairy tale village in her mind in anticipation of sharing it with Jackson and Lyall.

"Up that small incline is my Papa's restaurant, but it is closed today so he will be at home with my sister," Sarah said as she pointed at a sign beside the bridge saying Ristorante Terme.

"So is there thermal water here?" Aggie asked.

"Yes, that was the motivation for the location of the hotel. There is a cold artesian well bubbling up here under the bridge which flows down the valley, providing a rich source of minerals to the soil and everything that is grown in it. Hence the name of the town we first visited, 'Dolceacqua' meaning 'sweet water', where the river is used to irrigate the grape vines from which they make a unique ruby red wine called Rossese."

The women returned to the car and commenced the short but steep climb up to Castel Vittoria.

The narrow road was surrounded by a lush, green forest. Aggie was mesmerised as the fairy village came closer and closer and finally became real.

Sarah parked at the base of the village by an interesting 'ristorante' called 'Busciun': The Boar. The rest of the expedition would be on foot.

As Aggie opened the car door, the first thing she was aware of was the earthy bouquet of burning wood; this fragrance filled the air as she followed Sarah up the sloping walkway into the heart of the village. Large terracotta pots of aromatic herbs sat outside doors and up on balconies. Aggie observed that the houses in the first part of the village were relatively new, but as they walked towards the square, or the 'piazza' as the Italians called it, Aggie recognised the change in architecture; it was at least 14th century, perhaps even earlier.

When they arrived at the piazza, Sarah pointed out the plaque which was a memorial to the seventy-five civilians that had been killed by German soldiers during the massacre she had mentioned earlier.

It may have been because the sun wasn't shining in the square, but Aggie felt a sense of cold desolation in this place. It was very quiet, with very few people to be seen. Sarah reminded Aggie it was lunch time - the Italians always stopped for lunch.

They climbed the stairs above the piazza, passing the ancient church and the tall bell tower before arriving at Sarah's father's home. The house stood out from its rather drab neighbours, its colourful window-boxes brimming with red and white geraniums. At the front of the house was an immaculately painted deep-green door, fronted by a new, rattan "Welcome" mat.

Before they had time to knock, the door flew open and Rebecca rushed out, exuding so much warmth as she embraced her sister and then Aggie. The sisters stood in the street madly signing at each other, before taking stock, welcoming Aggie, and ushering her into the house.

The living room oozed with the welcome that only a well-lived-in family home offers. The walls had been impressively curated with an array of brightly coloured oil paintings of what seemed to be scenes of the village and a large vase of beautifully arranged fresh flowers sat on a corner table. In the centre of the room a dining table was perfectly set for four people for lunch. A delicious aroma of sage floated out from the kitchen beyond the living area.

An old man appeared at the top of the narrow staircase; he walked cautiously down the steep stairs, then directed a beaming smile at Sarah. His 90-year-old tanned face crinkled in delight, showcasing his lifetime in lines. All the people in the room were what Aggie would term 'short', even the old man who was shorter than both Aggie and his daughters.

Sarah introduced her new friend to her Papa who shook Aggie's hand with the grip of a much younger man, then kissed both her cheeks. "Welcome to our home, please call me Mario," he said in clear English. His firm handshake and strong voice were a contrast to his fragile build.

"Thank you, I am so happy to be here. Your English is excellent, did you live in England at some time?" Aggie responded.

"No, I have never left Europe but many of my customers speak English and I love watching American films. My daughters' mother was English and although we only had a short time together, she taught me many words that she felt were important all those years ago."

Rebecca ushered them to the table, then the sisters went out to the kitchen.

Aggie had never been offered such delectable Italian food. They commenced with antipasti, which was delicate crêpes stuffed with artichoke. This was followed by ravioli, a pasta stuffed with pumpkin and ricotta accompanied by a walnut sauce. Aggie was feeling very full when she realised there was still at least one more course to come. Thank goodness they rested between courses and chatted. Well, it was a slightly longer process than a regular chat. Sarah signed everything Aggie said to Rebecca. She read her Papa's lips and used a mixture of both to communicate with her sister.

Without going into detail, Sarah asked her Papa if he knew a person in Dolceacqua familiar with its history and who spoke English, who may be able to assist Aggie with her research.

"I do know someone," he said. "The man keeps his bees on our land up behind the restaurant. I haven't spoken to him in English, but I believe he speaks it very well. He knows a lot about the history of this area. Let me talk to him and I will come back to you."

"Papa and Rebecca are finally on email; it took me a while, but they love the internet now. So, I will give them your email address and they can pass it on and correspond for you if needed," Sarah added.

When the next course arrived, Aggie felt she had died and gone to food heaven. Finely sliced veal, briefly sautéed in butter and fresh sage, accompanied by lightly roasted potatoes sprinkled with chopped rosemary and ground pepper.

Rebecca's face radiated success as Aggie exuberantly expressed her enjoyment of the veal – she was the cook in the family, Aggie had learnt - and Sarah managed to translate the complimentary descriptions she offered.

After more conversation about the history of Castel Vittorio and the Nervia Valley, Rebecca went out to bring in the dessert.

"Oh my goodness, Sarah, I don't think I can eat anything else. I realise I have a pudding-shaped figure, but I will be barrel-shaped if I put anything else into my mouth!" Aggie exclaimed, placing her hand on her extended tummy.

"Nonsense, you are a beautiful woman, and you must have a taste, otherwise my daughter will be offended," Mario replied as he offered Aggie a wink.

The tiramisu again did not disappoint, and Aggie managed to stuff in more than one mouthful.

It took about thirty minutes to achieve the final farewell. Aggie was learning that Italians were long-winded folk and took their time with everything. Mario assured her he would come back to her very soon with an English-speaking contact who had knowledge of the history of Dolceacqua.

It was early evening as they drove back down the valley. Sarah pulled over to the side of the road when they reached Dolceacqua. "See how beautiful the castle ruin looks in this dusky light! Why not grab a photo?"

Aggie was able to get several shots with the bridge in the foreground. She would enlarge them later on her laptop screen and study them more closely, she thought to herself, wanting to keep a little bit of it private for now.

THIRTEEN

The day out with Sarah in Italy had been inspiring, entertaining, informative but emotionally and physically draining. As much as Aggie would have liked to share her discovery of Dolceacqua with her son, it would have to wait until tomorrow. She was too tired to do anything except go to bed.

She found herself beside the wall again. She knew she was in Italy and the village was Dolceacqua, however it was minus many of the more recent buildings on the other side of the river. Judging by the tempo of the 'dawn chorus' it must have been very early morning. The paths and roads were empty, there wasn't a soul about. The birdsong was punctuated by the gentle tinkle of the river beside her. Her nostrils were filled with the fragrance of jasmine and rosemary. She walked along the path, around the corner and abruptly stopped. The bridge! The sun had risen and brought with it a crystal-

clear sky; there was not even a breath of wind. Being on this side of the river and up so close to this majestic construction was extraordinary. Aggie felt its pulse in her bones, she was compelled to touch it, she walked forward with her hand stretched out...

Then puff! It was all gone. The hologram-like bridge in her dream had vanished. The bedside clock said it was 7am and Aggie lay there, now knowing the place she dreamed of was real. It was Dolceacqua, just over the border from where she now lived. But in another era; sometime within her family's history, she guessed, but when?

Aggie had decided to keep a small diary and a pen by her bedside. When she experienced a dream, she would write it all down before any of the details slipped from her mind.

She took her coffee out to the terrace and gazed into the foamy milk – noticing there wasn't a crescent in sight. Aggie had moved a big step forward in last night's dream. She had known exactly where she was. The bridge seemed significant. Perhaps this would provide her brain with the impetus to move forward.

She opened her laptop. Multiple emails popped up. Her first choice was the one from Dr Viner. She let out a 'whoop' as she read that the team believed that Aggie and her dreams would be a good fit for their research program. He asked if she would consent to a DNA test and if so, said he would courier a pack to her. He had attached a research form, which he asked her to fill in immediately after experiencing a dream and making her pleased she had a head start with her 'dream diary'.

The form had several headings:

Describe what you saw;
describe what you heard; describe what you smelt;
describe how you felt;

He also asked her to forward any hereditary information she may have now gathered, especially from her maternal side and then asked whether she would be available to make a visit to the USA at some point.

She replied in the affirmative to all his requests and told him that she was sure she had found the location of her dreams. Also, the crescent shape that had plagued her had now been revealed as an ancient crescent-shaped stone bridge.

Before she looked at her other emails, she wanted to speak to Jackson. It was only 7.30am in London but Aggie hoped she would catch him before he left for work. She called and told him all that she'd discovered.

"Oh Mama, that is all so exciting! Especially finding the actual location of your dream. I bet your grandma was from there. Now, I think in addition to the researchers taking your DNA, why not do a commercial DNA test with a company like Heritage.com - loads of our friends have done them with great revelations. You may have relatives still living there, who may have also submitted to the DNA database. It would be great to know and you might find out quicker this way."

"I will do that. I am hopefully being put in touch with a local historian and intend to search the birth, marriage and death register for anyone with my mother's name," Aggie chatted on, but Jackson had a meeting and needed to cut the call short.

Returning to her emails, Aggie ignored all four from her agent Penny. She left them unopened and decided she would read and reply to them when she had sorted her day out. Her life was on a whole new trajectory and she believed the days of dancing to Penny's tune were over.

Aggie went online and paid the hundred-pound fee for a DNA test at the company Jackson rated. The pack would take a few days to arrive and she would courier it back and wait for her emailed results.

Then just as she sat down to eat her lunch, her mobile rang with a strange number.

"Bonjourno Aggie, it's me Mario! I hope you are okay with my phone call. Sarah gave me your number; much easier for a 90-year-old to use the phone than that email machine!" he said.

Aggie laughed. "I agree Mario. It's wonderful to hear your voice!"

"I see my friend in Dolceacqua; he tells me he speaks English very well and he knows a lot about the history and the families of the area. He tells me it is good for you to join the Dolceacqua Facebook page and then meet him there. His name is Andrea. Do you know this 'Facebook' thing he talks about?"

Aggie laughed again. "Yes, I do know about Facebook, and I will do that. Thank you so much Mario, I am most grateful."

"My pleasure to help a beautiful friend of my English daughter. Sarah told me you liked the *'Ponte Vecchio'*. You know lots of people have painted pictures of it. One was a very famous artist."

"Do you mean the arched bridge? Who was that?" Aggie asked.

"Signore Monet! He loved that bridge so much he went for his holidays there every year just to paint it again and again. Anyway, I must go now and carve the meat, ciao Bella."

Aggie wasn't sure she'd been called 'beautiful' so many times by a man in her whole life. If only he wasn't 90, she thought absent-mindedly.

Aggie opened Facebook and searched for the Dolceacqua page, 'liked' it then looked in the admin section and found Andrea. She sent him a message asking if it would be at all possible to meet him for a chat.

She then Googled Dolceacqua and looked up Claude Monet's connection. She found a stunning picture of the bridge he had painted along with many others painted by different artists.

She was enjoying learning new Italian words and wondered if she should join an Italian language class, rather than French. Or at least try both.

Hearing a knock at her door, she peered through the peephole and saw Sarah's wide smile.

"I knew you would be checking; good on you as this building isn't totally secure," she said as Aggie ushered her in. "I'm not stalking you, I just wanted to say I gave Papa your mobile phone number - I hope you don't mind?"

"Not at all; he just called me," Aggie said, walking into the kitchen to turn the coffee machine on.

"The old devil! He loves to be involved!" she laughed, then noticed Aggie fetching two coffee cups. "Now, I don't want to hold you up – sure you have time?"

"I need a break; it's been a full-on morning."

Aggie went on to tell her friend about being accepted as a research subject in the USA, which may mean a trip over there and about joining the Dolceacqua Facebook page.

"May I ask about your books?" Sarah said, once they had sat down at the terrace table.

"Sure, ask away."

"Well, I put your name into Amazon books, but nothing came up, so I assume you use a pseudonym?"

"Yes, I do: 'Tabatha Heart'. But you must understand I developed a pseudonym because I am mostly embarrassed with the genre, I was fortunate to have success in. When my books started featuring on the bestseller lists it seemed silly to stop writing them," Aggie replied.

"What would you have preferred to write?"

"Well - my husband walked out on me when our son was only two years old and I had to support him alone, so this was a quicker and easier way to make money. But the book I really wanted to write was probably the one people would put down and wouldn't want to pick up again," Aggie quipped before she continued. "When I was young and naive at university, I was full of hope for a literary career. My secret wish was that I had the gift that would allow me to write a book that would be acknowledged as something very special. But those aspirations were short-lived when the reality of having to make a living struck home to me. So, using my passion for history, my yearning for romance and topped with an ability to articulate some rather graphic sex scenes, I found a way to use my literary education to make money."

"I am impressed! I may have to take a peek at some of Tabatha Heart's raunchy romance stories!" Sarah said as she stood up. "I won't keep you now."

Aggie was so happy to have this perceptive, calm woman as her neighbour and new friend. Their conversation had triggered the question of what her new book was going to be about and it felt a natural evolution that she should maximise her dream diary and build a fictitious story around the factual research she was involved in together with her family history. The manuscript could evolve at the pace of her discoveries. She wasn't interested in a biography and besides, the female protagonist would be tall and willowy, not short and dumpy. Aggie would enjoy visualising herself in a tall woman's skin.

She opened Penny's email and sent a very brief reply.

"Dear Penny, I must tell you the news that Tabatha Heart has died! May she rest in peace! Thank you for everything but that time of my life is over and I will no longer require your services as an agent. Agatha Sutcliffe."

FOURTEEN

Andrea, the beekeeper turned historian, although a little slight in his communication, agreed to meet Aggie for lunch in Dolceacqua. She had made it clear it was her invite and that she would be paying but had asked him to recommend somewhere nice to meet. Sarah had offered to drive her there, or for Aggie to borrow her car but Aggie really felt she needed to be independent. She would catch the train to Ventimiglia, which was only one stop, then catch the bus to Dolceacqua.

The bus was small and shaped like a pound of butter. It sat ten people, and everyone seemed to know one other; the noise level was high. They generously included Aggie in their conversations and to make life easier, she just nodded and said 'sì' at regular intervals which seemed to work. She was sure they were only half-listening and instead just wanted to talk. Italians loved to talk.

The butter-shaped bus arrived at Aggie's destination fifteen minutes before her meeting time with Andrea at Casa Bottega in the piazza.

Aggie walked over to the bridge; she now knew that 'Ponte Vecchio' were the words for 'old bridge' in Italian. As she had done in her dream, she leant over and placed a hand on the ancient edifice. Although the stone was cold, her hand burned hot at the touch and her pulse quickened. It was a defining moment. Her skin, her bones, her DNA shared a familiarity with this place; what was it telling her?

Aggie removed her hand, pulling herself together and checked the time. Then looking upwards, standing directly at the top of the crescent of the bridge above her, she noticed a man staring down at her. Their eyes met. Normally Aggie would have looked away. His face was somehow familiar. For a moment, she stared back but found the spell broken as the church bells pealed out midday. That was her cue and she walked off toward the restaurant, her hand still tingling from the returned touch of the bridge.

She recognized Andreaa immediately from his Facebook photo and she was pleased she had made the effort with a dress and grooming as he was very handsome, with a compelling smile.

He was a tall man and although casually dressed, he had a certain style about him. He sported an unshaven face, which Aggie and Jackson often joked was generally considered the "Italian stallion" look. Aggie figured he was about her age, early fifties. His hair was a bit wild, but then he did work with bees all day. His English was excellent, and he was very welcoming and proud to talk about Dolceacqua.

Aggie asked Andrea to recommend something local for her to eat. She had no idea what it was but was up for a new food experience and after he'd ordered for them, she took out her list of questions.

She now knew about the Italian way of going-off on a tangent and wanted to learn as much as possible by focusing on him. She told him her grandmother's name was Vera Balbo and that she was keen to confirm if she had lived in Dolceacqua. She said she wished to know anything about her ancestors and would love as much history on the bridge in particular as he could provide. She gave him a copy of the photo Lyall had enlarged for her.

The meal was delicious, it was called "baccalà mantecato": a salted dry cod enveloped in creamy mashed potato and served with fresh green beans. Andrea had recommended a glass of Rosesse, the local red wine Sarah had told her about. Although Aggie would normally drink white with fish the light red perfectly complimented her dish.

Andrea said he would go to the equivalent of the town hall and look up the family name for the date Aggie had given him, as well as seeing what else he could find out. He said it may take a couple of weeks as he was very busy moving beehives just now.

He spoke with such passion about his bees and told her that at different times of the year, the bees enjoyed different plants. They had been on rosemary and thyme through February but now had moved onto the heather and blackberries.

It was a joy for Aggie to hear someone speak with such enthusiasm and zeal. So refreshing compared with the commercial money-making bent with which people like Penny and her publishers infused every discussion.

Andrea had written several books on bees and didn't seem concerned if he made any money or not from them or the creatures themselves; it was all about sharing his knowledge and reaching the people that were interested.

Aggie excused herself to use the bathroom and on returning to the table, she noticed the man from the bridge was sitting behind her. She pretended she didn't see him. She felt uneasy with the idea he'd been listening to her speaking of her family to Andrea.

After enjoying a fabulous apricot tart and coffee, Andrea brought the lunch to a conclusion by saying he would come back to Aggie with as many answers as he could. She called for and paid the bill and as he kissed her goodbye on both cheeks, she was sure she caught the delectable whiff of honey.

The bus wasn't due for at least half an hour, so Aggie walked back to the base of the bridge and walked up it to the peak of its crescent shape. She took in the wonderful views that surrounded her.

To the rear of the bridge, a leafy slope bordered the fast-running river. It ran down a slight incline, sparkling as it caught the sun and in contrast to the other bank where the riverbed was flat and the water more sedate, barely appearing to move at all.

Aggie took out her phone and started taking photos, pointing upwards to the castle ruins, and including the foliage between the bridge and the ruins to frame the shots.

Aggie sensed a presence behind her and turned to find the mystery man who'd been on the bridge then in the restaurant behind her.

"The ruins were once the Castle Doria; it was built in the 12th century by Count Ventimiglia," he said in pleasant, lightly-accented English.

Aggie stared at him. He was marginally taller than her. He smiled.

"Bonjourno, I didn't mean to startle you, sorry. I am Leonardo, but everyone calls me Leo."

"Hi, I am Agatha, but no one calls me that. I'm really Aggie," she said, returning the smile.

"I don't wish to intrude, but before lunch when I saw you place your hand on the bridge, I was intrigued."

His voice was pleasant, without overt volume and it had a soothing clarity of tone. He was probably about sixty, and conservatively dressed.

"I am tracing my family's past," Aggie replied.

"Are you from here?" Leo asked.

"No, I was born in England of an English father and a half-Italian mother. So far, all the signs are pointing to the family coming from Dolceacqua. What about you, are you local?" Aggie's face flushed as she spoke.

"I was born and received my early schooling here. But we moved to Switzerland for my father's job where I attended the international school, which was all in English, then I completed my university studies in America."

"Oh, so you are here on holiday?" Aggie asked, still aware of the flush in her face. *What did that mean?* she wondered.

"Well actually I have recently semi-retired and decided to come back to my roots. I have rented a place in the village for a few months until I decide my next move. What about you? Are you staying here?"

His smile revealed perfect, white teeth which Aggie figured were a byproduct of his American life. Although short in stature and a little overweight, he was upright and impressive. If Aggie were describing him in written words, she would say that he "stood tall" and walked with a "sharp, firm" step. A snatch of thick white hair was cropped close at the sides of his head with a smattering of dark detail hinting at the black hair of his younger days.

"I live across the border in Menton – which reminds me, I better head off to the bus stop now as I think it's the last one of the day," Aggie said as she slung her bag over her shoulder.

"I realise this is a bit forward, but may I have your phone number - I may be able to assist with some translating of the history for you?" he said, his mellow brown eyes holding hers as he spoke.

They shone with significance and although he didn't tick any of the usual boxes, Aggie had to admit that she was attracted to him.

"I have a new French phone, but sorry I don't know the number off by heart yet. But you can have my email address," she said, fumbling in her bag for a card.

"Please allow me to walk you to the bus stop. I would offer to drive you home, but I don't wish to push my luck," he said, and they both laughed.

Aggie caught herself from blurting "push all you like" and instead just grinned. The chemistry was immediate, and this had not happened in years! She didn't want to blow it.

They arrived at the bus stop just as the butter shaped bus pulled in.

"It was so wonderful to meet you Aggie, I will email you," Leo said as she stepped onto the bus.

During the journey home, Aggie's brain whirred and stirred like a teenage girl's experiencing her first crush. Then the grown-up part of her kicked in. *He is almost as short as me and needs to lose a few kilos. Knowing my luck, he is married, and his wife is at home preparing his pasta*, she told herself.

Her thoughts zigzagged between lust and reason all the way home and before she knew it she was turning the key in her door with her phone buzzing indicating a text.

"Fancy coming in for an apéritif? Sarah x"

"Be there in 10," she quickly replied.

Aggie freshened up, then stepped across the hall, knocked at the door. Sarah handed her two courier packs; both the DNA tests, Aggie understood from the packaging. It appeared both companies had co-opted a French company to dispatch them. They had arrived together.

"We are both keen to hear about your adventure!" Sarah said as she handed Aggie a glass of wine.

Aggie reported on the meeting with Andrea and his bees, then started to say something about her encounter with Leo but stopped mid-sentence.

"I detect from the smile on your face that you saw something or met someone else at this village of 'sweet water' - maybe a sweet somebody?" JP teased with dancing eyebrows. His sexy French accent made the prospect sound even more amusing and both women laughed.

"JP! Don't be nosey!" Sarah said, slapping his hand.

"Sarah (which JP pronounced like "Seera") don't be so English, we French love to hear about love," he retorted.

"Okay, okay calm down you two. Yes, I did meet a mystery man on the bridge at Dolceacqua. I only spoke to him briefly; he wouldn't be the usual type I would go for, but I experienced an incredible rush of chemistry. I may be deluding myself, but it felt like it was a mutual thing. He was originally from Dolceacqua and had just returned. He is American-educated, so we could chat easily. But hey! He's probably a con man, or has a wife tucked away somewhere."

"Aggie, you must not fight chemistry! Trust me, I am a doctor!" JP said, roaring with laughter.

"My darling husband, your French humour doesn't always translate as well as you think into English," Sarah said, rolling her eyes at JP. Then turning to Aggie, she asked: "So when are you going to meet up with him?"

"I gave him a card with my email address on it, so let's see if he follows up," Aggie giggled.

As she crossed the hallway Aggie's head was doing a little dance from the wine. She'd had two large glasses of delicious chilled Vermentino and decided she'd run a lavender bath, put on the soundtrack to *The Bodyguard*, and slide into the water to daydream about love. And maybe a little bit about Leo, she admitted to herself with another giggle.

FIFTEEN

Despite the stimulation of her visit to Dolceacqua, Aggie woke the following morning after an extremely peaceful sleep without dreams and was confused.

Instead, she decided to get up and concentrate on the DNA tests. She took a swab from her mouth as instructed on both of them, then texted the courier company to come and collect them.

Aggie had planned to commence an outline of her new book this morning. The creative writing structure she had followed when she was Tabatha Heart was called 'The Hero's Journey'. She would outline the story in twenty points, spread over five pages which she would then 'blu tack' to the wall in front of her laptop. But before she commenced, she was very keen to see if there was a certain email in her inbox.

There it was! A message had arrived at 8pm the evening before from Leo Molinari.

He said he was enchanted to meet her and would love to visit Menton and take her for dinner. Would she be available on Friday evening; and perhaps she could recommend a restaurant?

Aggie replied that she would love to have dinner and would consult her neighbour about a recommendation. She added: "Would you like me to book it and if so what time?"

He must have been sitting on his computer because Leo replied immediately. "Yes please, I will be with you at 7pm. Please tell me your address and phone number. Mine is at the bottom of this email."

With the anticipation of a pubescent schoolgirl, her thoughts were immediately on what she would wear, whether Leo was for real and then – to Aggie's surprise – the question of whether they'd make love? It had been a while.

There was an email from Jackson directly after Leo's. He was asking if he and Lyall could come and stay in two weeks' time, as it was a bank holiday weekend in the UK, and he needed to quickly secure some low-cost airfares.

Aggie instantly replied that of course they could and signed off: "Let's chat tonight".

The next email Aggie figured must be spam as she didn't recognise the address. She was just about to push delete when she thought better of it. As she began to read it her heart did a somersault; it was from a solicitor's office in Manchester.

Dear Mrs Sutcliffe,

We found your card at the home of the late Mrs Karen Black. Our firm acted for Mrs Black as well as her father and her sister, Mrs Maria Sutcliffe, whom we also knew as 'Maria Black'.

We are assuming you must be a relation, perhaps her niece? If so, could you please contact us. Before Mrs Maria Sutcliffe passed away, she left a folder with us with your name on it. Until we found your card amongst your aunt's possessions, we had no way of being able to contact you. We look forward to hearing from you at your earliest convenience.

Yours faithfully
Robert S Allen LLB

Aggie felt both sick and excited at the same time. She immediately phoned the number on the letterhead.

"Ah Mrs Sutcliffe! I am pleased to hear from you. First let me say I am very sorry for the loss of your aunt."

"Thank you, but to be honest I couldn't stand the woman so there is no need to be sorry," Aggie admitted.

There was a pause and Aggie thought the lawyer had been disconnected.

Then he spoke more candidly. "To be perfectly frank, I can identify with that sentiment completely."

Aggie laughed.

"I am just glad we can forward you your late mother's folder of possessions. It has been sitting in our client's storage for over ten years. Where shall we send it?"

Aggie gave him her London address and said if he could ensure it would be there within the next ten days, her son could bring it over to France with him.

What a day this was! She'd been booked for a 'hot date' and her mother had sent her something from heaven!

Before she could commence her writing, she had one more thing she must do.

Aggie texted Sarah and asked if she could please recommend an appropriate restaurant for the first date of two people this Friday, and added a big smiley-face emoji for good measure.

Sarah swiftly replied. "Sit under the stars, beside the palms, looking at the ocean at the Panama Restaurant in front of our building. Walk down and check it out! Sarah x."

That evening when Jackson phoned, Aggie decided not to mention Leo. She would have already been on the date before the boys arrived in Menton and who knows which way it would pan out? Knowing how keen they both were on details, she decided to delay the news until they were in Menton.

Before her late afternoon dip, Aggie checked out the Panama Restaurant and saw Sarah was right, it looked perfect for a first date. She went in to book a table and felt a tingle of excitement knowing she'd see Leo there within a few days.

Back home, after her shower, Aggie pulled the bathroom scales out. She had been really trying with her food consumption and it was a great relief to see she had dropped a couple of kilos. A definite confidence booster for Friday evening's dalliance, she thought, with a smile.

SIXTEEN

All her dresses were piled on Aggie's bed and all her shoes scattered over the floor and she still hadn't decided which of either did her dumpy figure most justice. Leo would be at the restaurant in an hour and she needed to get sorted. Normally in a situation like this, she would call Jackson. One advantage of having a gay son was he was very much in tune with his mother's femininity, and very honest in his opinion.

Thinking strategically, she knew the best thing was to colour-block, as Jackson had said and not break up the lines. She now had a tan and weighed two kilos less, so decided on the floaty white dress, accompanied by her small diamond earring studs for embellishment. Earlier in the day, Aggie had made her first visit to a French hair salon, which Sarah had recommended. She had also treated herself to a manicure and pedicure.

Aggie had always been conscious of being short and Rubenesque on a good day, but plain-old fat on a bad day but she did feel okay about her hair and her feet - they were small, size 36, and delicate. Aggie took her dainty, elegantly diamante-studded sandals out of their tissue paper and slipped them on. They showcased her immaculate pedicure. She applied her makeup with great care, then liberally sprayed Mitsuko parfum over her hair and shoulders before leaving.

As she stepped onto the promenade to walk along to the restaurant, panic set in. What if he was just leading her on? What if her overactive imagination had misread the chemistry? What if he wanted to make love to her and he thought she was too fat? But before she realised it she was standing on the steps that led down to the restaurant. She breathed in, slowly exhaled, then walked down to the bar where Leo was waiting.

He beamed as she walked over to him, his mellow brown eyes crinkling with smile lines that made her feel wonderful. He wore smart navy trousers, teamed with a pure white linen shirt that had the sleeves rolled up perfectly to his elbows. As he greeted her, kissing both cheeks, she inhaled the lime notes of his aftershave.

They were shown to their table facing the sea and Aggie felt a soft breeze running through the otherwise humid evening.

"Shall we have a glass of Champagne?" he asked and she nodded in agreement.

The conversation flowed without effort or hesitation.

Leo was sixty, as she had guessed, and had been divorced for ten years. He had an unmarried thirty-six-year-old son. His ex-wife and son lived in America. He was an accountant, but his real love was poetry and history.

Aggie told him all about Jackson and Lyall and about her previous career as Tabatha Heart.

The food was impressive, and after a couple of glasses of wine they both were extremely relaxed.

"When I first saw you, touching the bridge the other day, I figured I must have known you from when I was a kid in the village. I thought I recognised you. I was on my way to have lunch at a different restaurant but I found myself following you to Casa Bottega. I have never done that before. I couldn't help overhearing some of what you and the gentleman were talking about. I felt envious of him," Leo admitted.

Aggie's writer's mind went into overdrive - she was imagining all sorts of scenarios now.

"Why would you be envious?" she smiled.

"It was a crazy notion, but I felt an instant attraction towards you. I can't say I have ever experienced it before." He reached across and held Aggie's hand.

Aggie forced herself to stay silent. She didn't want him to stop.

He chuckled. "If I wasn't Italian-born, and we weren't in France beside the sea and under the stars I would probably have been too reserved to have just said that," he said softly as he stroked her hand.

Aggie gulped - in fact she almost choked on the piece of olive that she hadn't quite swallowed.

"I must tell you I am a total romantic, but usually I can only write about it, not verbalise it. It sounds crazy, but I had a feeling of familiarity when I first saw you as well," Aggie said, then smiled.

Leo leant over and gently put Aggie's hand to his lips, bestowing a lingering gentle kiss.

By the time the dessert had arrived Leo had manoeuvred his chair closer to hers. The desserts were like art on the plate. Aggie had ordered sautéed fresh pineapple with kiwi coulis and a ginger foam. Leo had the key lime cheesecake with a crushed pistachio crust and panna cotta ice cream.

Leo laughed as he helped position the plates so Aggie could take some pictures to show the boys.

"You give out so much natural enthusiasm and joy, Aggie! It's so refreshing for me after the discontented women I have been around in America," he said.

They shared their desserts. Aggie experienced a strong sexual sensation as Leo placed a spoonful of citrus cheesecake directly into her mouth. He removed the spoon then sensually wiped a speck of cream off the side of her lip with his forefinger. Without taking his eyes off hers, he licked his finger and raised his eyebrows.

Aggie felt she really was a character in one of her bonkbuster novels, she was practically fizzing. She was so aroused she just wanted to get him back to her apartment and rip his clothes off. But civility prevailed.

Leo paid the bill, tucked Aggie's arm under his and led her down to the beach. As they reached the sand he flicked his loafers off, then bending down said: "Let me undo your sandals – it's so nice walking on the sand with bare feet."

It was an act of chaste intimacy as he undid the sandal straps, then traced his fingers across her perfectly painted toes.

"You have such small, beautiful feet; I must tell you I have a thing about feet!"

He looked up at her, then standing, drew her to him. Under the Riviera moon the mystery-man from the bridge at Dolceacqua kissed Aggie with such passion that she knew there was absolutely nothing medicinal about this mutual chemistry.

They were like giggling teenagers as they negotiated the stairs to her apartment; the final glass of limoncello had loosened their tongues and their legs as they tangled around each other in the dark on the staircase.

"Shush! I don't want Sarah and JP to think that I am up to anything," Aggie whispered as she fished in her handbag for the key.

"Why? Are you still a virgin?" Leo countered and they both roared with laughter.

"Verging on the ridiculous!" Aggie managed to get out as they both burst into another fit of giggles.

Once inside Leo was very keen to go straight to the bedroom.

"Slow down a bit, my Italian stallion; I am only a little bit tipsy and not that easy," Aggie said as she guided them to the kitchen.

Leo took stock. "Oh, Aggie I am sorry, I was just getting carried away." He looked genuinely embarrassed.

Aggie poured them both a glass of water. "It's been a long time since I did this; it's not that I don't want to. I really fancy you, and in my writer's mind I am confident, but in reality, I am a bit shy" she said, kissing his cheek.

He took her glass, placed it alongside his on the bench, then took her hand and he led her to the bedroom. "I am shy too, so let's leave the light off and keep our eyes closed until we feel happy about it."

Aggie pulled back the cover from her bed, removed her sandals and leant back. Leo was immediately beside her kissing her neck and stroking her leg. He sat up and swiftly removed his shirt, then helped her pull her dress over her head. Her ample breasts were neatly packed into her pure-white lace bra. Leo slid his trousers off and lay beside her. The kissing was intense and although he was a short man, she could feel his rather large rhythm stick hard against her thigh. He expertly unhooked her bra. "I love your full breasts!" he murmured as he nuzzled his face into her mountains of mammary.

Aggie had almost reached heaven, a man who loved her feet and desired her oversized boobs and now there was no holding back.

As the finale of their lovemaking reached its crescendo, Aggie's orgasm took her far, far beyond heaven. With Leo, her mind, her heart and her soul exploded into the ultimate nirvana.

Aggie slept like a baby, until she woke, slightly confused by a soft snoring sound next to her. The action the night before had been amazing, but the reality was that Leo was 60-years-old and snored. He had pushed the sheet back during the night and she could see at sober close-quarters a small roll of fat around his middle. Aggie slid quietly out of bed, grabbed her white satin nightdress, and went into the bathroom to brush her teeth. She had a quick splash before returning to the bedroom.

Back in bed, Leo was propped up against the headboard and had pulled the sheet over his tummy, but his hairy Italian chest was exposed. "I think you are a bit of a cheat, Agatha," he smiled dozily. "I know you have brushed your teeth!" He reached out and pulled her over. "However, I am very happy, as I take it as a sign you want me to kiss you again" He took both her cheeks in his two hands and gave her an exaggerated, loud kiss that made her laugh.

Aggie offered Leo a loose cotton dressing gown, a fresh towel and pointed him in the direction of the bathroom as she went to the kitchen to make coffee.

Yesterday she had felt like a bulky hippo at a water hole but overnight, this short Italian man had made magical love to her and this morning she was light as an ethereal fairy flying high on love.

Over breakfast on the terrace, Leo quizzed her in more depth about what she was currently writing. She hadn't yet told him anything about her dreams and where she thought that could be leading her writing. When she said it out loud it could sound a bit wacky, and she didn't want to cast doubts on her sanity at this early stage of the relationship.

"Come on Aggie, why are you hesitant to share? It's not a 'bodice ripping bonk buster' as you told me last night you have killed that author of. How bad can it be?"

He took his cup out to the kitchen for a refill. On his return he bent down, giving Aggie a little hug and a kiss.

"I want to know everything about you, what you love, what you hate, how you think," he said as he sat back down.

Aggie took a deep breath. She smiled across at him. Then she began at the beginning. How her half-Italian mother, displaying signs of mental illness, had left the family home when Aggie was only thirteen. She told Leo her grandmother's name was Vera Balbo and that she had gone to England and married her English grandfather. She added that she now believed the family had come from Dolceacqua and hoped to gain more conclusive information from local records.

Carefully keeping things as simple and logical as possible, Aggie told him about the dreams, the research company in America and the angle she hoped to take in the new novel she was preparing.

Leo listened intently and when she had finished said: "Let's see what this Andrea comes up with, but failing that I can have a look around for you as well."

It was 11am when Leo reluctantly made moves to go home. They were kissing goodbye at the door when Sarah opened her door opposite. She wore a large sun hat and dark sunglasses and had her big shopping basket slung over her arm.

"Oh, hi Sarah, this is Leo!" Aggie said, feeling like a schoolgirl just caught by her mother.

"Hello, Sarah! I just popped around for morning coffee," Leo said, offering her a little wave as he walked towards the staircase. "I will call you Aggie, ciao!"

Sarah beamed at her friend as she removed her sunglasses and pursed her lips. Ensuring that Leo's footsteps had reached the bottom of the marble staircase, she quietly said with a sly wink: "Morning coffee, that's one word for it!" Aggie couldn't contain the smile that spread across her face.

SEVENTEEN

Aggie had showered and dressed and spent most of the day savouring the afterglow of the previous night's lust-fueled activities.

Leo phoned her early in the evening full of compliments and affection and asking when he could see her again. Aggie was hooked but erring on the side of caution. She knew men - they needed to chase. She didn't want to be too available and although the sex was great and he made her heart leap, she had been at this place with a man before. They had wearied and the spark disappeared. Instead, she told him her boys were arriving that Thursday evening, and it may be a little soon to introduce him.

"Aggie, we are not a young couple with all the time in the world, we are grown-ups. Your son is a mature man in a relationship. I am no threat to him. I don't want to play games."

Aggie was a bit startled with his direct reply and took a step backwards.

"I guess you are right. I am a bit sensitive about certain things; it's because of what has happened in the past," she said. There was a pause.

"Okay Mi Tesora let's do this: for my part, I want as much of you as I can get but you have a day or two to gather your thoughts and come back to me if you decide you'd like us to meet each other again, with or without your son. It is your call."

Aggie felt quite deflated as she clicked her phone off. She quickly googled 'Mi tesora' and saw it meant 'my darling'. Then her phone buzzed in her hand.

"Mama, we are so happy, we will be with you in only five days' time!" Jackson exclaimed, full of excitement.

Realising he still knew little of her recent news, Aggie told him about the phone call from the solicitor and that a package would be arriving for him to bring her. She told him about the DNA tests and that she should know from Heritage.com next week. Then there was Leo.

"Actually, I went on a date last night!" Aggie blurted out.

There was a moment's quiet. "What?! Wow! That's fantastic. A French man? "

"No, an Italian. I met him in Dolceacqua."

"Great! We will look forward to checking him out," Jackson replied before he said goodnight.

Aggie gazed out of her window, as the bright blue of the sea-sky faded and was replaced by a blaze of rich red sunset.

A flock of small swallows filled the air, swirling and diving to catch their evening meal. The basilica bells rang out across the bay adding to the ambience. This picture of perfection reassured Aggie. Why hold back?

Reflecting on what had transpired in the last twenty-four hours, the meal, the romance, and the lovemaking, she recognised that perhaps it was her insecurity that was here holding her back.

Leo had been right. Jackson had been right. Of course, they wanted to meet each other. Aggie needed to be honest with herself - she was 52 not 32, why not just go where this was leading her.

She picked up her phone, scrolled to Leo and tapped in her text. "I would love you to join us for lunch at my apartment on Saturday. Love A x."

*

Aggie walked around the path towards the bridge. Every time she saw it, it was like the very first time. It radiated a presence of not only architectural brilliance, but a sense of passion, of romance, and of mysticism. It drew her in. The way it broached the river in a giant crescent - the curve appearing unsupported and magical. The bridge was the heartbeat of the village, the gatekeeper to the ancient castle above.

It must have been early morning as no one was about. There were no power lines, no cars, and no contemporary buildings. The café by the bridge, where she had sat with Sarah, was a villa. Aggie thought the time zone was maybe the late 1800s or early 1900s.

She was wearing a dark pinafore-type dress down to her ankles. Her black hair cascaded wildly over her shoulders. It all felt perfectly natural to Aggie to be in this body, but the angst and strong sense of loss she was feeling didn't sit well. She walked up onto the bridge, stopped at the top and looked directly down at an older woman, then called out and waved. Aggie heard a shout and the woman turned to look behind her.

Aggie woke and found it was 7am in current day France: 2022. She didn't feel frightened or frustrated on waking anymore, just curious. She documented the dream, then sent an email to Dr Viner telling him all about her latest experience in Dolceacqua.

Previously, he had explained that all her information and observations were collated on file, so each new update was important as it both increased the database for further research and filled in the picture of what she was experiencing.

*

By Thursday morning Aggie had prepared for Jackson and Lyall's arrival. The beds in the spare bedroom were made up with starched white cotton sheets, the cupboards and fridge were full of all the boys' favourite foods, and she was brimming with anticipation. She couldn't wait to share the experience of the Ventimiglia Friday market with them the next morning.

It was late by the time they arrived at the apartment and Aggie was disappointed that the spectacular views were limited by the darkness. But as she guided them up the marble staircase, they were more than impressed.

"The frescoes are wonderful, Aggie! Are they original?" Lyall asked as he craned his neck upwards to take them all in.

"I think they may have been touched-up at some stage, the humidity really affects the interiors in these old buildings," she said.

Once inside the door, Aggie hit the light switch and there was a collective "wow". The triple chandeliers offered a magnificent welcome to first time visitors and Aggie had a bank of perfumed candles burning, their flickering fragrance adding another dimension to the otherworldliness of the scene. The boys took in every painting and every piece of furniture with wide eyes.

They unpacked while Aggie made mint tea with fresh leaves she'd picked from the large terracotta herb pot on the terrace.

As they gathered around the table, Jackson handed her the unopened package that had arrived from the solicitor.

Aggie's hands trembled as she struggled to unseal the flap.

"Are you okay Mama? Here, let me get that," Jackson said as he took the package from her and ripped open the end of it to reveal a slim parcel of crinkled brown paper. He gently handed it to his mother.

Aggie grasped the tatty package in both hands. Her eyes glistened with moisture as she read the scrawly text.

"To be given to my daughter Agatha Sutcliffe in the event of my death. Maria Sutcliffe."

She carefully unwrapped the brown paper. Inside was a pile of A4 sketches. The first few seemed to have been drawn using both pencil and pastels. Aggie carefully removed it to study them more closely; her tears dripped down onto her hand; she wiped them just in time to avoid smudging the drawing that she had immediately recognised as the stone wall of her dreams. Her heart thumped so hard she clasped her chest with her hand and the tears fell.

Lyall handed her a tissue.

"Mama are you okay?" Jackson said, putting an arm gently around her shoulder.

"Yes, I will be. It's just after all these years my mother is communicating with me. I didn't understand how talented she was. This drawing is so precise."

"Have you been here?" Lyall asked.

"Yes, first in my dream, then in real life. It's part of the mediaeval village of Dolceacqua and this wall runs alongside the river. Just around the corner from this spot is an amazing crescent-shaped stone bridge, which I now believe is the catalyst for my obsession with crescents."

"Really? You have certainly made progress with all this!" Jackson said. He was animated.

"Yes, it's like a rope that is pulling me forward, the puzzle needing to be pieced together. If I look at how it all started, it was you introducing me to Sarah. I had noted Liguria was very close to Menton which I figured could be useful in finding any ancestors or family, but I hadn't worked out how I would identify the specific town or village. When we drove through Dolceacqua and I saw the bridge, it was total déjà vu, I had been there before!"

"So if your DNA has these memories somehow stored in your memory, do you have any control over accessing them to reveal their secrets? Lyall asked.

"At the moment, I don't know how. I need to be patient and keep submitting what I am experiencing to Dr Viner's team. They have vast knowledge of dream interpretation of this kind and Dr Viner has told me every case is different. At least now my dreams don't frighten or frustrate me anymore. I am just immensely curious to follow them. Seeing these drawings from my mother and knowing she most likely experienced the same thing is a quantum leap forward."

The boys sensed Aggie needed to be alone with the sketches. They kissed her goodnight and left her sitting at the table. There would be plenty of time for her to share with them. Tonight she needed the intimate, special experience of a mother sharing with her only daughter a revelation that belonged solely to the two of them.

Alone, Aggie saw there were several sketches of the stone wall, then one, near the bottom of the pile, of the bridge.

At this point Aggie's mind raced. Whilst she had written notes to document her dreams, her mother had sketched pictures.

There were eight drawings in total. The final one was puzzling; it wasn't something Aggie had seen yet but was just a pile of stones. It was as if one of the village walls had been knocked down.

She turned over the drawing, and on the back was written. "Very frightening!" Then, realising all the drawings had a text on the back, she turned them over and started reading them in the order her mother had placed them.

"Agatha, it is very difficult for me to explain, but I have strange dreams that don't seem to make sense. They keep coming back, sometimes night after night. So, I am sketching them to show you."

The next one read. "I am sorry I left you and your father, but I was so confused and frightened and didn't want to burden you as I lost my mind. As I write this, I now know I have a mental illness in which I have very bad hallucinations. The medication helps me cope a bit. I have left it too long now to come back and find you. You were such a beautiful child and I know your father will have been kind to you."

Aggie sniffed back the tears as she read the text on the back of the third picture. "Despite the doctor telling me my dreams are a part of my illness, I feel compelled to write to you about them, hoping you will read this one day.

I believe these dreams are a real place. Maybe somewhere in my mother's village in Italy. Sometimes, when I awake, I can even smell lemons."

As she read this line, Aggie's entire body shuddered. At the moment she absorbed her mother's words, a lifetime's perception of being an abandoned child was wiped away. Aggie completely understood her mother. From heaven or wherever Maria had gone to, she had reached out to her daughter and touched her soul.

EIGHTEEN

Jackson and Lyall were bowled over with Friday morning's adventure to Ventimiglia. Sarah had insisted she drive all four of them in her car; she missed her own son Nick and loved it that Jackson and he worked together.

The boys laughed as Nick's glamorous mother drove like a mad Italian, pooping the horn, swearing, and revving the engine.

After two hours shopping, they were a very happy party sitting in the shade drinking coffee at Sarah's favourite café.

Jackson and Lyall had given into the temptation of the copied designer handbags and had managed to barter for two Louis Vuitton man-bags before the local police appeared and moved the illegal vendors along.

The next day, Aggie, Jackson and Lyall spent time on the beach. After a light Saturday supper on the terrace,

Aggie declined their invitation for a walk through the Old Town. She was keen to do some initial preparations for tomorrow's lunch. There would be a party of six, as Leo, JP and Sarah were also joining them.

*

Aggie woke feeling refreshed after another dreamless sleep, grateful that she could focus on the day ahead, untired. It was going to be special.

She had pre-made a chilled, melon and ginger soup and the boys had gone off to the Sunday Menton market to buy fresh baguettes and choose a couple of cheeses. Her fish pie was made and ready to go in the oven when the guests arrived.

Aggie laid the table on the terrace, with a freshly starched and ironed white linen tablecloth and napkins. She had clipped some green ivy from the fence above the terrace and wound it around the small bowl of roses that Jackson had bought her. Aggie considered table presentation to be right up there with the quality of the food.

Under the boys' instructions, Aggie wore a perfectly fitting knee-length, chocolate-brown polka dot shift dress. She revealed a hint of cleavage and teamed it with her *chic* Charles Jordan sandals.

When she answered the door, Leo kissed her gently on both cheeks, then glanced at her exposed toes, raised his eyebrows, smiled, and returned to kiss her lips. Blushing,

Aggie ushered him out onto the terrace where the others were waiting.

Jackson went directly up to Leo and shook his hand. It appeared very welcoming, but Aggie knew this was her son's subtle way of stating that he was the number one man in Aggie's life – and Leo wasn't to mess his mother around.

When Leo offered to help bring out the food, Jackson made it quite clear he was the kitchen helper, and Lyall served the wine.

The first bottle of champagne went down well, so a second was opened before the lunch party proceeded to the excellent Bandol rosé. It was a perfect accompaniment to the chilled soup. By the time the fish pie and salad were served, the conversation had become lively.

JP made a few of his jokes; he was oblivious to the fact that the guests were roaring with laughter, not because of their content but because of the way he told them. His accent and misuse of English words sounded so funny.

Once her guests were enthusiastically tucking into the Tomme and Comté cheeses, Aggie relaxed; she leant back in her chair, her writer's eye surveying the attractive group. Jackson and Lyall looked young and fresh in their button-down linen shirts, designer shorts, and newly acquired coloured ICE watches. JP wore a slightly faded, but obviously favourite red polo shirt. Sarah, as usual, was immaculately groomed in a subtle blue and white striped dress. Then Aggie's eyes rested on Leo. Sitting down, he didn't appear short - all were of equal height at the table. He wore a navy and white striped shirt with the sleeves rolled to the elbow. He really did have a beautiful face. He caught her looking at him and winked knowingly, making a little kiss with his lips.

It was after 5pm when everyone finally left, Leo kissing Aggie passionately goodbye in the hallway, out of sight of her son.

"See that went quite well, didn't it? I think Jackson already likes me," Leo said.

"It was better for us being a larger group, and I will let you know what he really thinks when we next meet," she said coyly.

"Which will be very soon," he called out as he walked down the stairs.

Jackson and Lyall had cleared the table and all three of them were in the kitchen doing the dishes and clearing up.

"How old is he Mama?" Jackson asked first as he rinsed the wine glasses.

"Who, darling?"

"Who do you think, the Italian?"

"Oh, you mean Leo, short for Leonardo?"

"Yes, that one."

Aggie walked across to her son, took the tea towel from his hand and took both his hands in hers.

"My darling boy! He is sixty years old, unencumbered, and as far as I know, solvent and full of honourable intentions," she reassured, then kissed him on the cheek.

"For God's sake, Jacks, stop behaving like a jealous, spoiled child! Your mother is 52 years old and entitled to a lover!" Lyall said as he gave his boyfriend a hug.

Jackson laughed mischievously. "I enjoy being a spoiled only child! I'm not accustomed to competition. But if he makes you happy Mama, you have my permission."

"Surely, Jacks, you mean your blessing?" Lyall added.

*

The next morning the boys weren't due to fly out until after lunch and so they were enjoying a leisurely breakfast on the terrace while Aggie checked her emails.

"Oh look, Heritage.com has sent through the results of my DNA test; that was quick!" she said.

Jackson jumped up and stood behind Aggie so he could see her screen. It stated that full siblings can still have different percentages of origin DNA as everyone is individual and you can inherit different proportions of each parents' heritage. It showed Aggie was thirty per cent English (Viking heritage), sixty per cent Northern Italian and ten per cent European.

"I wonder if the European is French! You must talk to Grandad!" Jackson said.

"Ooh! You've always wished you were French," Lyall added, sounding momentarily very camp.

"I wonder how long my results from Dr Viner will take to come back." Aggie said, thinking aloud.

"I would imagine they carry out a series of tests, probably more comprehensive than these ones," Jackson replied, then looked at his watch. "We better pack up, it's getting on!"

Aggie had enjoyed their visit, but four days in her busy new life was long enough. She was keen to return her focus to her project and entertain impure thoughts of a short man called Leo.

NINETEEN

Leo had invited Aggie to spend Friday and the weekend with him in his apartment in Dolceacqua. Aggie sensed he was angling at dispensing with Andrea the beekeepers' services as researcher, wanting the job for himself. But Aggie wasn't going to be persuaded so easily. He may be great in bed, but historic research required someone with a broader knowledge of the families in the area. Aggie made it clear she would be happy to have some assistance from Leo but would also be meeting with Andrea. He would have to control the jealousy he felt towards the competition, she joked.

On Thursday morning Aggie opened an email from Dr Viner. It contained the DNA results, which were, as Jackson expected, a lot more comprehensive than the first set.

He said they had undertaken a deeper scan of the Italian percentage, and it could be pinpointed to the

Liguria area. They would circulate the results on a global shared database and see whether there were any matches from that region. He went on to say that his team were very excited with the progress they were making with her dreams and the breakthrough she was finding their location. He asked Aggie when she could come to America and how she felt about working with a skilled hypnotist. It was called "being regressed".

Aggie didn't reply immediately and instead Googled past-life regression but could only see courses on offer. One quote stood out. It was from a Danish philosopher called Søren Kierkegaard: "Life can only be understood backwards but it must be lived forwards."[1]

She replied to Dr Viner, thanking him, and asking him if he could give her a few days to consider this and she would come back to him.

Next, she phoned Jackson and read the email to him.

"I don't know quite what to say Mama; I agree it would be good to read some testimonials of other's experiences first. Let me have a look around online," he told her.

Aggie then sent a second email to Dr Viner asking if he was able to provide her with any testimonials. She said they could be anonymous but felt she would be more comfortable with a first party endorsement. Hypnosis sounded a little frightening.

---

[1] https://homepage.math.uiowa.edu/~jorgen/kierkegaardquotesource.html

She phoned Andrea to check his availability over the weekend. "I am glad you called Aggie; I was about to email you. Yes, I have found some family names that may be relevant." They agreed to meet on Saturday morning in Dolceacqua.

Although Leo had offered to drive through to Menton and collect Aggie, she preferred to catch the train and the butter box bus. She wanted to have a wander around the Ventimiglia market and pick up a few goodies for her stay over and was learning to love the time alone she had in this buzzy new place.

Aggie rolled a couple of dresses, a shirt, nightdress, and underwear into a large tote bag. She carefully selected an outfit suitable for travelling by bus and train, walking around the market in the heat and still arriving at her lover's place looking as fresh as ever. She tarted-up her lightweight white trousers and self-embroidered white shirt with a large amber-coloured bangle, her *chic* sun hat and large Gucci sunglasses.

Aggie was relieved it was only one stop from France to Italy as the train was packed with tourists with standing room only that day.

In Ventimiglia she discovered a comprehensive liquor shop where she bought an impressive looking bottle of Prosecco, along with some beautifully packaged chocolates. Her bag was now excessively heavy, so she walked straight to the bus station to complete the journey.

Aggie's heart skipped a beat when she spotted Leo sitting casually on a stone wall by the bus stop. He looked elegant in his pink and white finely striped shirt, beige chinos, soft leather loafers and aviator dark sunglasses. He may have been a bit short with a slight paunch, but to her he looked perfect.

"How long are you staying? This bag weighs a tonne," Leo said as he took Aggie's bag, then gently kissed her cheeks.

"'Always be prepared', is what my dad says," Aggie replied as she inhaled the familiar lime notes of his aftershave and returned his kisses.

They walked across the road from Aggie's bridge towards a large villa that sat at the edge of the central piazza. It appeared around the same age as Aggie's building in Menton - mid 1800s - and was called L'Agapantus. The creamy lemon-coloured villa stood three stories high with its tall windows framed by traditional pale blue louvred shutters. A large welcoming entrance was fronted by a stone path edged by rich lilac agapanthuses which stood as dignified as doormen for visitors walking towards the door.

"I am sorry there is no elevator, and I am on the third floor," Leo apologised, as they entered the wide chessboard-tiled entrance.

As they climbed the stairs Leo explained the local lady who owned the villa rented out the top floor as well as a couple of other rooms. The villa was built by a wealthy family in 1860 together with the small chapel next to the Ponte Vecchio - purely for the family's own use. "It was a statement of wealth - very *nouveau riche* back then," he chuckled.

They were both slightly breathless when they arrived at Leo's door but the apartment, she saw, was stunning. Leo immediately led her through to the main salon and pushed open the shutters.

A surge of electricity shot down Aggie's spine. There was her bridge in view of the window, perfectly framed by the rich blue, gold-fringed drapes. The river below danced with light as the midday sun lightly kissed it with its soft rays.

"I have been gazing out at this magnificent bridge every morning for the past month, and what magic spell it casts!" Leo declared as he faced Aggie and took both of her hands in his.

"Tell me about the magic," Aggie replied softly, savouring the tenderness of his touch.

"This bridge sent me an angel called Agatha who's known as Aggie."

If Aggie had known how to 'swoon', a superficial term she regularly used in her novels, she would have triple-swooned on the spot. This Italian was good – he might even be the smoothest man she'd ever met. But it felt genuine with him.

Leo showed her around the apartment; it had two large bedrooms, a bathroom with a large spa bath and a spiral staircase leading up to the space under the roof that the owners had developed into a studio. The table was neatly set for lunch in the small kitchen.

"I thought we would just have a light lunch here and go out for dinner tonight if that works for you?" Leo said as he opened the fridge door.

He took out a carefully prepared plate of thinly-sliced ham, a slab of cheese and gherkins, and placed them on the table alongside a fresh loaf of bread.

Aggie nodded with a smile when he offered her a glass of white wine. Once Leo was seated, he lifted his glass in salute.

"Here's to Aggie's first sleepover in Dolceacqua!"

The crisp white Vermentino slipped enjoyably across Aggie's tongue, offering an easy warmth to the simple lunch.

"You call it the Ponte Vecchio, I call it 'my bridge' but does it have an actual name?" Aggie asked.

"Ponte Vecchio just means old bridge in Italian and that's the only name I have ever heard it called. From now on I think we shall call it 'Aggie's Bridge'!" Leo smiled, popping a gherkin into his mouth.

"Now, I thought we would do a tour of the old town this afternoon, what do you think?"

"Yes please!" Aggie answered, returning his smile.

They crossed Aggie's bridge hand-in-hand, pausing at the top and Leo pulled out his phone.

"This is the famous place where local couples stand on their wedding day to have their photo taken; it's become known as a 'lucky-in-love' place." He put one arm around

Aggie and stretched the other one out as far as he could to capture the selfie.

"I'm not sure I believe you, and besides you barely have any of the bridge in the photo," Aggie said, laughing at what she thought a passerby would think of this slightly dumpy middle-aged couple taking a selfie.

Leo kissed her lips, then took her hand as they walked through the entrance to the mediaeval village.

An uncanny feeling of familiarity swept through Aggie as she took her first steps into the ancient, cobbled streets of the old town. She allowed the sensation to buoy her, becoming entranced by the sounds and smells that the village offered. Intimate courtyards afforded outdoor space to tiny stone houses. Large terracotta pots with plants sat beside an array of coloured doorways; drying clothes flitted outside windows, hinting to the characters that lived inside. It was a maze of stone and shadow.

Leo explained that this side of the river was known as 'Terra' and the other side, the modern part, known as 'Borgo'. He spoke knowledgeably of Dolceacqua's history as they wandered, poking around in the small artisan shops. Aggie purchased a small pencil sketch of the Ponte Vecchio from an over-enthusiastic vendor who conversed in rapid Italian with Leo.

After a steep climb, they came to what seemed to be the end of the main street and to the apex of the village - the Doria Castle ruins.

The then Count of Ventimiglia built the first part of the castle in the 12th century. Substantial fortifications were added in the 14th century. The castle was a comfortable residence during the Renaissance. It was damaged in the 18th century in The Wars Of Succession and again by an earthquake in 1887. The Castle and Dolceacqua were under French occupation from 1797 'till 1814 when the French province of Nice was partitioned. Leo spoke and Aggie listened, emitting an involuntary shudder.

"Are you cold?" Leo asked as he put his arm around her.

"No, I'm not cold, just experienced a spooky feeling as I looked up at the castle; it was as if someone just walked over my grave."

"Shall we leave the tour of the ruins until tomorrow?" Leo asked, still with his arm around her.

"Yes, that suits me. I am meeting Andrea for coffee in the morning. So perhaps tomorrow afternoon?"

Leo dropped his arm. His facial expression almost caused Aggie to laugh. He was going to trip over on his lower lip if he drooped it any further.

"Oh Leo! He has some information for me! It's only a chat over coffee, I assumed you would be joining us. Don't be jealous, it's your bed I am staying in."

Leo mumbled something in Italian that Aggie couldn't understand and stared down at his shoes with a shamed schoolboy expression.

They had walked about halfway back down the street when Leo stopped and cleared his throat.

"I guess I wouldn't have met you if you hadn't been visiting the beekeeper, so I should be grateful to him."

He then shook his shoulders as if trying to shrug off the moment of jealousy. Aggie was flattered in one way, but it planted a seed of caution in her thoughts.

Early in the evening the piazza of Dolceacqua was bustling with mamas shopping and chatting, children running around or riding scooters and bikes. Older men sat along the stone wall gossiping; more sophisticated younger people had taken the café seats and were sipping aperitivos and snacking on small bowls of crisps and pretzels.

"What is that orange coloured drink those people are drinking?" Aggie asked as they sat down at an outdoor table in the small bar by the fountain.

"Would you like to try one?" Leo said as he motioned the waiter. "It is called an Aperol spritz and is a cocktail of Aperol, prosecco and soda water; the secret to its success is a slice of fresh orange which gives it a citrus zing."

When the drinks arrived, Leo raised his glass to Aggie and she sipped her aperitivo, studying her lover with a fresh set of eyes. She hadn't figured jealousy as a barrier to a relationship in her fifties. Leo must have been able to read her thoughts.

"Aggie, I am sorry for my overreaction today over Andrea. I am sad to say that I am the jealous type, and as he is younger and slimmer than me, the old-school Italian pride overcame me," he said as his fingers stroked hers across the table.

Aggie smiled, allowing a few moments to pass before she replied. "In a way I am flattered, as, in case you hadn't noticed, I am middle-aged and a little overweight myself and I am sure there will be things about me that may grate on you as well over time."

This blip in their day soon passed as they moved across the piazza to the ristorante Leo had booked for dinner. The sun had set, the mamas had taken their boisterous children home, candles flickered on rustic tables as the soft sound of a classical guitarist playing in the corner established a perfect ambience for romance.

Aggie was happy for Leo to order for her, it seemed a subtle way to help boost his confidence. For the starter he chose a selection of antipasti to share, and after first checking with Aggie, he ordered milk-fed baby lamb, roasted in garlic and rosemary, and accompanied by sautéed potatoes.

The highlight of the antipasti was the stuffed courgette flowers. They had been delicately filled with a mixture of minced meat, rolled in a bouquet of Italian herbs and breadcrumbs, being lightly fried in the pan.

"Oh, my goodness! How divine, I have never tasted these before!" Aggie exclaimed. Both the waitress, who was the wife of the chef, and Leo beamed with pride.

"One day soon I will make you my own version," Leo added.

The lamb tasted like no other Aggie had ever eaten. Pastel pink, instead of a rich red meat, the lamb had only ever been fed milk, which explained why the taste was so delicate. However, she did experience a pang of conscience for the short life of the animal. The guilt soon vanished as she washed down the second mouthful with a sip of Rossese, the local specialty which seemed to match everything in this dream-like village.

After dinner they agreed on a short walk to allow their food to digest and crossed the river via the short bridge off the main road where they sat in the cobbled area in front of the Santa Antonia Church, looking back at the piazza and the hills beyond.

Maybe it was the bottle of wine or the liberal glass of limoncello with which they had finished the meal, but they could suddenly both feel romance in the air. A full moon had appeared in the sky and the sweet scent of frangipan wafted down from the nearby wall where it had intertwined with the ivy.

Leo took Aggie's hand and brushed it with his lips. "Aggie, my darling, someone famous, I can't remember who, once said: 'luce intellettüal, piena d'amore[2], which expresses how I feel at this exact moment here with you."

Aggie figured the limoncello had really got to him as he'd forgotten she didn't speak Italian, but then he added: "Light of mind, full of love!" and kissed her passionately.

---

[2] http://dantelab.dartmouth.edu/reader?reader%5Bcantica%5D=3&reader%5Bcanto%5D=30 - Translation Light intellectual replete with love

"I realise I am a bit tipsy, but I really want to make love to you. It's just whether we can make our way up all those stairs without doing too much damage to ourselves!" he smiled.

*

Daylight was streaming through Leo's windows when Aggie woke and realised there had been absolutely no action the previous night.

The bed was empty, and she could hear the splash of the shower. She desperately needed to pee and was relieved when Leo swiftly wrapped the towel around himself and provided her with the privacy of the bathroom.

"That spa bath looks enticing!" Aggie commented, as he gave her a damply clean hug.

"Let me fill it for my princess," he said as he turned the taps on. He added some lavender oil and a drop of bubble bath.

Aggie lowered herself into the deep wide bath of fragrance and froth and then found Leo directly behind her.

"I am not sure there is room for two!" Aggie commented.

"We will snuggle up close, and I will be here to wash your back," Leo responded, as he slid in the bath, facing her.

Leaning forward to kiss her with his freshly-cleaned teeth Aggie felt at a disadvantage but it clearly didn't bother him. As they kissed, she could feel his excitement beneath the bubbles. Things became very active; stroking her breasts, he leant forward a bit too far and Aggie slipped down in the bath almost going completely under the water. They were laughing so much they could barely manage to get out of the tub. Once they were on their feet, safely wrapped in large white fluffy towels, Leo led her briskly back to the bedroom. He hurriedly closed the shutters and straightened the sheets.

"Now let me rub some of this lavender body cream on your back," he said.

In the sober morning light, Aggie was relieved to be able to lie face down, her back and bottom had not yet experienced any of the ravages of cellulite. Leo gently rubbed the fragrant cream onto her back, then moved down around her buttocks. It was all she could take, she turned over and pulled him toward her. The sexual harmony between them eclipsed any of Aggie's inhibitions. They made delicious love with the fervour of a couple decades younger.

They were both wearing the same loved-up look when they sat down with Andrea at the café. Leo took the chair closest to Aggie, then gently brushed against her arm in an obvious motion of ownership.

Andrea had done a search of births, marriages and deaths in the local church registry, and it looked as if he had located Aggie's great grandparents' marriage certificate. They were Sofia and Claudio Balbo, he told her. Her grandmother's birth certificate showed she was Vera Balbo. He handed her copies of what he had found.

This was great news, as now Aggie was sure of her mother's heritage for the first time.

Aggie explained briefly to both men about her dreams, and the research that was to be undertaken. Nothing more than Leo already knew - she knew better than to reveal any new facts in front of Andrea. Before he left, Andrea reaffirmed he was pleased to help in any way. Aggie thanked him and said she would get back in touch when she had moved forward with the project.

Leo and Aggie wandered over to the Saturday morning market; they leisurely chose from an array of appealing foods that the locals offered. After gathering a selection of salami, stuffed olives, sun dried tomatoes, cheese, and a loaf of fresh bread they made their way back to the apartment.

Leo brought two chairs from the kitchen and placed them on either side of the small table that sat in front of the window overlooking Aggie's bridge. Aggie sliced the bread and they placed what they wanted on their plates and sat down looking out at the river and the bridge beyond.

Leo took a closer look at the papers that Andrea had given Aggie. "I see there is an address for the house your great grandparents most likely lived in when they registered your grandmothers' birth. I don't recognize it, but we can look on Google maps and go and have a look this afternoon if you want?"

"That would be great, but we better be a bit careful as maybe there are some of my family still living there; you never know what skeletons are in family closets and who may or may not be welcoming," Aggie said, nervous.

Leo raised his eyebrows.

"Well, consider that my grandmother left this rural part of Italy nearly eighty years ago to go to England, which would have been a big deal for a young Italian woman back then. Who knows why? I think I should cautiously feel my way, to begin with," Aggie said, offering a smile. "Just in case," she added.

TWENTY

"Leo, I would like to tell you more about my dreams, the journey I am on, and the book I am hoping to write about them, if you feel it's something you still want to hear about," Aggie said as they sat sipping their espresso after lunch.

"I want to know everything," he replied as he squeezed her hand.

Aggie told him more about her mother; how she had always felt she had been deserted by her; how this had affected her own self-worth. But now, after all these new discoveries of her mother's mental illness and having been given the sketches with the notes describing how much her mother had loved her, her feelings had changed from a deep anger and disappointment to compassion and love.

"My mother left us because she was very aware of how unstable she was; she believed for me to have one sane, stable parent was so much better than being drawn into her mixed-up world," she said as a single tear rolled down Aggie's cheek. "When I saw her sketches, I immediately recognised my dreams - they were her dreams too. Not the same but her drawings of her dreams are definitely of Dolceacqua, too."

Aggie then told Leo about Dr Viner and the US research program and that she would be going over there soon.

"I haven't finally decided about being regressed through hypnotism; I have asked if they could share with me the testimony of someone who has already experienced it."

She let out a big sigh and stood up but Leo was immediately beside her. He took her in his arms.

"Whatever it takes, I am here for you," he said.

Leo pulled up the map of Dolceacqua on his phone and typed in the address. "The house your relatives might have lived at – or might still live at – is just across the river in the Old Town," he said.

It felt very familiar now, walking across the Ponte Vecchio. It had taken months of struggling with her dreams to reach this point, so far away from Bayswater in London and her regular life with Jackson and Tabatha Heart. This bridge was the key to her family's past, a past that would play a key role in her future.

The address was very easy to find; it was located just within the walls of the village and now operates as a B&B called Le Gemme.

"Shall we knock at the door?" Aggie asked, her skin prickling all over.

"It's not as if it's a private home; we can book in if we have too!" Leo said as they walked up the steps to the entrance. He pulled at the small iron bell which gave out an indelicate clunk, reverberating around the stone wall surroundings.

The door was opened by an attractive, middle-aged blonde and Aggie was immediately put at ease when the woman offered a big smile and ushered them into the small entrance hall. Leo explained in Italian who he was, and that they believed this house used to be in Aggie's family. The woman switched to speaking English and introduced herself as Bettina.

She had owned the house for twenty years; the woman she had bought it from was called Nonna Rosa and as far as the new owner knew, Nonna Rosa was still alive.

"Nonna Rosa must be in her late nineties now," she said using the Italian word for 'grandma'.

Aggie could feel her heart beating, maybe this old woman was a great aunt of hers? But before she could ask a question, Leo was already talking.

"Would it be at all possible for us to have a look around? Apart from Aggie's possible family connection, I have friends coming from America to visit soon who would adore to stay in such a beautiful house," he said, offering Bettina one of his most charming smiles.

"Yes, it would be my pleasure; three of the rooms are vacant as the guests are not due till late afternoon. Follow me!" she replied.

As she turned, Aggie flicked Leo's leg and scrunched her face at him. "You are such a liar!" she whispered.

"Yes, but it worked!" he grinned.

The house was built in the 14th century and had very low ceilings, steep stairs, and no bannisters. It was beautifully decorated - almost curated, Aggie thought, describing everything as always as she would in a novel. Bettina was clearly very proud of the place. She had strategically placed smaller beautiful antique pieces, so they didn't clutter the smallish rooms and clearly had an eye for it. The walls were adorned with paintings of contemporary scenes of the surrounding area as well as old sepia-tone photographs of local interest that had been upcycled in ornate gilded frames.

The first room they stepped into had rendered walls painted white, a double bed with a puffed-up old-fashioned eiderdown and cushions, which looked so deliciously comfy. All the furnishings had a splash of pale Wedgewood blue. The second room was similarly decorated, but with a lemon-coloured theme running through the furnishings.

"Are you up for another flight of stairs?" Bettina asked. "Because I promise you our top room is worth the climb!"

They both nodded and followed her upwards, Aggie keeping one hand on the wall for balance and pleased Leo was behind her - just in case.

"I tried to keep this room in as similar a style as it would have been a hundred years ago," Bettina commented as she opened the very low door. She walked ahead and briskly threw open the rustic wooden shutters.

Being in the room, Aggie felt the now familiar shock overcome her and felt as faint as she had in Sarah's car. Her brow dampened and Leo noticed immediately the change in her demeanour.

"Aggie, here, sit down, darling," he said, guiding her to a chair.

"Oh no, were the stairs too much?" Bettina asked.

Aggie, concentrating on just breathing, eventually managed to speak.

"I am so sorry - I didn't mean to scare you. No it wasn't the stairs. It's just - I have been in this room before."

The owner looked puzzled, assuming she hadn't grasped Aggie's English correctly. She'd fetch her some water, she said, expecting her to be more coherent after that.

Leo knelt beside Aggie. "Tell me!" was all he said.

"I am assuming these stone walls have been left exposed as they would have been a hundred years ago. The fireplace still has the iron grate and those implements to stoke the fire. I have seen them all before! I visited this room in one of my dreams. It was winter and the fire was lit and there was a man sitting at a table," Aggie clenched her fists and pressed them to her mouth. "The bed wasn't in here but Leo, I can almost smell the same woody scent I experienced in my dream," Aggie mumbled, then stood up, suddenly desperate to look around the room and out of the window she'd seen so many times before through somebody else's eyes.

"Do you feel frightened, my darling?" Leo asked protectively, putting his arm around her shoulders.

"No, no, not frightened; it's a weird feeling, like what I experienced when I first saw the bridge. It's like a shock that whatever is happening in my brain, in my memories, is real and now proved. I am confident I am following the right path by searching for the meaning of all this."

Bettina returned with a glass of water. Aggie didn't wish to expand on what had just happened to a stranger and so took the glass and drank, then asked if it was okay to take a few photos.

Once they reached the door, Leo took the same initiative he'd displayed downstairs.

"Bettina, you have been very generous to show us around and I know my American friends will love it here. I will ask them to be in touch and in the meantime do you think the old lady, Nonna Rosa, would agree to meet with Aggie, as it looks like she could be a distant relative?"

"Well, I am not sure if she still lives with her niece, but I will write down the name and number and you can phone and ask," Bettina replied as she walked to a set of drawers and pulled out a small, well-used address book.

Aggie was lost in her thoughts as they wandered back across the bridge. Leo guided her to a café in a quiet corner of the square.

"Thank you, Leo, you handled me very well then," Aggie said as she sipped green tea from the porcelain pot Leo had ordered.

"Apart from a bit of a blip yesterday, we seem to have a real affinity. It was very apparent that the sudden reaction you experienced when we walked into that ancient room was something otherworldly, almost supernatural," he said, staring intently at Aggie.

"It's more than that, to me. It's as if it's always been there, nestled in my brain somewhere. I have now read pages and pages of opinions and research on this subject, as well as seeing my mothers' sketches. I do believe these are memories stored in me, in my DNA. What I don't understand is, why they are surfacing now, and what I should be doing with them."

Leo listened intently.

Aggie was so relieved he didn't think she had a screw loose like people less open and knowledgeable about the now-developed science had assumed of her mother.

They went home, and at dusk once they were dressed for dinner, Leo liberally sprayed Aggie's legs and arms with pleasant, scented mosquito spray.

"Exactly where are we eating? Are we going into a forest?" Aggie was fascinated.

"No, not a forest but somewhere very close to a stream that leads to the river, where the little blood thirsty mozzies cruise in the evening."

After a mystery walk alongside the river and across the small bridge on to the Terra side of the village. Leo had booked an outdoor table in a tiny restaurant that was in fact the ground floor and garden of the owner's house. Their table was under a large olive tree with tealight candles flickering all around its ancient trunk. The table was draped with a vintage damask, self-embroidered tablecloth in an old gold; mismatched, gleaming cutlery and heavy crystal glasses adorned the rest of it. A small glass jar of delicate field flowers sat in the middle of each of the five tables.

"This is so beautiful, Leo!" Aggie exclaimed as she reached across their table to squeeze his hand.

"I am so pleased you like it. I have never been here before but I came across it when out taking an evening stroll when I first arrived and figured it was too romantic a location to eat at alone. It's Dolceacqua's best kept secret - only for those who belong here!" He leant over and brushed her lips with his then whispered. "Just like us - we belong here."

They ordered and ate in a daze of affection, but Aggie was focused on the main course of crumbed-veal served with sweet courgette that was beyond anything she'd ever imagined in taste. As she savoured it an elderly man with an ample grey moustache and ancient dark brown eyes appeared with a violin. As his first shaky notes were drawn out from the ancient, worn instrument, a silence embraced the restaurant. Aggie's first thought was that it was going to be a musical disaster, but she was blown away when he played a few more notes and came into his stride. The sound emanating from the violin, on this perfectly calm evening under a half-moon surrounded by the twinkling tea lights, was the most beautiful Aggie had ever heard. Tears welled in her eyes. The pitch, and the soar of the bow on the strings was pure and clear, and somehow, she recognised the tune.

When he finished, all five tables erupted into applause and "bravos". The old man beamed beneath his bushy moustache, took a little bow, and returned to the house.

The waiter offered Aggie and Leo a glass of grappa, which they graciously accepted, then he went on to explain the old man was his 89-year-old grandfather who, as a young man, was an acclaimed virtuosa and had gained a place at the Florence College of Music only to turn it down in favour of staying in Dolceacqua and supporting his family after WW2.

"Things were very difficult here directly after the occupation; the people of this valley had resisted both Mussolini and Hitler. They were very active in the resistance and suffered dire consequences," Leo said.

"I think that's when my own grandmother went to the UK to get work. If she was alive, I think she would now be nearly 90," Aggie replied. "This must be high in alcohol; I feel a warm glow from head to toe," she added.

"Hold that thought! I am going to pay the bill and we will go home," Leo said, taking his wallet out and heading into the house to pay.

Aggie felt as if she was awake in her own dream as they walked back to the apartment on the cobbled street under the golden glow of the half-moon, accompanied by the inner glow from the grappa.

That night Leo made slow passionate love to her with the window open so they would feel the magic of the moon. Afterwards, as they lay holding hands, he turned to her and said: "Us meeting has been like two small stars colliding and knowing they were always destined to become a constellation." Then, he closed his eyes and began to snore.

Aggie pushed him gently onto his side and closed her eyes.

*

She immediately knew where she was but it took a few moments to understand it wasn't quite real. The bed was gone, there were no electric lights. A glass table lamp of some kind offered some light to the dimly lit room. She was sitting in a tatty armchair next to the fire. Aggie got up and walked over to a cracked mirror that hung by a clothes rack; she was the young girl with black hair again; this time it was pulled back in a chignon at the nape of her neck. She studied her new face for a while then went back to the chair. It was an odd feeling, like being a voyeur, a ghost from the future. Her hand rested on her tummy. A faint sound of music began to waft into the smokey room. Aggie got up out of the chair and smiled as she walked to the window. She threw open the battered shutters and allowed a melody drifting in the air outside to fill the room.

Aggie gasped! She immediately recognised the violin melody. She could also now see she was heavily pregnant, and her eyes were wet with tears.

The fear shot through Aggie's being.

"Aggie, Aggie wake up! It's okay, it's only a bad dream!" Leo's voice was somewhere in the background.

Aggie opened her eyes. Tears poured down her cheeks as she sat up, confused. After a few moments of orientation, she wiped her eyes.

"Wow, that was spooky! I know it was a dream as I am awake now, but it was so real."

"Why were you crying?" Leo asked, as he put his arms around her.

"I can't say for sure, but there was a very young pregnant woman up in that room we were in today; It was as if I was her; I was so sad. Then the same music we heard this evening came wafting up from the street; it seemed to comfort me; then as it played on, I began to sob and hold my stomach"

Aggie looked up, there was sunlight peeking through the edge of the curtains.

"Is it morning?"

"Yes, my darling it's around 7am," Leo replied, then got up and went to the kitchen to make coffee.

Aggie took out her small diary and wrote down her notes about the dream. Leo didn't say much. Aggie could feel he was doing his best to be supportive, but it was a very strange situation.

A period of six months had passed now since she experienced her first disturbing dream. It was, of necessity, a solo journey; she could only go through it alone. Those close to her had to have blind faith and be her supporting cast.

Leo attempted to persuade Aggie to stay another night, but she really wanted to get back to her own place and take stock of all she had experienced in the past two days. She agreed to him driving her back to Menton. He was very sensitive to her change of mood. Once they pulled up in front of her building, he undid his seat belt and took both her hands in his.

"Darling, say no if it's not what you want, but perhaps I could follow up on locating Nonna Rosa and see if you can chat to her. Also, the old violinist with the big moustache may be able to offer some information?"

"Oh Leo, thank you! Yes please, that would be wonderful."

She leant forward and kissed him as passionately as she could muster, then stood waving until his car was out of sight.

TWENTY-ONE

Aggie hadn't opened any emails for the two days she had been in Dolceacqua. Amongst a lot of junk mail, she spotted one from Dr Viner and, unusually, one from her father which she opened first.

Aggie inhaled, her father was telling her he had experienced some pain in his arm, and went to the doctor who had sent him straight to the hospital for heart monitoring. They had diagnosed angina and that his heart was "weary". He would need to rest and have regular checkups. He hadn't phoned because he didn't wish to panic her. His partner Barbara was staying with him, and he would call Aggie if things got any worse. The email had been sent on Friday afternoon; today was Monday. Aggie felt sick.

She phoned her father's landline, but it went straight to voicemail, so she phoned his mobile. It rang for quite some time then was answered by a female voice.

"Hello Aggie, this is Barbara. I am sorry, but about an hour ago I had to call an ambulance as your dad was in distress. I had just found his mobile in his jacket pocket and was scrolling through to find your number; thank goodness you have called." Her voice was on the verge of breaking. Aggie was dumbstruck. "Aggie, Aggie are you there?"

Finally, Aggie could speak. "Yes, I'm here. I'm sorry, I am just so shocked; I never knew he had a bad heart; is he conscious?"

"Yes, he is, and he knew I would be calling you. He told me to tell you not to come back. But in my opinion, if he were my dad, I would say "best you come soon."

Aggie went straight into organisational mode; she went online and purchased a seat on the last flight out from Nice at 8pm, then called Jackson to tell him the news. He said he would be at the airport to meet her, and the spare room was all made up. Then she phoned Leo, who offered to drive her to the airport. Aggie thanked him but declined. She didn't wish to add any more emotion into the situation. She knocked at Sarah's door and asked if she would mind booking the taxi service for her as Aggie's French was still a little shaky. Sarah immediately said how sorry she was, adding: "I am sure he will be okay," at which point Aggie burst into tears. Sarah guided her into her kitchen and made her a strong cup of tea.

By 9pm UK time that night she was walking through the arrival gates at Heathrow into the arms of her tall, strong son. They both promptly burst into tears. Jackson took her small case, and they made their way to where the Heathrow Express departed; after a twenty-minute train ride they pulled into Paddington Station.

"Let's not get a cab son, I would like to walk if that's okay," Aggie said as they took the Praed Street exit from the station and walked towards Connaught Village, then out onto Bayswater Road.

The hum of London traffic, and the sight of red buses and black cabs offered a sense of familiarity and comfort to Aggie as they walked beside the park.

"I will go to the hospital first thing in the morning; it's a bit of a trip out to Chase Farm Hospital but the tube will probably be the quickest route."

"I shall come with you Mum," Jackson said.

"No darling, I feel it's best I go for the first time on my own to see what's what and, from what Barbara said when we chatted this afternoon, he mustn't have any stress or excitement."

Aggie felt a little odd arriving at her own home and taking her things into the spare room. The apartment was immaculate, and Jackson had lit a scented candle and placed it beside the bed - he was such a thoughtful man. Lyall was away on a course for work, which suited Aggie as she had her precious son all to herself.

In the morning, Jackson appeared beside Aggie's bed with coffee in her favourite cup on a small tray. "Now Mum, are you sure you will be alright going to the hospital on your own?"

"Darling, thank you I will, and Barbara will be there. I don't know her that well, but she and Dad have become very close."

"Well, I will get off to work then! Please keep me posted as soon as you have seen him."

Aggie inhaled Jackson's delicate cologne as he kissed her cheek.

On arrival at the hospital the only entry option was the tall revolving door, not a process she enjoyed. She experienced a sense of dread as the moving door slowly pushed her into the hospital entrance. A cleaner immediately placed a yellow floor sign in front of her, while he fervently mopped the linoleum floor; the heavy pine scent followed her all the way to the lifts.

Once she had arrived on the fifth floor, she sanitised her hands then pressed the button which opened the door to the ward.

A mature nurse void of any expression greeted her and led her through to her father's cubicle. He lay very still in the bed, his face was ashen, blending with the sheets that encased him. His body was hooked up with various wires that led to a bank of screens on one side of his bed. On the other side, Barbara had dozed off in the chair. She woke with a jolt, her normally immaculate grey bob a little dishevelled and her lips without the rich red lipstick she had worn on the two other occasions Aggie had met her.

"Oh, Aggie! Sorry, I must have dozed off. I am so glad you are here."

She stood up, walked over to Aggie, and hugged her. That was just enough to set her off; tears streamed down Aggie's face.

Both women moved into the hall.

"Thank you, Barbara, I am so grateful! Sorry I am crying, it's a shock," Aggie whispered.

"Of course, it is, and for me as well, but I have had a bit longer to adapt." She squeezed Aggie's hand then added: "I need to go and freshen up and grab some breakfast in the canteen, so you sit with your dad. He is waking intermittently."

She went back into the room to collect her purse and left. Aggie stared down at her sleeping father. For so long he had been all she had - a solo father was a bit of an oddity back then. She had never known him to have any girlfriends; Aggie had been his total focus. He looked so much older today; there were dark grey half-moons under his eyes. He coughed, then opened his eyes. After a few confused seconds his eyes rested on Aggie. He slowly lifted his hand and pulled down his mask, revealing blue tinged lips.

"My darling Agatha, please come closer!"

Aggie sat up on the bed and took his hand. "Dad, please don't call me Agatha, you only call me that when it's serious. I know you will get through this and get well," Aggie said, struggling to hold back the tears.

Her father managed a smile: "I hope so, but I have to say, it's pretty scary not being able to breathe."

Aggie took turns with Barbara throughout the day sitting with her father. He seemed to rally. He sat up and ate some soup. They had to leave the room at times to allow the staff to deal with him, so they grabbed a quick lunch in the hospital café.

"When your dad had his first lot of pain last week, he debated whether to call you or not. I didn't feel it was my place to interfere, but I am so pleased he emailed you. He pulled a big box out from under the bed and spent Saturday morning rummaging through it. He said if anything happened to him to make sure you take a look," Barbara said in between mouthfuls of the limp salad they were sharing with their salmon sandwiches.

"That's strange! When I was a teenager, I used to poke around when he was out, looking for clues about Mum; he must have had it well hidden!" Aggie replied.

"It may just be birth certificates and documents; I don't think it's anything to be concerned about," Barbara said as they left the café.

"Please Aggie, go home now! I will still be here tomorrow morning. Have some supper with my grandson and a good night's rest. Barbara will be back for a couple of hours this evening," Aggie's dad said as he held her hand.

"She is a good woman; you lucked out there!" Aggie smiled.

"Yes, and I may even marry her once I get out of this bloody place!"

Rather reluctantly, Aggie kissed her father goodbye then navigated her way out through the revolving doors to a waiting cab to take her home.

On arrival at the apartment a delicious aroma beckoned her to the kitchen. Jackson stood resplendent in one of her aprons at the bench, he had the whole cooking thing going on.

"Dad seemed to get better as the day progressed, he had a light lunch and sat up without his oxygen attached. He even said he might ask Barbara to marry him!" Aggie told Jackson as they sat at the table enjoying lasagna and salad.

"That's great news!"

Then, to take his mother's mind off her father, Jackson asked: "How is the research going into your dreams?"

He raised his eyebrows and smiled. Jackson was enthralled as Aggie updated him on the visit to her historic Dolceacqua house, how Leo had ingratiated himself into playing a role in the research and what a beautiful town Dolceacqua was.

"So, is this Leo a bit pushy then?" Jackson asked.

"I know where you are coming from, son!" Aggie said, narrowing her eyes. "But no, he was very subtle, he stood back and only stepped in as a support mechanism, then gently offered his help."

Later, Aggie drifted off to sleep in the spare room, heartened at what she felt was her father's recovery and with warm thoughts of her loving son.

The next morning, she arrived at the hospital at 9am; Barbara was standing at the door to the ward. The grief on her face said it all. "Oh my God what's happened?" Aggie cried out.

"He's gone!" Was all Barbara could get out.

"Gone? Gone where?"

"Aggie, your dad died an hour ago! I have been trying to call you, but you must have been on the tube, underground, no signal."

Aggie glanced at her phone; the sound was turned off.

She shuddered; her entire body shook as the shock set in. How could he be dead, when 24 hours ago he took his oxygen mask off, sat up and ate soup and said he was going to marry again? Aggie could not cope. The next few hours were a blur. Then it seemed as if Jackson just appeared at her side.

"Barbara called me Mum; it's okay I will deal with everything. I am going to take you home now in an Uber." He placed his arm around Aggie and gently guided her to the cab.

Over the next few days, Jackson dealt with everything, he liaised with Barbara who informed him which undertakers Aggie's father had specified, the old man had thought of everything which made it easier for both women.

Three days passed before Aggie began to see through the fog of her grief. She realised she hadn't communicated with Leo or Sarah; in fact, she hadn't looked at any emails or phone texts. There were three texts from Leo and two from Sarah. She texted Sarah a quick update, then Leo and said she would call him soon. Next, she opened her laptop to a deluge of emails. She noted one from someone in the USA, titled 'My Regression Experience' and one from Leo. She would deal with those later. Many were from long term friends who had seen the death notice in the Daily Telegraph newspaper. After she had sent as many responses as she could muster, she called Leo.

"My darling, I am so sorry you lost your Dad. I nearly jumped on a plane to be with you but then decided better of it, I am sure you have a lot of support from Jackson. I can come for the funeral if you wish?"

"Thank you, I appreciate the offer, but no, I will be okay; Dad only wanted close family and friends, absolutely no fuss. I am going over to his place tomorrow to start sorting everything, then after the funeral next week I will fly back to France."

Aggie was very taken by the delicate way Leo spoke to her; his words offered her comfort. He mentioned the email, it was to do with her research but could wait until she returned. Everything else felt different now.

TWENTY-TWO

Aggie's father had been a very organised man but clearing the house that he had lived in for over fifty-two years was a massive task. Jackson had already taken a lot of time off from work, so Aggie was relieved and felt it entirely appropriate that Barbara had offered to help.

Her father's will contained no surprises: the house was to be sold and everything would go to Aggie apart from two gifts of ten thousand pounds to Jackson and Barbara.

"Oh, Aggie! I am so embarrassed about this; it isn't necessary; I am financially okay; please let's give it to Jackson," Barbara said when Aggie informed her.

"No, my dad loved you; one of the last things he said to me was that he was going to marry you and knowing him the way I did, he would have put a lot of thought into this," Aggie replied.

Barbara took a fresh white cotton hanky from her sleeve and dabbed her eyes.

The women were at the house; they had made a plan of attack, agreeing they would commence in the kitchen, working together then go room by room. Aggie put the kettle on; in the absence of a coffee machine, instant coffee was not an option for Aggie. Barbara retrieved the old tea pot from the place it had been housed for at least the past 40 years and they nostalgically sat chatting while the PG tips brewed.

"What about that box you told me about?" Aggie asked.

"I thought we were working room by room?" Barbara replied.

"Well, plans are meant to be changed; I will go get it," Aggie said as she went into her dad's bedroom.

She placed the box on the table and proceeded to go through the documents. As suspected, there were all the relevant certificates - Aggie's birth certificate, her father's parents' birth, marriage and death certificates, then surprisingly her mother's birth certificate and what appeared to be a copy of her mother's parents' marriage certificate - Vera Balbo to Jack Black. That may prove useful in her research!

Then, at the bottom of the box was a small jewellery box with a handwritten note wrapped around it, secured with a rubber band.

"I'm pretty sure your father only wrote that last week," Barbara said.

Aggie carefully took the band off, unfolded the paper and smoothed it out.

Dear Aggie, if you are reading this then I am most likely no longer with you. I harbour some guilt that I didn't give this to you earlier, but it was the only piece of your mother that I had wholly to myself. I loved her with all my heart. She was wearing this when I met her, she never took it off. When she left us, it was sitting in this box on the table on my side of the bed. I didn't want to consider what that meant, but deep down I knew she no longer felt she had control of anything. I believe it was her great grandmother's and I am not sure what it symbolises. If you can trace its origin it may help your research on the lost memories you and your mother have suffered from. Dearest Agatha, I may not have been the most demonstrative father, but I must tell you, your mother gave me the greatest gift I could ever have - you are the best thing that has ever happened to me.

My love to you always and forever.
Dad xxxx

Aggie wiped her eyes with the back of her hand, grabbed a tissue, blew her nose, and handed the note to Barbara.

"No Aggie, it's not my place to read this."

"I would like you to, I feel we are in this together; many years ago he loved my mother, and now I am so grateful he found love again with you."

The pendant was a very small delicate silver cross with a loop at the top; Aggie was pretty sure it was called an "ank", but it wasn't anything she recognised.

It took three full days to empty the house, Aggie kept very little. She took a box of photos, the certificates, and the pendant.

Although Aggie's sorrow hovered very close to the surface, the funeral offered her a sense of completion. The haze lifted and the grief shifted.

At the lawyer's suggestion she had given Jackson power of attorney to deal with the house sale.

Then it was time for her to return to France.

She was doing the last of her packing when the doorbell rang. Assuming it was probably more flowers being delivered she opened the door without checking through the peephole.

"I understand you are grieved Aggie, but we have some unfinished business to discuss," Penny said as she pushed past Aggie and strode towards the sitting room.

Aggie was aghast! She followed in Penny's wake. The woman was on a mission. Her narcissistic oratory went into full flow.

"How dare you ignore all my emails and calls! How dare you not honour our contract! You are taking the food from my mouth! You are contracted to write four books a year for Random Publishing! All I have done for you, and this is how you treat me! Agree now, to stop this nonsense or I will sue you!"

Aggie found her voice. "All you have done for me! What about all the money I have made for you, you ungrateful cow! This is my life! Sue me!"

The agent's face boiled into a mottled shade of red.

"You bitch! Look at you, you may have lost a bit of weight and flickered your hair about, but you are still the dumpy frump you have always been. I've a good mind to slap your ugly fat face!"

She stepped forward towards Aggie, then stopped in her tracks as Jackson shot into the room holding his phone. He walked directly up to Penny, wielded his hand, and slapped her face.

Penny recoiled, clutching her face. "That's assault, I am calling the police, you perverted poofter!" she roared.

Jackson still had his phone in his hand. "Go ahead, call the police. I recorded everything you said, abuse, fat shaming and physically threatening my mother, then, I turned the phone off when I whacked you. I must say, I really enjoyed doing that. I turned the recording button back on while you were verbally gay bashing me, I am sure the Daily Mail would love a copy of this conversation with the famous literary agent 'Pushy Porno Penny'!"

Penny glared at Jackson, then realised he was serious; she was savvy enough to know too well in these woke times she was at a disadvantage. She spat on the floor, then stormed up the hall and slammed the door.

"Are you okay, Mama?"

Aggie had sat down on the sofa; she held her hands to her face. As she dropped them, she burst out laughing. "That was truly one of the most magnificent moments I have ever witnessed! I have been dying to slap that woman for years."

They were still giggling as Jackson said his final goodbye at the station. "I am pretty sure she won't be suing you anytime soon," Jackson said as he kissed his mama goodbye.

Sitting on the Heathrow Express reflecting on what had transpired since her father died, Aggie felt some of her zest had quietly returned; she was looking forward to reconnecting with her research, Menton, Dolceacqua and her lover.

She didn't have to wait long. Despite booking the taxi service to collect her at Nice airport, the man standing at the arrival gate with a sign saying "Aggie" was a shortish, Italian with deep brown eyes and fabulous shoes.

"I took the liberty of talking to Sarah and cancelling your taxi; I hope you don't mind?" Leo said as he took her case.

"Not at all," Aggie smiled.

Leo let go of the case, pulled her to him; wrapping his arms around her, he engulfed her with the delicious lime notes of his aftershave as he kissed her with the passion of a twenty-year-old.

It was good to be home.

TWENTY-THREE

During the ride to Menton, Aggie shared with Leo the details of the house clearance, the funeral and mentioned the pendant. He was a good listener and kept giving her knee a squeeze of encouragement as he navigated the monstrous juggernaut trucks on the motorway. They both laughed when Aggie told him of Jackson's assault on Penny.

"Remind me never to upset your son," Leo said as they turned off the motorway at Menton.

As they parked the car, the sun was on its way down; Aggie looked out at the view. The enchanted light of dusk cast a peaceful dusty hue over the old town as a few lights haphazardly, adding a sparkle to the shuttered windows. She was back in her happy place!

As Aggie put her key in the tall heavy front doors of Maison Manera and pushed them open, it was a safe feeling of belonging that greeted her.

Sarah and JP had offered Leo and Aggie a light supper when they arrived, depending on how Aggie was feeling.

Once she had refreshed herself in the shower and slipped into a new dress she had picked up on a rushed visit to Zara, they knocked at Sarah and JP's door.

Sarah enveloped Aggie in a loving hug; she and JP were very genuine and tender with their supportive words about her loss.

"I am the only one of us who is not yet an orphan. Thank goodness I still have my Papa," Sarah said, as she served a wonderful spinach and feta pastry pie - the pastry was exquisitely light; accompanied by a green salad and washed down by a chilled bottle of rosé.

Once back in Aggie's apartment, Leo chose his words very carefully. "Aggie, I don't wish to presume anything as I'm aware you didn't invite me to collect you or to be here in your home," then he stopped not quite knowing how to phrase the next bit.

Aggie bit her lip. She purposely allowed a somewhat lengthy silent pause before responding. Leo shifted a bit on his feet.

"For God's sake, of course I want you to stay, but maybe in the spare room," then she stopped and raised her eyebrows before continuing. "Or maybe in my bed if you promise to give me a good time!"

Leo took the bottle of Limoncello from the freezer, while Aggie lit a bank of tea-lights on the dresser beside the bed; candlelight was a lot kinder to her wobbly bits.

She had slipped into her cream, satin nighty, which was edged in soft, intricate French lace; it had a concealed stretch strip across the bust line which assisted Aggie with a much-required uplift.

Leo stripped to his boxers and hung his clothes over the chair. They sat between the crisp white sheets, sipping their Limoncello with Leo intermittently nibbling Aggie's ear; it drove her wild! He continued to tease her for a bit longer, then, after sliding his deft hands up and down her satin gown, the proceedings heated up.

The candles had completely burnt out by the time they had reacquainted themselves with their slow-but-sure magnificent, middle-aged orgasms.

Before Leo left the next morning, he discussed with her what her immediate schedule was. He told her to have a read of the email he had sent, and they agreed she would go through to Dolceacqua on Friday to spend a few days with him.

Pleased she could now focus on her work, Aggie was glued to the email from the woman called Mandy in the US who had recounted her experience of being regressed by a specialist at the Denna Institute.

Mandy introduced herself as a 55-year-old woman who worked as a journalist. After suffering with inexplicable dreams, she decided to work with whom she believed were the best in the field to help her. Like Aggie, after various questionnaires and DNA profiling, she had been selected to be part of Dr Viner's research program. In addition to repetitive dreams, she had, on several occasions, experienced déjà vu type incidents. Mandy had been brought up in a Midwestern town and as a young girl her parents thought she had a mental illness as she would wake up screaming in the night. She kept dreaming the same dream of seeing a man brutally murdered. It was always in the same place, by a river under a big tree. She couldn't see the murderer's face but felt the victim's pain. Then one day as a teenager on a school field trip, she recognised the river and the tree, so started doing her own research, looking up old newspaper articles in the library. It turned out it was where her great, great grandfather had been murdered and her great grandmother, as a young girl, had witnessed it. She had suffered such severe shock she could never speak of it. When Mandy was regressed the hypnotist was able to take her back, so that it felt as if she was physically present, seeing everything in real time. They had somehow tapped into her great grandmother's traumatic memory. That trauma had impacted on her great grandmother's brain and been repressed. They reasoned that it had been passed through her DNA and taken residence in Mandy's own memory. She went on to say that after the regression and the discovery of the full circumstances, her dreams ceased. She reassured Aggie, given her own experience, she had nothing to fear.

With this information swirling in her mind, Aggie opened the email from Dr Viner who had obviously anticipated a positive response from her after connecting with Mandy.

He was asking if Aggie would be able to commit to a date in three weeks' time to come to New York, as the schedule with the specialist regression hypnotist and the backup assistance the process required was tight. They had a subject who was unable to attend, and they were keen for Aggie to fill the now vacant slot. The Institute would meet all the costs of her airfare and accommodation.

Aggie texted Jackson and asked if he was able to have a quick chat. Ten minutes later he had phoned her.

"Mum, I believe you have a very strong mind and will, so I am confident you will deal with the regression process fine; my only concern would be that you may still be grieving over Grandad's death," Jackson replied, after Aggie had told him about the email. Then he added: "Also, I am wondering if it would be preferable if someone goes with you to give support?"

"I had the same thought myself, but I believe someone with me may be a distraction; I don't mean in a bad way, but I need to wholly focus on the process the Institute is going to be subjecting me to."

Aggie sighed as she clicked the phone off from the call. Her brain was strained. She threw open the ceiling-to-floor windows that faced the sea; the road noise was a bit annoying but after a few minutes it just became a light hum. She pulled her comfy chair so that it sat within the window cavity, and sliding into the chair, she spent a few moments appreciating the spectacular view of the azure blue sea fronting the 14th century Old Town.

She then opened her notebook and wrote a list of pros and cons of how this journey into her memory may impact her life.

When she had written down all aspects of the process, she wrote the real question haunting her.

Should I be going to visit my past, when I have just found so much happiness in my present?

TWENTY-FOUR

That evening Aggie phoned Leo to discuss the content of his email and asked why he hadn't told her these things when they were together.

"I felt you had a lot going on; I like to process things in order, so I thought it best you read the email first. Besides I wanted to be the centre of your world on our first night back together – sorry if that seems selfish."

Aggie didn't get his logic, but she thought better of challenging it.

In the email he said he had located the old peoples' home Nonna Rosa was in. The contact, a local lady that he had been directed to, said Nonna Rosa was now 98 and had some memory loss but on matters of the past she still had good recall. He had spoken to the old violinist from the restaurant, who had told him that his grandfather had written the tune for a girl he was madly in love with; he would play it outside her window. He said, from what he recalled, the subject of his affections had some troubles in her life, so he married someone else, but always hankered for his lost love.

"If you wish, I can phone the old peoples' home and see if we can visit Nonna Rosa on Sunday?" Leo offered.

Aggie updated him about the emails from Mandy and Dr Viner. She asked him if he would ask the old violinist if she could record that tune on her phone, as she had a feeling it may be a useful tool in the regression process.

By the time Friday arrived, Aggie had caught up with everything to do with her trip to the US. She would be away seven days, five of which would be spent with the team at the Institute.

She was intrigued at what might be revealed with meeting Nonna Rosa and she was keen to be with Leo again.

Aggie had agreed to join Sarah on her early morning trip to Ventimiglia market on Friday, then Leo would collect her from there mid-morning.

Sarah's driving was as entertaining as ever and the excursion reinforced how fortunate she was to be in this unique situation with new friends in a wonderful location.

With the idea of cooking Leo parmigiana di melanzane for lunch, Aggie purchased two large aubergines, then, under guidance from Sarah, chose some creamy looking mozzarella from the cheese vendor. Sarah insisted that Aggie should use sundried tomatoes rather than fresh.

Once they had completed a full lap of the veggie market and made a quick perusal of the clothes and bric-a-brac, they sat down for coffee.

"You are a brave woman cooking an Italian dish for the first time for an Italian!" Sarah said as she bit into her half of the panini.

"I have made it before for Jackson."

"Ah, but he is your English son and wouldn't know any better, and if he did, he wouldn't say anything anyway," Sarah laughed then added: "In my experience, Italian men don't roll like that; food is first and foremost!"

Aggie raised her eyebrows. "Okay, so I may just feel my way on this!"

Sarah waited in the car park with Aggie where Leo said he would meet her. He arrived precisely on time.

"That's a good sign!" Sarah whispered as she gave her friend a small nudge.

"What's this?" Leo said, once they had arrived at his apartment, peering into the bags. Aggie had placed the bag from the market on his table and proceeded to put things in the fridge.

"I had intended to cook you lunch, but Sarah has put me off," Aggie grimaced.

"Put you off, why?"

"She tells me Italian men are very fussy about food, especially Italian food."

"Well, she is correct, let me see what you have bought," Leo said as he examined the produce.

They horsed around and laughed about the dish. While Leo didn't agree with Sarah or Aggie's recipe, he did say that the aubergine and mozzarella were of the highest quality and, with Aggie's permission, it would be his pleasure to make the dish with his own hands for her.

Leo took Aggie step-by-step through the process of making his version of parmigiana; it was simple, but he was very precise about how slim he sliced the aubergine, and the quality of the olive oil he fried it in. Then attention paid to the layering and the proportions of the mozzarella, parmesan, tomato, basil, and aubergine in the baking dish. He allowed Aggie to make the green salad to accompany it whilst he popped out and bought a fresh focaccia, which Aggie now knew was Italian for "soft bread". They sat at the small table in front of the window in the bedroom to eat, which enabled them to have a view of Aggie's magnificent bridge.

"I am so pleased Sarah discouraged me from cooking this for you!" Aggie announced after her first mouthful of the creamy aromatic parmigiana. Leo beamed with the overstated pride of a typical Italian man.

He told Aggie he had booked a visit with Nonna Rosa this afternoon. Then tomorrow after mass, the old violinist, whose name was Tommaso, but went by Tom, had agreed to bring his violin to Leo's apartment and play the special tune for Leo to record for Aggie.

The old peoples' home near Ventimiglia where Nonna Rosa was resident was tucked away up a narrow street and while it appeared to be in disrepair from the outside, the interior was spotless. However, Aggie's keen nose detected heavy notes of a pine disinfectant concealing more human type odours.

They were greeted by the matron, a woman who clearly enjoyed her pasta. They followed her bulky body as she swayed along the narrow corridor and into a large studio room. There were many shelves of impressive ornaments each seated on its own white lace hand-tattered doilies, a thick Persian style mat covered most of the terracotta tiled floor, and old black and white photos of families from the past watched out from slightly battered gilt frames. Then Aggie's eyes rested on the old woman sitting in a wheelchair in front of the window on the far side of the cluttered room. The woman's face was edged with spidery lines, but her eyes shone as bright as sunlight from behind large-framed spectacles that perched on her nose. She stared intently at the visitors.

Leo immediately walked over, thanked her for agreeing to their visit and introduced himself and Aggie. Nonna Rosa appeared not to pay him much attention, her eyes held their gaze on Aggie's face.

She motioned for the matron, who was still hovering in the background, to pull up a couple of chairs for her guests. Aggie was aware that, although cluttered, there was an opulent ambience to the room and, given the servility of the matron towards the old lady, that Nonna was held in some esteem in this domain.

Once they were seated, Leo explained that Aggie only understood a little Italian and he was there as a translator; he assured her that anything that was said would be treated confidentially.

Nonna flicked her hand towards the matron and told her to close the door on her way out.

"So, you are Vera's granddaughter, finally come home to find your family? Well, it's a bit late, most of us are dead, or in my case nearly dead!" Nonna said, gesticulating her hands in the air, then with an exaggerated manner, plopping them down on her lap and letting out a sigh.

Leo was momentarily taken-aback, so a bit slow on the uptake. Aggie poked him, then he translated. Nonna watched intently for the younger woman's reaction.

A tear caught Aggie's eye; the statement was a surprise, but not a shock.

"Were you friends with my grandma, did Leo tell you her name?"

Leo swiftly translated.

"No, this American didn't give me information about your visit. Your grandmother and I were best friends, as well as being cousins, so that makes you a niece of sorts. The minute you walked into the room I knew who you were, too young to be Maria, she would be your Mama."

Leo continued to translate.

Nonna Rosa told Aggie how Vera left Dolceacqua suddenly in 1949; her parents said they were never sure of the real reason, but thought it was something to do with a man from the nearby village of Apricale. They were all devastated, but Rosa said she felt reassured when she wrote that she had met and married a nice Englishman. When they heard she was pregnant they sent the family the christening gown and started saving for a trip to England. But then Vera's mother Sofia had a fall and never recovered. She passed away and Claudio, Vera's dad, died a year later from a broken heart. Vera had been an only child. I never heard from Vera again, and Maria never made contact."

Then, as bright and alert as Nonna Rosa had been when they first arrived, she suddenly stopped speaking and dozed off. This coincided with the matron's return, and Aggie suspected she had been listening at the door the entire time.

"Nonna Rosa needs to rest now please," she stated.

The old lady looked up from her doze and reached out for Aggie's hand. "Maria, my little one, I have so much more to tell you; please come back again!" Then she dropped her hand and closed her eyes.

The old lady's touch left a lingering sensation on Aggie's hand; she gently fingered the spot. Rosa was her great aunt of sorts; she was sure there was far more for her to tell.

"She gets confused sometimes," the matron said as they walked back down the corridor.

Aggie graciously thanked the matron in Italian and Leo said they would phone in advance for another meeting very soon.

"She was getting your name mixed up with your Mama's there at the end," Leo said as they drove back up the valley.

"Yes, she was, but, like a lot of old people, she was taking herself back to the past. She has been around for 96 years - it's a long time."

Back in Dolceacqua, Aggie and Leo ate out in one of the popular ristorantes in the piazza. Aggie was mindful to be vigilant about her food intake; being in love made every activity so enjoyable, but eating too much just made her fat.

The next morning, with some encouragement from Leo, they walked across Aggie's bridge to the Church of San Sebastiano and slipped into the back row. Aggie had been given a basic Christian upbringing but wasn't Catholic, however, she was keen to absorb her surroundings as the rituals proceeded.

The church walls were painted two shades of blue with salmon pink panels. Aggie figured this must be a modern spin on the décor. The space was very tall and long with only minimal natural light, but the magnificent chandeliers created a hue of golden light from overhead which danced with the more subtle illumination of the flickering candles from the altars below. Like most 14th century Italian churches, the decoration was opulent with gilt, impressive marble altar tables and extravagant holy statues.

Aggie was enthralled listening to the group of older women seated in the front two rows singing unaccompanied in total harmony. Their song responded to the parts of the service the priest sang in a chant like tone. The melodic sound reverberated around the high vaulted ceilings. Adding to the ecclesiastical ambience was a fragrant waft of musky incense that added a final touch to the drama of the ceremony. It reminded Aggie of the saying about Catholic services being all "bells and smells!"

They scooted out of the church before the priest and his procession reached the door; this is where he would greet his flock and make a cursory check as to who was attending mass.

Old Tom arrived at the apartment ten minutes after Leo and Aggie. He carried his violin and a small bag of pastries.

"A few sweet 'vaginas' to go with our coffee!" Leo said in English as he opened the bag and laughed.

Aggie thought she must have misheard him. "Don't worry I will explain later!" he laughed again.

They listened as Tom talked; Leo had to keep stopping him so he could translate for Aggie.

Tom said that he was 89, and his memory was a bit hazy, but he would do his best to tell them about the history of the melody called 'Triste per Amore', which translated to 'Sad for Love'. His great grandfather, who was also called Tommaso, was in love with a girl whose name he couldn't remember or maybe he was never told. They were both very young. Tommaso, his great grandfather, was a music genius and wrote the melody when he was only 16. Old

Tom knew this part of the story was true as he still had the original sheet of music that had been dated and kept in the family. The year was 1885 and it was the same year that the painter Monet painted the Ponte Vecchio.

Leo had to keep prodding the old man to stay on track. He said at first the young girl returned his great grandfather's affections, but then, for some reason, she finished with him and broke his heart. That was when he wrote the melody.

For months he stood outside the window of her home playing it to her on his violin. Then about two years later in 1887, Dolceacqua experienced a large earthquake and that was when the girl either died or left the district. There were a lot of rumours.

As Leo translated this part of the old man's story, a shiver passed through Aggie; from her head to her feet, as if death had just paid her a passing visit.

"Do you know if the girl got married? Did she have children?" Aggie asked.

"He doesn't know if she ever married, only that she rejected his great grandfather, who eventually married a girl called Katia - they had two daughters, Isabella and Marisa, and a son called Angelo, who was my grandfather," Leo translated.

Aggie wrote down Tommaso details and asked for the names of his parents, siblings, grandparents, and great grandparents.

Tom had become distracted, the way old people do, and couldn't seem to focus; it was just illegible scrawl he responded with almost. He retrieved his violin from the case and started twiddling with the strings. Then spoke three soft words, "Triste per amore". Leo equally as quietly said: "Sad for love".

Leo beckoned for Aggie's phone and pressed the record button, as well as on his own phone. They closed the window to block out the noise from the Sunday lunch bustle in the piazza below.

Tom placed the ancient violin on his shoulder. It slotted into position as if it was an extra limb. The body of the violin was made of a rich polished piece of maple wood. When he lifted the bow and grasped the neck of the violin and played the first three notes, the sound reverberating around the full height of the salon, Aggie knew for sure this violin must have been made by a master and was now played by a master. With her writer's cap on, she tried to capture in words what the music meant to her. The combination of notes suggested lost love and heartache, but simultaneously reaffirmed its sincerity and virtue. Aggie struggled to find any better description than "pure" to describe this transcendent experience, and she knew deep within herself that it was a part of her DNA, a part of her history.

When Tom finished, he appeared tired and sat down on the chair. Aggie wiped her eyes then went over and kissed his cheek.

"Grazie, Tom", that was beautiful, bellissimo," she said.

The old man gave a wide stained-tooth smile from beneath his grey bushy moustache and said: "Lo suonerò ogni volta che vorrai baciarmi!"

Leo smiled and translated: "I will play it anytime you wish to kiss me!"

After Tom had left, although Aggie was keen to discuss the melody and her instincts about the old man, her curiosity about the "vagina cake" quip was more pressing.

Leo was in his element; he was in full story-telling mode. "In 1300 the Count of Doria introduced a law that allowed him to 'de-flower' any bride the evening before her wedding. A young woman called Lucrezia was in love with a young man called Basso. She did not want to spend the night with the Count and lose her virginity, so Basso and Lucrezia decided to marry in secret. Unfortunately, the not-so-secret festivities got noisy, and the count's soldiers arrived, capturing Lucrezia, and taking her to the castle. The young girl resisted the Count's advances, so he had her locked in the castle prison until she changed her mind. But Lucrezia was of a strong mind and would never give in, eventually starving herself to death. Basso was hollowed with grief at the death of his beloved. He broke into the castle and threatened the count's life, forcing him at knifepoint to write a new law in which he abolished his right to a bride's virginity. The next day the whole village had mixed emotions over the sadness of Lucrezia's death and the happiness of the new law giving more freedom to women. For this reason, the women of Dolceacqua created a new cake in honour of Lucrezia, to remember and thank her forever. It was called "michetta"; Dolceacqua is the only place in the world where you will find it."

Leo paused and raised his eyebrows at Aggie.

"So, what does 'michetta' actually mean?" she asked.

Leo said, a little sheepishly: "It is essentially a slang word for a 'vagina' – the cake is made in the shape of a vagina. The story goes that the women of the village who had initially created the cake sang as they distributed it around the village, 'Men, we can now give our michetta to whomever we want!' And ever since, in August, we celebrate the occasion with a michetta party here in Dolceacqua where we drink our unique Rossese wine and enjoy the special cake."

Leo cooked Aggie a wonderful Sunday supper of ossobuco made from cross cut veal shanks. He initially browned them, then placed them in a heavy iron oven dish with lots of chopped vegetables, herbs, and white wine. After two hours of slow cooking in the oven, he served it topped with finely chopped garlic, parsley, and lemon zest together with a generous helping of polenta. Aggie ate everything on her plate.

Then Leo spent quite a long time extolling the virtues of slow cooking and the importance of fresh local ingredients.

Next, he moved onto the subject of Aggie's trip to America.

"I am very pleased for you having this opportunity, and I shouldn't really say this to you...," then he stopped.

"I can hear a 'but' coming? "Aggie replied.

Leo placed his knife and fork on his plate and kept looking down as he spoke.

"I told you one of my failings was jealousy, or probably, if I am being honest with myself, it's insecurity. I keep thinking you will meet someone else and get emotionally connected to them."

Aggie took an involuntary breath; she heard his words but couldn't fathom the logic.

He continued: "I am short, a bit overweight, with not a lot to offer. In America I have probably been overexposed to all the 'beautiful' people and never felt I really matched up. At heart, I am a boy from a village in Italy. So, meeting you, a sophisticated, educated beauty who wants to spend time with me has been the best thing that has happened. I have a fear of losing you."

As hard as Aggie tried, she could not suppress her need to laugh; she managed to keep it at just a big smile. A proper Englishman would never have been so frank and raw with his feelings.

"Oh Leo! You are so perfect! As I have mentioned before, you may not have noticed, I am a short, overweight, middle-aged woman. The attraction I have for you is a once-in-a-lifetime occurrence for me; I can assure you my head won't be 'turned' and I won't be seduced by George Clooney during my seven days away in the States." She leant over the table and kissed him. "Well, that's not entirely correct, I feel sure you would allow me one night with George, but he is probably at his mansion on Lake Como!"

Leo finally cracked a smile.

They relaxed on the big soft sofa; another first for them as a couple - film night! Leo had found an Italian film with English subtitles, called *Cinema Paradiso*. As Aggie snuggled into her short, cuddly, but perfect lover, she sent the universe a silent prayer of thanks.

TWENTY-FIVE

Aggie was a bit flustered, Leo had stayed in Menton with her so he could drive her to the airport. It had been a bad move; she was used to sorting herself out ready to travel. He had been a distraction. She was feeling sure there was something she had missed in her packing. Then there was a knock at the door, it was Sarah, who immediately spotted Aggie's dilemma. She went into the kitchen and made three cups of coffee; she placed Aggie's on the bedside table where she was finishing her packing, gave her a wink and ushered Leo out onto the terrace to drink theirs together.

In the bedroom Aggie calmed; she checked off her "packing" list and realised she hadn't included her phone and laptop chargers. Thank goodness for Sarah, who was still engaging Leo in distraction-chat when Aggie appeared on the terrace.

"Okay, I am all packed and ready to go!"

Sarah accompanied them to the car and gave Aggie a warm goodbye hug.

Leo navigated the car through the morning rush in Menton and once they were up on the motorway, they both relaxed.

"I am so blessed to have met Sarah; she reads me well," Aggie said.

Leo patted her leg. "She is special, and I am so happy to have met you both."

Checking in at the Air France business desk, Aggie was pleased she was wearing her new streamlined leisure top-and-trousers look that Jackson had sent her from Selfridges. It was a posh tracksuit designed by Eric-Way Lovemore and made in a classy silk mix fabric. She had teamed the soft bronze ensemble with a pair of pristine white trainers and carried her newly acquired Louis Vuitton tote bag. She felt suitably important, blended in appropriately as well as being "comfy" for her journey to New York via a quick change in Paris . She was extra pleased after the chap at check-in looked her up and down, then reissued her ticket to a first-class upgrade.

Leo dragged out his goodbye, kissing her on the lips with the ardour of a teenager before she managed to wrangle from his embrace and swipe her ticket at the departure gate. Just before she finally moved out of his sight line at the security queue, she gave him one last wave.

Aggie decided long-haul first class was the way to travel, especially as she wasn't paying for it. She accepted the glass of champagne and had a look around at her fellow first-class passengers. She gave a silent chuckle, as across the aisle sat a George Clooney look-alike, a well-groomed attractive middle-aged man with George's trademark "salt and pepper" hair. If only Leo could see her now!

The plane meal was wonderful and after her second glass of champagne Aggie fell asleep.

She awoke with a desperate need to pee; as she moved to open the door, out stepped George Clooney holding a very flamboyant sponge bag. He smiled and with his free hand, held the door open for her. The loo reeked of a very sweet fragrance, not at all masculine, Aggie chuckled again. Leo would be pleased.

On arrival at JFK Airport, there was a man holding a sign that read "Aggie" to greet her as promised by Dr Viner's assistant Jacqueline. He was tall with bright blue eyes and had platinum blonde hair poking out from under his chauffeur's cap. Aggie felt almost embarrassed when she saw her mode of transport was a limo; but this was America, and everything was big!

Aggie was thrilled to be cruising up Fifth Avenue in a limo, but a nagging angst hung in the background; how would she react with the regression process? They had spent all this money on her, what if it didn't work? What if she couldn't be regressed?

Her angst dissipated as the limo pulled up outside the Langham Hotel; the doorman arrived immediately at the car door and a bellboy took her case from the trunk. As

Leo had suggested to her, she had a stack of $5.00 bills for tipping. The first one was dispatched to her blonde driver and the second to the doorman, once he had accompanied her to the reception desk. They gave her a warm American welcome as they handed her the key. The bellboy travelled with her up to the 7th floor; her room was wonderful with a fabulous view of New York.

Jacqueline had said it was only a 15-minute walk from the hotel to their offices, but maybe on the first day it would be best to catch a cab.

Aggie hardly slept; her brain was all over the place. As she dressed, the seeds of anxiety kept prodding at her thoughts. The possibility of unravelling the past, which may upset her, versus the status quo, where she was exceptionally happy, was the dilemma. Then her writer's brain and her natural sense of curiosity won over, this was a great opportunity, and she would see it to its conclusion.

Catching a yellow cab was just like she had seen on TV; it smelt of stale cigarettes and she struggled to understand what the cabbie was saying, who spoke in what she figured to be a broad Brooklyn accent.

The DENNA offices had a very clinical feel; the reception area sat within pristine white walls that displayed a series of black framed pictures of complex-looking DNA models, stylized and coloured for what Aggie suspected was artistic effect rather than educational direction.

Jacqueline greeted her. She was a tall woman with short black hair, a rich smile, and a strong New York accent. She immediately put Aggie at her ease as she led her along the corridor to Dr Viner's office.

"Agatha, we finally meet. I feel I know you already as you write such wonderful descriptions of your dreams, and such comprehensive interpretations," Dr Viner stood up from behind his desk and offered a firm handshake.

He was a doctor of genetics. There were framed certificates and awards displayed on both walls of his office confirming his credentials and achievements. He was a tall thin man, if Aggie was giving a written description she would use the words, "slim" and "bony" man. He towered above Aggie. He sported a thatch of thick white wiry hair, which gave him a mad professor look. His horn-rimmed specs were circular and perched on his pointed, aquiline nose. He wore a caramel-coloured roll neck sweater and chocolate brown corduroy trousers.

"Please call me Aggie, everybody does, and thank you for the luxurious flight over, and my wonderful hotel room," Aggie said and offered a smile.

"Well, you will be earning it; we have a lot of work planned!"

Jacqueline took over and explained that on this first day they would take blood samples, skin samples, and monitor Aggie's heart and brain activity. Then she ushered her through to the lab and introduced her to the team. Aggie put on a loose gown, which made access to her heart easier, then they hooked her up on several monitors. The young man taking her blood also lightly scraped her skin;

he explained they would see if they could match her DNA to those on non-commercial databases which were held by the medical profession for diagnosis purposes, also to the police database which they had discovered provided all sorts of interesting connections. Italian and European bases would be their primary focus.

Aggie was most intrigued when he told her about a historic database they were building in collaboration with various researchers around the world. Taking DNA samples from groups and individuals such as royals, aristocrats, famous artists, and writers; it was then used to help determine issues such as primogeniture, provenance, ownership of art works and inheritance.

Dr Viner had arrived in the room and joined in the conversation, saying that using this database, they had been able to retrieve a series of paintings that had been stolen in Paris during WW2 by the Nazis and sold on. Also, a Jewish baby boy who had been born in the Dachau concentration camp and survived, had never known who his parents were. He had spent most of his life searching for his identity; eventually he did a DNA test which after several years of not revealing anything, finally matched him to a DNA sample taken from the bones of a famous sculptor. This not only gave the now-older man his identity and some distant cousins, but also proof that the sculptures that his great grandfather had crafted were legally his property.

It was such a full day of "brain strain" for Aggie, she opted for some exercise by walking back to the hotel, navigating with Google maps. It was a pleasant evening and she enjoyed taking in the sights, sounds and smells of downtown New York.

Around 7pm she received a text from Leo asking if she was in her room and could he call her. He wanted to hear everything that had happened. Aggie felt a sense of comfort, knowing he was interested and offering comments.

Aggie had opted for the room service menu for her evening meal. When she said she would cut the conversation short because the meal trolley was being wheeled in, Leo seemed very pleased to hear she was eating alone.

For her first day of hypnotherapy Jacqueline had recommended Aggie have only a light breakfast and not to drink any stimulants, so no tea or coffee. She also said to wear comfy clothes as she would be on a reclining chair. Aggie opted for her smart travel outfit.

On arrival Dr Viner took her into a room with soft beige-coloured walls, dark wood floor and a rich linen drape shading the floor-to-ceiling window. Aggie guessed it had been designed to cocoon and relax the patient as opposed to the bright clinical feel of the rooms she was in the day before. A modern Scandinavian soft-leather recliner and footstool sat in the middle of the room; a bank of monitors was positioned on either side of the chair; two upright office chairs and a table sat at the end of the recliner.

A stocky African-American with tight curly grey hair appeared in the room. He sported a grey, well-trimmed beard and frameless glasses. He looked Aggie directly in the eyes as he put his hand out to her.

"Hi, I'm Clive Greenwood, I am a therapeutic regression hypnotist, and I will be working with you over the next three days."

His voice was deep, mellow, and charismatic, and his eyes were as rich as melted chocolate. He motioned for Aggie to sit down on the recliner then proceeded to carefully tell her what was about to take place.

"Dr Viner and his team will hook you up to these monitors, they record your heart rate, and other more complex reactions, similar to what a lie detector measures. The data collected helps us to discern what is truth and what is imagination when we regress a subject. After the sessions we endeavour to cross check locations, dates, and people as quickly as possible through internet search engines. In this first session I will take it very slowly and see how you react, and how far we can go without you showing signs of distress. I have read all your notes so I will initially be encouraging you towards revisiting the Italian town of Dolceacqua."

Two assistants placed sticky suction cups on Aggie's arms and forehead, these were connected to the monitors by wires. Clive asked Aggie to get as comfortable as she was able in the chair and put her feet up on the foot stool. The action will be occurring in your subconscious, but I will be asking you to tell us contemporaneously what you are seeing, feeling, hearing, and smelling. He asked Aggie to focus on his fore finger as he rhythmically moved it back and forth; the last words she was conscious of hearing were: "…We are going back to Dolceacqua in 1924, the year your grandmother Vera was born…".

Aggie looked around the room, there was no fire in the hearth and the window was open; it must have been spring; she could hear the trickle of the river below. The strongest sense she was experiencing was how warmly cocooned she felt. She was all wrapped up in a soft blanket on the bed. "Oh, my darling little flower, look at those big eyes!" Aggie stared up at a huge woman who loomed over her. It took a while to register, but once she smelt the delicious aroma of mother's milk, she realised she was a baby and her mother had picked her up and was cradling her in her arms. It was a most heavenly, secure feeling. The love permeated her body, it soothed her skin and was the purest sensation she had ever experienced. Her mother's melodic words danced in her ears, "My little Vera, I can tell you have been here before, haven't you? You have the most perfect baby face, but a very old soul."

Then the moment passed. Aggie was now standing face-to-face looking at her mother, but she had aged. This woman had lines etched in her forehead and around her lips. She was crying.

"Vera, you don't need to leave; England is a lifetime away. What that beast did to you will pass; you will heal; please stay

here with me." Aggie experienced a feeling of fear, of finality; she kissed her mother's soft cheek, picked up her case and walked down the stone stairs to the light, the salty taste of her mother's tears still lingering on her lips.

Then Aggie heard three clicks and opened her eyes. The eyes she now looked at were like liquid chocolate. Clive was smiling at her: "Welcome back!"

Aggie took a few moments to gather her thoughts. "How did that go? It seemed like a very short time."

"You were impressive! We know your memory was your grandmother Vera's experience. You spoke to us as it was occurring in your subconscious. Could you hear me asking you questions?" Clive asked.

"No, not at all! I wasn't aware of anything here in this room."

Aggie sat up.

"Do you speak Italian Aggie?" Dr Viner asked.

"Hardly any at all, why?"

Both men smiled. Then Dr Viner replied.

"Well, you articulated all your observations, as a baby and as a young woman in perfect Italian."

"No! I don't believe you!" Aggie said as she took her feet down from the foot stool.

Dr Viner motioned to his assistant to play what they had recorded. Aggie was mesmerised as she heard her own voice speaking. She now realised they were her great grandmother's and her grandmother Vera's words in fluent Italian.

"We anticipated that you may speak in Italian, so our recording has instantly translated it. You know what you said but we will listen to it now in English," Dr Viner said as his assistant switched the recorder back on.

When the recording finished, Dr Viner was silent for what seemed an age. Then he stood up.

"Aggie, what is most remarkable and important to us is that you were able to describe so many sensory perceptions; the ripple of the river and the smell of your mother's milk are particularly poignant."

Clive cleared his throat and spoke.

"I have to say you would be the most responsive subject that I have ever regressed. It will be interesting to see how far back we can go."

Then Dr Viner continued: "I believe you just happen to have an extra dose of what we call ESP - extra sensory perception - within your DNA; both these events you channelled from historic memories were significant life experiences; Vera, hearing her mother's voice as a tiny baby, then recalling the very last time she saw her mother, after a bad experience with a man. Your mother Maria most likely had heightened ESP as well, but given her bipolar disorder, and lack of education, it disturbed her and eventually pushed her over the edge. Whereas, you appear to have harnessed the memories and have been able to develop a process to deal with them; but we must be very mindful not to push you too far."

He then advised her that they had done enough for today and reminded Aggie not to drink alcohol, or other stimulants while they were conducting the regression sessions. Her mind and body needed to be calm and have the exact same temperature and body vitals as she had today, to make the sessions as effective as possible.

While Aggie stood up to drink the cup of tea Jacqueline had brought her Clive informed her: "While you were under, I asked you not to dream again until you were back here at the clinic; however, given we haven't encountered anyone as sensitive as you before I am not sure it will work."

Aggie remembered the way back to the hotel, so was able to soak up her surroundings better without having to focus on her phone map. Her mind was buzzing with what the day had given her.

Taking advantage of being directly beside Central Park, she wandered in and walked around; it was reminiscent in a way of her beloved Hyde Park, but not as vast and with perhaps a few more dubious characters than she had noticed back home. She returned to the street and spotted a sign in a small alley off the main street. It was advertising dining and jazz that evening.

Arriving back at her hotel, she flicked through her music app and played Randy Crawford singing "One Day I'll Fly Away" as she sunk into the large hot bath scented with an abundance of Jo Malone body oil. Aggie was on such a high, she decided not to ruin the moment by checking her emails. She had decided to go to the jazz bar for a meal. Slipping into a pair of black tailored trousers, a bright orange, fine-knit roll neck and her precious Ralph Lauren black jacket that had been her go-to favourite for the past 10 years.

Aggie was still on her regression high as she stepped out onto Fifth Avenue.

She wandered about a bit, retracing her steps to find the alley where she had noticed the sign; eventually she found it and walked down the steep stairs to what was called the jazz cellar. Aggie perused the tables, she didn't want to sit anywhere too obvious; she wanted to be a voyeur, to observe the surroundings and not have to talk to anyone so she could indulge her own private thoughts. She secured a small table at the rear of the room and ordered scampi and fries with a green salad on the side. As she sipped her lime and soda, her handbag vibrated. Grabbing her phone, she realised she had not turned the sound back on from before the session at the clinic. There were two missed calls from Jackson, three from Leo and a text from Sarah.

She returned Sarah's text first, assuring her she was okay, and it was all going well. She then called Jackson and gave him a quick abridged version of what she had experienced and said she would call with all the details once the regression process was over. Leo wasn't so easy to fob off. He insisted he call her back directly, so that she wouldn't be concerned about the cost of the call. He questioned her on every detail, which irked her; he didn't seem to grasp the subtleties of an English woman attempting not to have a discussion. But she knew well enough that he would take offence if she said anything, so she just subtly adapted some of the details. She wasn't ready to share the experiences of seeing her great grandmother through her grandmothers' eyes; it was an almost supernatural experience and was deeply personal; Aggie would go as far as describing it, if she had been writing it down, as a spiritual awakening.

Aggie breathed a final goodbye to Leo as her food arrived. It was the largest plate of fried food she had ever seen, the salad being an afterthought in a small bowl on the side.

The jazz trio consisting of piano, saxophone and double bass, arrived on the tiny stage. To grab the customers' attention, they opened with "Fly Me to The Moon", then moved on to some more abstract and long-winded numbers that only true jazz fans would love.

A rather odd-looking chap wearing a cloth cap, at a nearby table started smiling and nodding towards Aggie, between stuffing jumbo chips into his mouth. Aggie decided this was her call to pay and leave.

TWENTY-SIX

The following morning Aggie woke up relieved by the absence of dreams. After a light breakfast and a cup of boring herbal tea she opted to walk to the clinic. She may never be offered the opportunity to step out of a five-star hotel and walk along Fifth Avenue again, so she was determined to savour all the great moments.

Dr Viner's team were ready for her, and she was all hooked up to the monitors when Clive arrived. "I am going to take you back further today and for longer; we have Sophia as your great grandmother but don't know that for sure; we feel there may be a deeper trauma, further back. We believe we can allow you some stress as you seem to have the mechanisms to deal with things, but if the monitors rise above what we believe is reasonable we will wake you."

Aggie was in another world. She looked across at the man sitting opposite her; he looked angry and smelt like freshly cut grass; he wore a tattered white shirt, frayed at the collar, a brown waistcoat and sported a bushy brown moustache that completely shaded his upper lip. "That menace from Apricale won't ever bother our Vera, or any other girl, again. We saw to that last night!" *he said.*

"Oh Claudio, what did you do?" *The words seemed to be coming from Aggie, but she realised they were her great grandmother Sophia's words.*

"Best you don't know!" *Claudio replied, then lit up his pipe before continuing,* "We don't want what happened to your great grandmother happening to Vera now, do we?"

"That was all rumour, and it happened such a long time ago; why say that now? Our Vera is not pregnant, and it breaks my heart that she is leaving us tomorrow." *As her great grandmother Sophia turned her back on her husband, Aggie was able to see out the window of the stone-walled room; it was springtime.*

The intensity of Sophia's angst tore through her entire body. It was so strange, Aggie knew somehow, she was still Aggie, but in this moment, she was feeling everything that her great grandmother was feeling. The thought of Sophia losing her only daughter, Vera, was too much.

Then Aggie was gone.

Next, she experienced a moment of blackness; not unpleasant, it was if her thoughts were taking a pause.

Now, she was somewhere very different; she was sitting on the side of a bed in a room she didn't recognise, her small legs didn't reach the floor. She had a sense that she had moved a long way back in time. A young woman who she seemed to know to be her mother, stood at the door in heavy debate with someone Aggie couldn't quite see on the other side of the door. Her mother was dressed in a long black frock with a patterned apron pulled over it. Eventually the other person left, and her mother flopped down on the bed beside Aggie.

"My sweet Isabella, my Mama says you should never have been born; what a cruel thing to say, you are my life, we must find a way to stay together! He will never come back for me; he is too important, and I am nobody, but I won't give you up!"

Aggie was now seeing everything from Isabella's perspective, she felt so warm, so cherished to be enveloped in her mothers' arms. Her voice had a soft gentle sound that fluttered over her, leaving a gentle warmth like the morning sun on her face. She drifted off to sleep.

She woke to the delicious smell of cooking. It was dark outside. There was a bank of candles glowing on the table. The room was tiny, it had only a single bed, a small table with two chairs and a small cast-iron stove, all cramped into a pocket-sized space. Aggie jumped off the bed and went over to the window; she could just peek out if she stood on her tiptoes. They must have been in the country as she couldn't see any other buildings, and no lights, just a big moon.

"Isabella, you are not yet two and look at you, full of curiosity; I do love you so!" So, Aggie knew now; she was seeing this life as Isabella, a two-year-old; what a lovely name!

Her mother scooped her up in her arms, put a big cushion on the chair and sat her down at the table with a bowl of *food in front of her. Just one bowl between them. Her mother blew on a spoonful of food to cool it down then put it in her child's mouth.*

It tasted divine; Aggie could taste potatoes and spinach; then her mother had a spoonful herself.

Aggie recognised it straight away; the violin struck out the first few bars of the crisp melodic melody of Triste per Amore; it wafted through the silent night and in the partially open window.

"Oh Tommaso!" Her mother said out loud and got up from the table; she opened the window and gave a gentle whistle. The playing stopped and moments later a young man appeared at their door.

"Quick, come before anyone sees you! They all will have heard you playing that song."

"My Sienna! I must try with you one last time, My Love; I don't care if little Sophia isn't my blood; I forgive you; you can still be with me, we can go away to some place where nobody knows us. You can't keep living in this dreadful room with no one to care for you both."

Aggie now knew that Isabella's mother was called Sienna.

"Life used to be so easy; you and I slipped from one summer to the next without effort. But we were children, we were innocent. We have both grown up. You know I care for you; you have been so kind to us, we would not have survived without you. I am now forced to agree with you and my mother, who was here today yelling at me, that 'he' would have returned by now if 'he' wanted me. I can't bring myself

to say his name. I think I now want to accept you, but I feel it would be so unfair to you," Sienna declared.

"We have lived side-by-side since we were children and I have always loved you; to be seduced by such an important man was a terrible thing, but in a way, I can understand it. If I had been a woman, I am sure I would have been seduced by him. We will never say his name, ever!" the young Tommaso said as he took Sienna's hands in his.

Sienna hung her head, and tears simultaneously emptied down both their cheeks.

Aggie rushed over and hugged her mothers' knees. Sienna stroked the child's head.

"I need to think this over for a while," Sienna said, deep in thought, *"I will give you my answer tomorrow. Let's meet when I come to town, up by the entrance to the castle Doria ruins; at lunch time when everyone is at home."*

Then Aggie heard three clicks and opened her eyes.

It took her a little longer this time to get her bearings. She felt a sense of confusion before she said, "How long was I away?"

"About thirty minutes, which, judging by what we have witnessed with other subjects, is about average," Clive said, as he gave her a reassuring smile.

Aggie sat up and took the cup of tea Jacqueline offered her.

"If you are comfortable with it, we thought you might like to join us for a light lunch and we can talk through what you experienced," Dr Viner said.

Aggie felt a little unstable as she stood up. Jacqueline was quickly at her side and walked beside her to a room with a sideboard and a table set for lunch. The sideboard had serving dishes with two different salads, bread rolls and cold meats.

Aggie was back to normal now and ravenous. She topped her plate up and they all focused on eating before chatting.

She related what she had experienced; the other three listened intently; then Dr Viner responded.

"Well Aggie, having a descriptive writer's mind seems to naturally enable you to speak in a documentative way about your historic memories. It seems that you may have skipped a generation, as Sienna, Isabella and Tommaso sound as if they were living in the mid to late 1800s, whereas we know for a fact Sophia and Vera were around 1924 to 1949."

Jacqueline poured the coffee.

"Is it okay if I have a coffee? I am dying for one," Aggie said.

Clive laughed. "Yes of course, we won't be regressing you again today. Tomorrow will be your last day. You are articulating memories which we would term 'traumatising' experiences. All of which have happened to the women in your female line. You have dealt with them well, so far. However, we haven't studied a person with your strength of mind and acute responses to stimuli before, so we must tread carefully."

They went back to join the rest of the team who had been searching online for any Sienna, Sophia, and Tommaso in Dolceacqua back in the late 1800's. It appeared all three names were quite common in the area, but the birth, marriages and death records had not yet been made available online. Aggie would need to look in person when she returned.

That evening, Aggie felt the need to be alone, but not staying in her room. She didn't want to talk to anyone including Leo. What she was experiencing was so personal and overwhelming she needed to digest it in her own company. Sharing with Clive, Dr Viner and his team was integrated with the process, but she couldn't disclose any of this to anyone else just now. Aggie wanted to update her diary with everything while it was fresh in her mind.

She found a small table-for-one in the hotel Grill Room and ordered a Caesar Salad. A glass of white wine would go down so well, but Aggie managed to get that urge under control. She messaged Leo and Jackson with a firm statement, saying she was still involved in activities with the clinic, and she would call them on Friday before she left. She could almost feel Leo's frustration in his return text; she only replied to thank him for the offer of collecting her at the airport; she would look forward to that.

Going through her diary and the pics she had taken of her mother's sketches, she kept thinking about the stone walls; then her thoughts wandered back to the dream where she stood behind the artist with his easel painting the bridge. Bingo! That's where she remembered the black dress and the patterned apron.

Aggie was in a state of excitement by the time she arrived at the clinic the next morning.

"I looked at my notes for a dream I experienced a few months ago; I was standing behind a couple of painters with an easel; at that time I couldn't see what they were painting, but I now realise that it was the bridge at Dolceacqua! I am sure that was Sienna as well!"

Dr Viner answered: "I had picked that up from your notes, but didn't say anything, as the worst thing we can do is place any hint of suggestions or direction in your mind. Everything you can see must be a genuine historic memory."

"I will take you today back to the time of Sienna, Tommaso and Isabella; we are not sure of the exact date, but it is probably mid-1880s," Clive said, then as Aggie was still quite hyped up, he worked her through some deep breathing exercises.

It seemed to take longer this time as Clive moved his forefinger back and forth, Aggie got to the count of ten then she was gone.

She knew who she was, she was two-year-old Isabella. What a joy being two! She skipped along the cobbled path holding her mama's hand. Her mama was her world, she was so happy being with her, the only other person she knew was Tommaso. The streets were empty. Mama said everyone is inside having lunch. She has given me the most wonderful apple to eat, it's my treat for being such a good girl.

We are walking up the steep path towards the big castle. I must run to keep up with Mama; she has such long legs and seems to be in a hurry. We reach the top of the path. Mama says Tommaso will be here soon and for me to have a seat on the bench where the old ladies usually sit. I look up at the castle, it is the tallest building I have ever seen.

It's strange as I can feel my seat shaking and no one is there; Mama is over by the wall that takes you up to the castle. There is a loud rumbling noise like a large cart coming down a cobbled street. She looks over to me; she has a scary face then she starts to run to me, but my seat shakes so hard I fall on to the ground and when I look up the walls are falling, the big stones are crumbling. Mama, Mama where are you!

I am getting up, but the ground shakes again. I can hear a scream then realise it's me screaming; I run over to the pile of rocks, I can see Mama's head, and her legs but her middle has big rocks covering it. She is not speaking; she must be asleep. Mama, Mama wake up!

One, two, three clicks. "Aggie come back to us!"

She can hear Clive's voice, but she can't see anything.

"Now gently open your eyes and remember you are Aggie; you have regressed, you are safe."

Aggie opens her eyes; the room seems too bright, and she lifts her hand to shield her eyes.

"My mother is dead isn't she!" She feels sick.

Someone puts a plastic bowl on Aggies lap; she vomits; this seems to help; she sits up. A few minutes pass, she recognises Dr Viner who is standing beside her; he takes the bowl and returns.

"Sienna, your ancestor, must have been killed in an earthquake; her two-year-old daughter Isabella witnessed the event. You were seeing it through her eyes. Her trauma has been passed down through her DNA to you," Clive states very clearly.

Aggie still feels puzzled. "But I was there, I could see and feel everything, and I know it's real as I stood in that exact spot with Leo only a month ago!"

"It was real, and it was traumatic; just give yourself time to adapt back to the present," Dr Viner said, then he sat down beside Clive, facing Aggie.

Eventually Jacqueline brought in cups of tea, and Aggie seemed to rally after a few sips. "I feel better now," she said.

Dr Viner asked Jacqueline to send his assistant back in. They looked at the monitors then took the suction cups and probs off Aggies arms. "Your vitals are nearly back to normal, but you had us going for a bit; we thought you were going to have a stroke; Clive was challenged getting you back; the pull on Isabella to wake her mother was so strong. Death doesn't feature logically in a two-year old's psyche, it's total confusion," Dr Viner said.

His assistant handed him a paper. "Here is the online search, the earthquake at Dolceacqua killed one person, it doesn't say who, but it was on the 23rd of February 1887.

Aggie was very quiet; she was in a strange world; alive in 2022 and standing over her dead ancestor in 1887.

"My mother Maria drew a picture of a pile of stones; I think I included it in my notes to you. Do you think she saw the same thing?" Aggie asked.

"Yes, I do. I feel sure all four generations carried this traumatic memory, channelling it down to you. Isabella most likely hid it in the recesses of her two-year-old mind, and if no one ever talked to her about it, then she may have believed it to be a dream. It would have caused some long-term damage, not being addressed," Dr Viner replied.

"How would my mother have seen what I saw? I am pretty sure she hasn't ever regressed," Aggie said.

"No, she wouldn't necessarily need to be regressed to experience the memory. Each person processes things differently. That's why so many people have been wrongly diagnosed with a mental illness when in fact what they have been seeing, was not a psychotic episode, but a historic memory. That's why our research is so important," Dr Viner stated then asked if Aggie would like to join him and Clive at a restaurant for lunch. "It will be good for you to get out of this environment to help you move forward to the present," Clive added.

The restaurant was what Aggie would have imagined from watching American TV shows. It had a revolving entrance door, faded decor, and a very over-enthusiastic host who had seen younger days. The oblong tables sat within "booths" with banquet seating on two sides. Aggie slid comfortably into the soft, well-worn leather of the banquet.

Once they had ordered, Clive opened the chat. "I would have loved to have delved back even deeper into your history Aggie; you have been by far the most responsive subject I have ever regressed."

Dr Viner then took over the conversation. "We also need to understand where to draw the line; your vitals were showing a lot of distress, which reaffirms to us just how traumatic it is for a small child to witness such trauma as their parents' death. And then, from what we think happened, she was never allowed to work through it. It is my opinion; we ceased the regression at the right time."

"It was the most traumatic thing I have ever experienced! And confusing because I was a small child watching my mother being crushed; then within seconds I also knew I was a 52-year-old who was witnessing something from the past. That part of the process is what exhausts me. Now I am firmly back in the present, my big question is who was Isabella's father? It is clear she was born out-of-wedlock and a prominent man of some kind," Aggie said.

"When the team looked online at the records for births, deaths, and marriages in Dolceacqua, they didn't go back that far, so that is something you will need to look up in person. In the meantime, we will be searching through as many DNA databases as possible to see what else we can find," Dr Viner replied. Then added: "You mentioned writing a book about this process, will you do that as non-fiction or as a novel?"

"I haven't decided yet. I need to work through a grief process - not like when my father died, but grief for my great and great, great grandmothers. It would be impossible to unsee what I witnessed," Aggie replied. "I also feel the sorrow for my mother tied up in this emotional mix. I need to solve the mystery of Sienna's lover, Isabella's real father. Did he bring her up after Sienna's death? Why was her name not mentioned in the article on the earthquake? There seems to have been some reason at that time to hide those facts," Aggie took a break and had a few mouthfuls of her tuna salad and a sip of the delicious Californian white wine, which after her enforced abstinence tasted so good.

"During my university education where I read English, I also focused on research, as something I wanted to incorporate into my writing on historical subjects. However, I found myself in a position where I had to support my baby son and myself; I didn't have the luxury of being able to choose what work I did and ended up writing erotic romantic fiction, which I don't even like. But it gave me income and financial security. I would like to write now using my own name and produce something I can feel proud of," Aggie said, then took another sip of her wine.

Both men smiled: "How fascinating, you are full of surprises. I do hope you solve the mystery of Isabella's father; I feel sure our team may turn up some DNA to help. Please keep us posted," Dr Viner said.

They agreed, if Aggie found out more details via her Dolceacqua connections, or Dr Viner through the DNA bases, they would pass it on.

On her last evening in New York, Aggie had planned to go out, but the regression process had taken its toll. After responding to Leo's text that he was looking forward to collecting her at the airport, she sunk into her bed and for the first time since her disturbing dreams commenced, she slept peacefully.

TWENTY-SEVEN

Aggie felt a little guilty that, while in the US, she hadn't been as communicative with Leo as he would have preferred. He liked to talk, but what she had experienced had been too personal; other than with Dr Viner and Clive, it wasn't an experience she had wished to share. Now she was back on an even keel, and in a place where she would be happy to talk about it. She was excited to know Leo would be waiting for her at the airport. The plane swooped out over the Mediterranean and then turned to land at Nice airport on the seafront. It gave Aggie a great view of the Riviera, Cap d'Antibes, and Cannes on one side and Villefranche-sur-Mer and Beaulieu-sur-Mer on the other. This vista conjured the visions of glamour of this region that dominated so many magazines, books, and movies.

She had refreshed her makeup, brushed her hair and given herself a generous spray of Chanel no 5 before she disembarked. She was surprised that Leo wasn't waiting in the arrival hall; maybe he had been caught in traffic. She turned her phone on; she would give it ten minutes before she called. She needed to use the loo, so dashed off not wanting to miss Leo. He still wasn't anywhere near the arrivals door when she returned. When she called him, it went straight to voicemail. A big knot formed in Aggie's stomach. Where was he? She tried his number several times and it went to voicemail each time. It had been nearly an hour now since she had landed. She left a message on his phone saying she would get a cab home.

The cab driver practically flew along the motorway, overtaking everything in sight; Aggie was relieved when she finally got out the cab door, still in one piece. Once in the door of her apartment her phone gave a shrill ring from within her handbag. Leo's name flashed up.

It was a female voice speaking French; Aggie responded in English saying she didn't speak French.

The voice switched to English. "Madame, I am sorry to call you from this phone, I am an officer with Nice Police, there has been an accident, and the gentleman is unconscious; he only has an American licence as ID. I can see you have attempted to call him several times over the past couple of hours."

Aggie was dumbstruck.

"Madame, madame can you hear me," the policewoman's voice sounded ghostlike from the handset Aggie was still holding.

"Yes sorry, I am here; I just got a shock. He is Leo Molinari; he is Italian but has been living in America. Where is he?" she finally managed to say.

"He is in the emergency department at Nice hospital; if you are coming here, we will get all the details then?"

"Yes, yes I will be there as soon as I can."

Aggie left her case in the apartment hallway and walked across to Sarah and JP's door; Sarah answered immediately. "Aggie you are home! How wonderful!" Then she saw Aggie's face. "Oh, dear God! What has happened?"

"Leo has been in a car accident! The police retrieved his phone and my number showed up, so they called me. He is unconscious in Nice hospital; would you mind helping me get a cab?"

JP had joined them at the door. "No cab, we will all go together; I know my way around the hospital; let me get changed and we will take you straight away."

JP was very calm and collected. Aggie hadn't seen this side of him before. He drove as fast as was legal, but very cautiously, compared to her trip only half an hour earlier. He pulled straight up at the hospital, scanned a card and they pulled into the parking area, in the doctors-only spaces, very close to the hospital entrance. JP walked over to the front desk, retrieved the information he needed and came back to the women and ushered them to a quiet spot at the edge of the entrance hall.

"Leo is still unconscious; he was in an accident on the motorway very close to the airport. The police are waiting for us up on the ward," JP informed them; Sarah put her arm through Aggie's.

Leo had been moved from the emergency ward up to the critical care ward, JP explained as they rode up in the lift; this was usual practice; they would have ascertained his injuries and would be monitoring him now.

As JP navigated, they made their way to Leo's ward; Aggie could hear her own heart beats; she was thankful Sarah and JP were with her. There was a clear sign saying: "No Visitors Without Prior Permission". One word from JP and they were ushered in. When they arrived at Leo's bedside, he was hooked up by three lines to a beeping screen; Aggie felt some relief as she could see his heart was still beating.

This scene was so reminiscent of the last time she saw her father, but he had been sitting up chatting to her from his hospital bed. Leo was pasty-faced, with a bulky bandage around his head; it appeared that the main injury was to his forehead. Aggie burst into tears. Sarah was immediately beside her with a tissue. A young, dark-haired police woman had entered the room.

"Bonjour, I am Officer Laurence, I assume you are Monsieur Molinari's family?"

JP explained Leo's family were in America, but they were his close friends. The policewoman nodded then continued.

"Monsieur's car was hit from behind; we suspect the culprit was high on drugs; he has now been arrested. The accident pushed Monsieur's car into the side-railing, and he knocked his forehead on the dashboard."

She went on to ask Leo's full name, age, and Italian address, then enquired if JP would prefer to call his family in the US. She offered them Leo's phone back and a card with her details before saying goodnight.

"Aggie, I think we should just wait a bit longer before you call Leo's son. I will go and speak to the duty Doctor and find out what tests have been done and what they showed," JP said, then gave Sarah a nod and went out into the ward.

Sarah pulled up chairs on either side of the bed and motioned Aggie to sit down. Aggie picked up Leo's hand and kissed it.

"Talk to him, Aggie, they say unconscious people can often hear, even if they can't respond," Sarah said as she squeezed Leo's other hand.

"Leo, I have so much to tell you and I was so looking forward to seeing you again. Please wake up soon my darling," Aggie whispered very close to her lover's ear.

The two women sat chatting quietly about New York without going into the details of the regression. Sarah was very diplomatic with what she asked. They both understood it was an exercise to keep Aggie distracted as well as offer Leo comfort, hoping he was able to hear them.

Eventually JP reappeared. "They conducted a brain scan just before we arrived; it showed mainly normal activity, but a small amount of swelling where the main injury is, in the frontal lobe. The x-rays showed Leo also has several cracked ribs and a broken fibula; they are coming to set the leg soon, at which point we will have to leave. It is probably a good thing he is unconscious for now as the pain would be immense. His body will readjust to cope, and hopefully he will wake soon."

Two, gowned medics arrived and asked the trio to leave; they explained they needed to set Leo's leg in the room as it would be inadvisable to move him. They assured Aggie she may visit after breakfast in the morning. She prayed he'd be awake.

TWENTY-EIGHT

Aggie woke up the next morning very disturbed; she had dreamt that Leo was calling her name as his car was shoved off the road. In the dream, no matter how hard she tried, she couldn't reach him. It was early morning; she got up and showered; she needed to call Leo's son, James, then leave for the hospital as soon as possible.

Aggie found James's phone number on Leo's phone. He was shocked to hear the news; Aggie explained their friend was a doctor and his advice was that Leo would wake up soon, so best to wait a day or two before travelling over. James agreed to this, and Aggie assured him she would message him daily and call him as soon as Leo woke up.

Sarah had offered to drive her to the hospital, but Aggie said she would catch the train. There was a station within a 10-minute walk to the hospital. Aggie was grateful for

Sarah and JP's help last night, but that was an emergency and she now needed to be self-sufficient.

In usual circumstances, travelling by train along the Riviera would be an absolute delight. But today, the scenery just flew by, unnoticed. Aggie was distracted, flashes of guilt swept through her at her lack of sharing with Leo during her trip away; she feared he may not recover.

After taking a few wrong turns trying to navigate her way from the station to the hospital, with anxiety levels running high, she finally arrived. She found a loo in the hospital foyer and managed to refresh her makeup.

JP had thankfully sorted things so when Aggie arrived at the ward, she was down as Leo's next-of-kin in France.

Leo's leg was encased in plaster from the knee down. As Aggie looked at his still body and listened to his soft, easy breathing, she thought she could see more colour in his face than yesterday. She sat down beside him and placed his hand in hers and started a conversation as if he was awake. She told him all about Dr Viner and Clive and each stage of her regression.

Nurses came in and out, checking his vitals every half hour and when they left the room, Aggie would whisper a description or comment about them to Leo. It was about 4pm when Aggie's tummy began to rumble; she had been at his bedside all day; she would have to go and find something to eat. She kissed Leo's cheek and told him she would be back soon. The ward receptionist directed her to the café a couple of floors down.

She was gone for only about thirty minutes but when she returned to Leo's room two nurses and a doctor were standing over the bed. Aggie's heart took a dive.

"Leo, Leo" she called out as she bolted to his bedside. "Is he dead?"

"No Madame, he is not, but he has been calling out for the past half hour, so the nurse requested me," the doctor said, in heavily accented English, then went on to reassure that Leo's vitals were fine.

"What was he saying?" Aggie asked.

"Apparently nothing the nurses could understand - a mixture of Italian and English they think; anyway, he may calm down now that you are here; we will leave you; please press the buzzer if you are concerned," the doctor said, as he and the nurses left the room.

Aggie sat down beside the bed; Leo's eyes were closed; she picked up his hand. "My darling, it's me Aggie. If you can hear me, please squeeze my hand."

A few minutes passed with no sound or movement; then Aggie felt the gentlest of movements from Leo's hand.

"Oh Leo, well done! Do that again so I know I'm not imagining it."

She kept very still and waited a few minutes more; this time he squeezed harder.

"How wonderful! I know you can hear me; keep pushing through the fog, I need you to come back to me."

There were signs of movement on his face. He made a grunting sound then she heard the word "water". She pressed the buzzer; he was on a drip, and she didn't know if it would be okay to give him a drink. When the nurse arrived, she said it was, and fetched a drinking beaker. She didn't speak much English but conveyed to Aggie by pointing at one of the lines on the beeping screen that Leo was slowly regaining consciousness. The nurse propped him up and Aggie held the beaker to his lips; he took a sip; then lay back on the pillow, his eyelids flickering, then, he opened his eyes. Aggie was transfixed. He mouthed the word "Aggie" and squeezed her hand tightly, before closing them again.

The doctor returned and explained he was regaining consciousness, but it would happen slowly, and it would be best if Leo rested now, and that Aggie should go and get some sleep. He said she would be welcome to come back after 9am tomorrow. Aggie reluctantly kissed Leo goodbye but was reassured that he could hear her.

On the train home, she messaged James with an update. He responded straight away, saying he was in the process of booking a flight to Nice and would message her as soon as he had the details.

Aggie had barely undressed and lay on her bed when she fell straight to sleep.

The following morning, she was back on the train again. Once she sat down, she turned her phone back on and was greeted by a barrage of texts from James, Jackson, and Sarah. She quickly responded to her son and Sarah with a short update, then took time to digest what Leo's son James was saying. He would arrive tomorrow and had booked a room in a small hotel near the hospital. He said for Aggie not to meet him at the airport, but to stay with Dad.

When she walked into Leo's room he was sitting up in bed, his eyes closed; the monitors had been removed. As she sat down, he opened his eyes, and after a moment of focusing he offered Aggie a huge smile.

"Oh Leo, thank God you are awake!"

The tears streamed down her face as she stood up, leant over, and hugged him.

"My darling Aggie! I have been waiting all night for you to come back," he said and returned her hug. He went on to explain that he could hear her, but wasn't able to respond, but when she had said to "pull himself out of the fog" he had found the strength to do it.

Aggie told him that James would be arriving tomorrow and that he seemed like a very caring young man. They chatted for about ten minutes before Leo drifted off to sleep.

The doctor explained that, although Leo was conscious and talking, they would need to observe him for a few more days, as the swelling was still present in his frontal lobe.

Later that afternoon when Aggie felt Leo was as comfortable as he could be, she returned home, keen to soak in a bath and take up Sarah and JP's offer to share a glass of wine.

She had had a good phone catchup with Jackson on the train journey back to Menton and felt a massive sense of relief as she slid into her lavender-scented bath.

Later, over the much-anticipated glass of wine, JP concurred with all that Aggie had told him and agreed that Leo was on the best path possible to recovery.

The following day, Leo was dozing in his hospital bed, and Aggie was scrolling through the internet on her phone when a swarthy young man appeared at the door.

"Hi I'm James you must be Aggie," he said as he reached out to shake her hand; at the sound of his son's voice, Leo immediately woke up.

"Oh son, I am so happy to see you!"

Tears poured from both father and son as James bent over the bed and embraced his father. Aggie stayed for a bit and exchanged pleasantries, but then said she would go for a walk and give them some time together.

She found a seat in the park close to the hospital. Now she could begin to relax, knowing Leo's son was present and able to offer support. Aggie began to refocus on the results of her trip to the US and her regression.

TWENTY-NINE

The hospital was quite strict about the one visitor rule, so Aggie agreed to visit in the mornings and James in the afternoons. James had taken two weeks off from work and said, depending on what they all decided, he was OK to extend his leave. He would spend his mornings being a tourist.

"Aggie, I remember you telling me when I couldn't respond you were sorry for something that happened in America; I don't remember what it was you were sorry for?" Leo said once he was back from his bathroom visit.

"Oh Leo! It was only George Clooney; he happened to be on the same plane as me and I just had to agree to go to dinner with him!" Aggie said with a straight face. "Seriously, I just felt I didn't share with you enough when you called me in New York, but I didn't talk to anyone, including Jackson. It was the most emotional experience

I have ever been through. If you can imagine some sort of supernatural time travel, that begins to explain it," Aggie said.

"I can't imagine it, but I believe you. So, what's next?" Leo said as he shifted back onto his pillows then moved his heavily plastered leg into a comfy position.

"Well, I need to go and look at the birth, marriage and death records in Dolceacqua and see if I can find Sienna who was four times my great grandmother in 1887, then work forward from there. I don't think whoever it was she was pregnant to, was from Dolceacqua, and, for whatever reason, didn't stand by her," Aggie said as she popped a small pillow under his plastered leg. Leo grimaced.

"Did I hurt you?" Aggie asked anxiously.

"No, not my leg, my heart! I assume you will be asking the beekeeper to help you?"

Aggie suppressed her laugh. "No, not necessarily; if I can't manage myself, I will wait until you are back on your feet, you crazy, jealous Italian!"

They were continuing to hypothesise about the stigma of being an unmarried mother back in the 1800s when the doctor came in.

He explained that Leo was doing well and if he had someone to stay with him, and could manage the crutches, he would be able to go home in a couple of days. James arrived while the doctor was talking.

James said he would commit to staying with his dad for two weeks, and during that time they could reassess the situation. Aggie added that after that she would be happy to stay with him.

On the train home, Aggie smiled as she looked at her phone - a text from Leo.

"I am grateful to have James with me, but it's you I want more than ever."

Italian men really knew how to lay it on! Aggie promised Leo that she would visit him every second day in Dolceacqua whilst James was staying with him, specifying that during these visits she would also be searching for information about her ancestors. Then, when James left, she would move in with him for as long as he had the plaster on his leg.

For the first time since Aggie arrived back from New York, she had an entire day at home which included Sarah joining her for a casual lunch on the terrace.

"Are you sure about moving in with Leo?" Sarah asked after her first sip of rosé.

"Leo's plaster will only be on for four more weeks and with no lift in the building I would feel terrible if something happened to him; and I feel it's a bit much to ask James to take more time off work," Aggie replied.

Sarah laughed, "I can imagine how very happy Leo is about it!"

The conversation moved on to Aggie's experiences in New York. Sarah sat transfixed as Aggie took her through each session and described what she witnessed from the past.

"You haven't commented! I guess it is all a bit hard to believe," Aggie said, then took a long sip of her coffee.

"No, quite the opposite! I experienced an ongoing abnormal anxiety for years; it was only after my husband died and I had counselling that I opened myself to understanding it all," Sarah said then paused.

"Do you want to talk about it?" Aggie asked, offering a smile.

"I'd love to share, but only if you have the time?"

"Yes, I have the next 24 hours and I absolutely want to hear!"

The friends simultaneously leant back in the white cane terrace chairs, cradling their coffee cups.

"I was adopted as a baby and enjoyed a very happy upbringing with a younger brother. I never felt the need to ask about my biological parents; I had been told my birth mother was dead. As a child I had a special friend; she spoke to me using her hands and her heart; although my mother told me she was imaginary, to me she was very real. Then when I was about five and going to school, she disappeared," she paused, then went on. "After I finished high school, I studied as a speech therapist and especially enjoyed working with the deaf. When I met my first husband, we agreed he would work, and I would bring up the children. Although I was very happy with my family life, I continuously harboured a 'feeling' that something was missing. I can only describe it as an ache in my heart. I figured it may be some sort of longing for my birth mother. When my husband died the 'missing' feeling morphed into anxiety attacks. I spent time with a grief counsellor who encouraged me to consider changing my lifestyle, perhaps doing something I had always wanted to do. I decided to try and find out about my birth parents," Sarah paused as she put her cup down on the table.

Aggie smiled, "please go on!"

"I had always fancied living in France and had friends in Nice, so ended up here in Menton. Whether it was a coincidence or preordained, my birth parent search led me to a hospital that was just across the border in Ventimiglia. Around that time, my friends invited me to a restaurant they knew up the Nervia Valley, Terme Ristorante in Pigna. As we drove up the valley I began to perspire; it was a frightening feeling, as if all the anxieties in the world were sitting on top of me. Then, when we arrived at the restaurant, I almost collapsed from this overwhelming sensation. I managed to pull myself together to eat lunch, but popping outside to get some fresh air I looked up at the hill above the restaurant; there was Castel Vittorio, magically hovering in the sky. The vista engulfed all my senses, it was compelling! I felt such a strong need to go up there but didn't share any of this with my friends as I thought it was part of me going mad."

Sarah's phone buzzed, she glanced at her watch. "Oh! It's JP - he's home, I had better go." She stood up, then added "It took me weeks to put all the parts of the puzzle together. JP was a great help. You probably have deduced what eventually was revealed. When I saw my twin sister for the first time, my heart nearly exploded with joy. Then I went through a series of very confused feelings peppered with anger at the deceit that had taken place by my Italian grandmother, and in turn by my father. But once I understood the entire background I accepted it, and we three are making up for lost time."

Aggie had so many questions she wanted to ask. What was the deception and why had it taken place? Why was one twin adopted? But Sarah needed to leave, and she didn't want to push her. Then, as they arrived at the door Sarah added: "I can tell you hand-on-heart, extra sensory perception is very real, and memories are stored in our DNA for sure. I always felt my sister's presence; she was with me as a child, the imaginary friend. I believe I was 'guided' towards learning to communicate with deaf people. What is happening with you and your dreams just confirms to me we need to open our minds to the amazing complexities and wonder of human beings and how blood and love tie us all together!"

The two friends hugged, and Sarah promised to come up to Dolceacqua for a visit while Aggie was nurse-in-residence.

THIRTY

Aggie was distraught to hear Nonna Rosa had passed away. Leo had phoned the retirement home to make an appointment for Aggie to visit her, only to be told that Nonna had died the previous week. The manager of the facility had phoned Leo back the following day and informed him that Nonna had left a letter addressed to Agatha Sutcliffe as well as a box of old letters, and could she please come and collect it.

When Sarah came to visit Aggie in Dolceacqua the following week, she offered to drive her to the retirement home. James had returned to America and Aggie was settled in Leo's apartment; she had taken over the spare bedroom as Leo, with his plaster cast, took up most of his double bed and Aggie didn't want to accidentally knock him during the night.

"Aggie my darling, I love you being my nurse, but I prefer you being my lover. Please, I am not sick, I have a broken leg and my ribs are almost healed, please sleep with me," he whined.

Leo was beginning to irritate Aggie with his constant need for attention. She had shared with him the scenarios she had discovered in her regression sessions and the names and approximate dates of the people she had encountered. But her visit to the council building where the records were stored did not bear fruit. Everything was in Italian and the woman who worked there spoke minimal English and had a bad attitude towards Aggie.

Aggie would have loved to have engaged the beekeeper to assist but thought better of it. Now, after three weeks without being able to leave the apartment, Leo had become exceptionally grumpy and frustrated. She kept telling herself she had offered to care for him, so there was no pulling out. If the situation was reversed, she was sure he would step up to the mark.

It was such a relief when Sarah came to visit; Leo rallied and laid on the charm. The three of them shared lunch and a glass of wine together before the two women drove off to collect Nonna Rosa's box.

On the way back Aggie stroked the faded advertisement for crème caramels that adorned the lid of the old, battered cardboard box which sat on Aggie's lap. Her writer's mind wandered to thoughts of what family spirits would be released once the contents were revealed.

"Seeing my name written here in this spidery writing, it seems Nonna Rosa must have sensed she wouldn't see me again. It's a pity all the letters inside are written in Italian as I would have preferred to read them by myself," Aggie said.

"Well, I could ask my father to translate them to you if you wanted, I feel sure he wouldn't mind," Sarah said, keeping her eyes on the road as she navigated the winding road back to Dolceacqua.

"I think we would see a grown man cry if I did that! Leo will translate them, and if I am being honest with myself, I do love and trust him; but thank you for offering," Aggie said, uttering a small sigh.

Once they had parked, they decided to sit for a while at a café and continue chatting before Aggie returned to Leo's apartment.

"So, tell me Aggie, did I hear correctly in the car that you are in love?" Sarah chuckled.

"Well, I guess I am! I haven't given this much of myself to any man, in the romantic sense since my marriage. Annoying as he can be in an Italian sort of way, it feels very normal for me to be with him. I guess my Italian genes are strong. I sense he would always be loyal," Aggie replied, then took a bite from the cake they had agreed to share before she continued. "In light of your experience of finding your birth family, I think you will understand when I tell you that I believe there may be an element of the 'predestined' to Leo."

Aggie stood a minute as Sarah drove off. She was near Leo's apartment, facing the bridge where this quest had begun. The strong arch that had haunted her subconscious, the precise formation of the stones, and the accompanied sounds of the soft ripple of the shallow water over the rocks, still filled her with both a sense of belonging, and desire to resolve the unanswered questions.

"What were you thinking about?" Leo called, once Aggie was in the door. She went through to the bedroom; he was sitting on a chair looking out the window.

"What do you mean?"

"I was watching you gazing across at your bridge, I tapped on the window but of course you couldn't hear me," Leo said and offered a smile.

"Oh, it's good to see you smiling again!" Aggie said as she placed Nonna Rosa's box down on the table in front of him. "I have some work for you to do now, work we can do together."

Leo smiled and opened the box; a slightly musty smell wafted out.

"This box has been closed for a while," Leo said.

"Let's read this first!" Aggie handed Leo the separate letter. It had her name written in the same spidery writing as was on the top of the box; the writing was in proper ink, no doubt from an old-fashioned fountain pen. He cleared his throat then began to translate.

"Dear Agatha, I am sure I must be on my final journey as I cannot even get out of bed now; I regret I didn't share more with you when you visited me. You look so much like your grandmother Vera; she was my first cousin and my dearest friend. It took me back to the time before she left for England. I assume the American Italian is translating this for you, which does make me feel a little uncomfortable, but I am unable to write in English. I believe if you trust him, then I must as well. The letters in the box I have saved from various family members. They seem to be of no interest to my family anymore, no one would take them. Many are very old, so I am leaving them to you; your and my family have been connected for many generations. Please understand, in the distant past shame was a very destructive element in our society and an unwed mother was treated in a very bad way. Thank goodness this doesn't happen today.

I hope these letters may help you find the answers you seek.

With respect and love
Rosa

Aggie sniffed back her tears, then looked across at Leo who still held the letter but had dropped his hand onto his lap. A tear rolled down his cheek and he quickly moved the letter so the ink wouldn't smudge.

They sat in silence for a moment before Leo spoke.

"She was clearly a well-educated, articulate woman; what a shame we didn't get back to see her." He reached across and laid his hand on Aggie's.

"I felt that too; but I am so grateful she made the effort to write to me and leave me these; I think we have had enough emotion for today. How about I make us some supper and we start translating the letters tomorrow?"

"Memories can be rather unreliable friends," Leo stated as they sat opposite each other eating supper at the small table that looked across at Aggie's bridge.

"What do you mean by that?"

"I remember my mother telling me an incident in her life that happened with her and her sister; my mother always harboured a grudge about it. They never spoke about it and Mum did all she could to avoid my aunty. Then, when Mum died my aunty expressed her sadness at not having a close relationship with her sister. When I mentioned the incident, she was totally puzzled; her memory of it was so different and was of no consequence to her. So, I guess my comment is that whatever is spoken about in these letters is just the writer's perception of any given situation and we must look at the narrative from various perspectives."

Aggie was slightly taken aback but impressed at Leo's comment; she felt she had a kindred researcher with her.

The next morning Aggie was up early and surprised to see Leo had already made his way to the kitchen and prepared breakfast.

They decided to commence with the latest letter and work back. They checked the letters were in chronological order as best as they were able - some of the postmarks were either faded or torn. Nonna had mostly organised the letters into decades and tied each bundle with a ribbon. The postmarks were predominantly from within the Liguria area and mostly from the five mediaeval villages that were situated in the Nervia valley.

The first letter was dated 1950, 72 years ago and was postmarked London and sent from Vera to Nonna Rosa; from Aggie's calculation her grandmother Vera would have been 20 years old.

> *Dearest Cousin Rosa, London is such a large, busy city and, although there are still many destroyed buildings, the famous ones that didn't suffer from the bombing, like Westminster Abbey and Buckingham Palace, are most impressive. They say the King and Queen stayed at the Palace during the war; they must be very brave. I have a good job as a maid at a hotel in Piccadilly. (I can hear you making a comment about me being a maid!). I will just do this work until my English is good*

enough to get a better job. I have made friends with a girl in the hostel I am living in who is teaching me English and I am teaching her Italian as she has an Italian boyfriend. I miss you very much, but I really want to make my life here.

I love you always.
Cousin Vera x

Leo diligently read two more letters line-by-line which mostly gave descriptions of life in London, then the third letter said she had met a wonderful Englishman who wanted to marry her. The last letter in the bundle was the most enlightening.

Dearest Cousin Rosa, Jack Black and I are married now, so I am Mrs Black as they say in English. I wrote to Mama and Papa to tell them the news and Mama wrote back very angry as they hadn't met him and because it had happened so quickly; they suspect I am having a baby. Mama also sent me my Christening gown and said if I do have a baby, I must promise her it will be Christened in the Catholic Church. I have not told my parents yet that I am pregnant so please keep my secret until Mama announces it. She will no doubt work all the dates out and make her own truth. I am suffering a bit though. It's strange, at

night time I keep having disturbing dreams about rocks falling, then other nights I dreamt about men sitting by the river in Dolceacqua painting pictures. Jack tells me I cry out in my sleep. I do hope the dreams stop soon.
If it's a girl, she will be called Maria and if it's a boy he will be called Jack. I will post you a photo when he or she is born.

Love
Cousin Vera

"Well, that is fairly clear, my grandmother was having the 'dreams'! It seems this was the first time it happened, when she was pregnant. From what I can work out about when my mother's disturbances started, it was when she was pregnant with me," Aggie said as she got up to make them both a mid-morning coffee.

"But yours didn't start 'till you were fifty; so how does that work?" Leo replied.

Aggie returned to the living room with the small espresso cups of coffee.

"My thinking is, when I fell and knocked my head about twelve months ago it caused some sort of disturbance in my brain. I was only out for a matter of seconds, but the doctor insisted I rest for a few days and avoid looking at screens." Aggie took a sip of her coffee then continued. "According to Dr Viner's research, DNA can store certain memories just like it passes on certain ailments, determines your eye colour and various other traits. In his opinion the female line in my Italian family appears to have acute extra sensory perception as well as these inherited memories. The memories are predominantly of trauma events that weren't properly processed at the time they happened. Pregnancy alters the enzymes and many other things in your body and can act as a trigger to activate these memories; similarly, a brain injury could act as a trigger."

"So, what about your mother's mental illness?" Leo asked.

"Dr Viner said he believed she had a predisposition to puerperal psychosis which is a mental illness triggered by giving birth and the six-week period after the birth where the body reverts to a non-pregnant state. My mother's psychosis, probably due to the dreams, was extreme and morphed into a bipolar disorder diagnosis, from which she never recovered properly," As Aggie spoke, she felt a lump in her throat and her eyes welled up.

Leo reached across and took her hand. "We can stop for a while if you like?"

But Aggie dabbed her eyes and was keen to move on with the next bundle of letters.

The next was postmarked in the Nervia Valley and was from Sofia, Vera's mother, who was living at the time in Pigna, a village a few miles away. It was addressed to Marisa in Dolceacqua who was Nonna Rosa's mum. It was written in 1951 and reiterated what they had learned from Vera's letter, that Vera was married to an Englishman and expecting a baby and Sofia had sent the Christening gown.

There were a few more letters in this bundle spanning the years, mainly about daily life and gossip that didn't appear to relate to anything relevant to Aggie. Then they came to a letter from Sofia to Marisa written in 1929. It must have been delivered by hand as there was no postmark on it.

> *Dearest Sister, I hope you receive this. I am sending it with Cousin Angelo as we both trust him. He is coming down to Dolceacqua to buy wine for his brother's wedding next week. Being married isn't quite what I expected, so you must be prepared when it happens to you. What happened on our first night was quite painful, but I am getting used to it now. I guess I should know soon if I am going to have a baby or not. I tried to talk to Mama about having sex before the wedding when I was still living in Dolceacqua, but you know what she is like, she ignores the question. I heard a rumour today from that dreadful old witch with no top teeth who always gossips that Mama was adopted. I wasn't even sure what that meant at first, but then I wondered if it was true? Maybe that is why she is so difficult. Do you think you could ask her?*

I hate to think other people know things about our family that we don't know.

Your loving sister
Sofia.

The following letter was a reply to Sofia from Marisa, which Nonna Rosa must have rescued somehow. It also had no postmark.

Dearest sister Sofia, Angelo is proving useful being our personal 'go-between'. I seal mine to you with glue so you will know if he reads them. I think he quite likes me.

I managed to be with Mama on my own and built up the courage to ask her if she was adopted. It did not go well. She yelled at me that Tom and Katia were her parents as much as she was our Mama. Then she stormed out of the room and banged the door shut. It was horrible, not like when she would ignore us, or when she would cry out in the night with a bad dream and Papa would nurse her. She was hurt and angry at what I said, and I deeply regretted asking her.

I went to my bedroom and cried. She must have heard me as she came in and sat on the bed. She didn't say sorry, neither did I. She said there were things in life which we didn't know about, as it wasn't important to our happiness. Then she left. So, I have been thinking about what she said, and I think Mama is right. This adoption and the problems it has caused shouldn't make you and I unhappy, so best we ignore that stupid old witch who told you.

Your loving sister Marisa
P.s I think I would like to marry Angelo!

"Bingo! My great, great grandmother had bad dreams as well and there was an adoption! Now we are getting somewhere!" Aggie leant over and kissed Leo's cheek.

THIRTY-ONE

As well as the letters there were various receipts, birth, and death certificates in the old box. Leo was vigilant and as Aggie put things in various piles of priority, he read every line, translating where he felt it was relevant. After three intense days scrutinising most of the letters and documents they agreed, they would need to visit the town hall and check some of the names on the registered birth certificates.

The research would need to go on hold as Leo was due to go back to Nice hospital to have his plaster removed. Aggie had agreed to drive him in his newly repaired car which had been delivered the day before. If Leo picked up on her fear of agreeing to do this, he said nothing.

It took Leo quite a while to negotiate the three flights of stairs, wearing the massive heavy plaster. Aggie had retrieved the car from the carpark and pulled up as close as she could to the front door of Leo's apartment building.

Aggie had driven on the wrong side of the road before on holidays in Europe so navigating the road out of Dolceacqua wasn't too bad. Leo was very quiet. Even going through the toll gate to the motorway was straight forward, but once they were on the motorway Aggie began to sweat; she was driving in the slow lane, but cars were hurtling past her and it all seemed too fast.

"Darling you will need to go a little faster," Leo said.

Aggie could detect the fear in his voice; this was the same motorway he had crashed on. She tried to look relaxed, but her hands were sweaty as she clutched the steering wheel, and her face was flushed. She sped up and kept at a steady 95, before she began to calm down. From the corner of her eye, she caught Leo making the sign of the cross and relaxing his shoulders.

When they finally pulled into the hospital car park Leo took a deep breath and looked over at her. "This truly must be love!" he said then opened his door.

Leo was able to have his plaster removed - the bone had healed well. He was given a set of exercises he must do to strengthen the leg and he would need to go to physio weekly.

Back at the car, Leo, who now had a walking stick, was keen to drive. He had convinced Aggie that because the car was automatic, he would only need to use one foot. Aggie figured the risk of Leo driving outweighed the drama of her back at the wheel.

During the hour's drive back, Leo was very pleased to be back in control; he was relaxed and happy. They stopped in Ventimiglia to buy fresh food. Leo carefully picked out a bunch of colourful courgette flowers, some creamy looking white cheese and four pots of fresh herbs. He would need his walking stick for a while but at least he was independently mobile.

Once they had navigated the slow walk up the stairs to the apartment Leo took Aggie in his arms and gently kissed her lips.

"Let's leave the research for today and I'll cook our dinner," Leo said, raising his eyebrows and smiling; then he added, "Hopefully now my plaster is gone there will be room in my bed for both of us!"

Dinner was a taste sensation. For the starter, Leo stuffed courgette flowers with cream cheese he had blended with the three different finely chopped herbs, basil, oregano, and flat leaf parsley. He delicately drizzled the flowers in olive oil.

The main dish was very simple spaghetti pasta for which he made a tomato, garlic and sage sauce and served with green salad on the side. This was accompanied by a glass of what was Aggie's favourite Italian wine - a chilled, crisp white Vermentino.

Leo's post-plaster lease of life continued as after dinner, he led Aggie to the bedroom and with some strategic manoeuvring on both their parts, made gentle love to her, after which they both fell asleep.

There was no echo from the surrounding habitation, just the clack of her and her Mama's shoes on the cobbles as they walked up though the hushed village to meet Tom. Aggie knew she was seeing this through Isabella's eyes, her three times great grandmother, aged two. She had been here before. She knew the villagers were indoors eating lunch and napping. She was snacking on a soft apple. Her mama's meeting with Tom was very important. When they arrived at the area beneath the castle, Tom wasn't there. He must still be on his way. The deafening roar of the quake heading down the valley, the ground shaking, her mama calling her name, the wall crashing around her pushed her young brain into total confusion and shock. She ran to her mama; her head was lying flat on the ground with a pile of rocks on her chest and arms. Mama, Mama please wake up!

"Aggie it's okay, it's a dream."

Aggie could hear the soothing tone of her lover's voice somewhere in the distance. She forced open her eyes. Leo put his arm gently across her.

"Do you want to tell me where you were?" he said softly.

"I saw my mama dead, or rather Isabella saw her dead, no wonder she was a distant mother in Sofia and Marisa's letters. What a terrible thing to witness," Aggie said as she sat up. "I saw it when Clive regressed me at the clinic, it was much worse then."

"Maybe we should slow down with the research if it is bringing up all this past. It was safer in the controlled environment you had with Dr Viner and his team," Leo said as he propped their pillows up behind their backs against the bed head.

Aggie was quiet for a few moments, then she took a deep breath and gained her composure. "No, I am okay. I need to see this through to some sort of conclusion. To repress trauma, to not face things and not move forward, causes more damage. I feel I need to resolve this for my own sanity and for all my female ancestors who passed it down to me."

She got out of bed and took her notebook from her bag and recorded what she had seen and felt.

It was 3am, Leo limped out to the kitchen and managed to bring them both a cup of herbal tea.

"Let's see if we can go back to sleep; I will hold you in my arms," he said, once they had finished their tea.

Aggie slid down into the cotton sheets; they were refreshingly cool on her skin. She embraced the contrasting warmth of Leo's muscular arms around her and thanked the universe that she wasn't alone.

The next morning, they had emptied the cardboard box, and the contents were in piles that Aggie had made on the floor on one side of the salon. There were still a few faded letters without envelopes they hadn't got to, but they were both keen to see if they could find Isabella's birth certificate.

Whilst Aggie believed she had faced the death of Isabella's mama through her two recalls of the trauma of the earthquake and had dealt with it, she still didn't know who Isabella's mama was.

The dumpy assistant in charge of births, marriages and deaths at the Dolceacqua town hall was a middle-aged woman with garlic breath who scowled at Aggie.

Leo handled her with his natural charm, and they gained access to what they needed.

The earthquake was in 1887 and Aggie figured Isabella would have been at least two years old then, so they began their search in the files for 1885. It was a laborious process which showed two Isabellas being born but both to parents with completely different family names and Leo was able to cross reference their marriage and death certificates which made it clear they were not Aggie's Isabella. They did, however, find a marriage certificate for Isabella and Carlos Raimondo; it named Isabella's parents as Tomas and Katia Peron; however, there was a small, smudged scrawl beside their names. The dumpy record keeper had been hovering nearby and could see Leo was struggling to decipher something. She appeared beside them with a magnifying glass and imparted a garlicky comment to Leo. He peered through the glass, as he translated for Aggie – the word 'custode' which means 'guardian' in English came up. She took a photograph on her phone of the certificate and decided, as they had been in the records office for a full five hours, they would call it a day.

The next morning, back at the cardboard box research, Leo managed to read a faded letter which opened with "My Dearest Daughter".

> *My Dearest Daughter, I have made an official will with the advocate in Ventimiglia that my wife and your Carlos will get to read when I die. But I needed*

to write this to you privately and unofficially as, because of the circumstances of your birth, my wife and your husband do not want to acknowledge the real truth. I understand why they are like this, but you must not carry any shame. What I told you when you turned 16 was a very difficult thing to grasp, and at times I have doubts if I should have told you at all. But as I am now getting very old, my views are strong on this point, I believe we should not have wiped your real mama from your story. It is so important to know, no matter what anyone says, you were always loved. Your real mama was called Sienna, and she was the love of my life. She adored you and you spent the first two years of your life with her. Then, after her tragic death, you appeared to have no memory of her at all. My wife agreed to be your Mama and she loved you as much as she could. We agreed never to mention Sienna and we moved to Apricale for a while in the hope that the gossip would be less. But there are still evil people who will always point the finger. Be strong, my precious Isabella, like your mama.

*Love forever
Papa Tom*

"It would seem Tom had an extramarital affair?" Leo said, looking to Aggie for comment.

"This letter seems to indicate that. But my gut tells me that might not be the case," Aggie replied.

After lunch, they were nearing the end of all the documents, when Leo picked up a frayed, faded piece of paper which was stuck to the back of a receipt which had been for the delivery of a cart full of firewood. The receipt was dated 1886.

He used Aggie's hairdryer to heat the paper then, very deftly peeled the second piece off. The writing was scrawly and faded but legible.

There was no 'Dear' or 'Dearest'; this was a curt letter.

> *Sienna, what you have done to our good family name is disgusting and sinful. Hiding out in Pigna with that child won't solve the problem. You need to move away from here or accept Tom's proposal of marriage. We don't want you living in this valley with your bastard daughter. If you don't marry Tom, you will be dead to us. To throw yourself at that man from Paris was wicked. He will never come back for you.*
>
> *Mother.*

Aggie thrust her hands to her mouth as she abruptly stood up.

"Oh my God! Isabella's father was French, this is a whole new twist!"

THIRTY-TWO

"There can't have been many men from Paris here in Dolceacqua in 1885!" Leo stated.

Aggie was already tapping into her Google search.

"Just because he was from Paris doesn't mean he was French. Dolceacqua attracted many painters during that time including Claude Monet. I don't recall any French blood being mentioned in my DNA, but I will email Dr Viner tonight with this latest information and see what he can add."

"With all this research we are doing, I think I will send for a DNA test as well just to see how closely related we are," Leo added, laughing as they chatted through the possibilities of why Isabella's lover didn't return to her.

"Maybe he was killed; maybe he didn't know he left her pregnant," Aggie said.

"Or maybe he was married, and it was a one-night stand," Leo added.

Dr Viner acknowledged Aggie's email and said he would submit her updated information to his team and do a new search of her DNA sample to establish any French connections.

Aggie needed to broach the subject with Leo about her moving back to her own apartment. They were enjoying their after lunch coffee when she mustered up the courage.

"I feel we have made big steps in our research. I can now comfortably say that the trauma of Sienna's death, which Isabella witnessed, has been resolved. I am confident the second time I observed the horror has allowed me to deal with it on behalf of all my female ancestors. However, I now have a sense that the love affair which Sienna had and the lover she became pregnant to, hurt her deeply. All this secrecy and silence around his name does suggest he was most likely married. She would have been a virgin; she would have been naïve; and she would have been vulnerable; at the time of her death she would have been living life in a high state of anxiety," Aggie said, then paused to take a sip of her coffee.

"I can hear a 'but' coming?" Leo clutched his cup and raised his eyebrows.

"It has been wonderful having you share all this with me, and we will keep sharing, but I need to go back to my own apartment for a few days."

Aggie averted her eyes as Leo's bottom lip trembled.

He quickly recovered. "I know you do, I have just got so comfortable with you being here," he said.

"We won't stop the search now, I will do all I can to find out who this 'bounder' was who preyed on such a young girl, then deserted her. I don't have to imagine how she felt because her hurt, and trauma are residing within my memory. I can feel what she felt but could never express. If she had lived longer, maybe, as she matured, she would have found a way to overcome her pain and all the guilt. Imagine, during her entire pregnancy she was berated by her mother and shunned by her community. It would also have had an adverse effect on her unborn baby. So, my three-times great grandmother had a lot to deal with."

Leo took Aggie's hands in his.

"As you speak you radiate love for this ancestor the same as if she was a friend living with us now, and, by association, I am totally drawn into her world with you."

Aggie smiled and kissed his cheek.

The following day as Leo drove to Menton, Aggie silently reflected that her quest was also a catalyst for her relationship with Leo. There weren't a lot of men who would volunteer for such a mission. They agreed he would come and stay with her for the weekend which allowed Aggie three days to herself.

That evening it was comfort food she craved; she settled on baked beans on white toast and a cup of frothy hot chocolate; then she enjoyed a long leisurely phone call with Jackson.

The next morning full of the joy of a new day, Aggie opened the word documents page on her laptop and commenced typing:

The hurt from my mother's desertion, and the shock of her death left me staggering along through life, full of self-doubt for far too long. I now know that my mother loved me. It was the right time for her to walk out of the shadows, and for her soul and her memory to walk tall beside me. I will accept the privilege that I have been lucky enough to be born in a time when science is able to explain the previously inexplicable; a privilege my ancestors never had. My mental health and my life won't now have to be 'afflicted' by the memories stored in my DNA. I have the tools to understand them. Sienna, Isabella, Sofia, Vera and Maria this book is for you......'

Her phone beeped a text.

"Do you fancy a light supper with us tonight, 7pm?" S x

"Great, thanks, see you then. A x"

Aggie still wasn't quite sure where this new manuscript would take her, but she had a beginning and almost had the middle part; it was just the ending that was still a mystery.

She continued writing on and off for most of the day. To establish credibility early in the manuscript, Aggie understood the importance of setting up the scientific validity of the journey. So, she included validation excerpts from the various different institutes she had researched regarding "stored memory" DNA:

Psychology, genetic memory is a theorised phenomenon in which certain kinds of memories could be inherited, being present at birth in the absence of any associated sensory experience, and that such memories could be incorporated into the genome over long spans of time[3].

Aggie needed to be wary of saturating her reader with too much science; it was a process of balancing it with the real-life action to keep the reader turning the page.

By 7pm she had changed and was ready for company. It was so easy socialising with Sarah and JP; Aggie only had to step across the hallway; they both always seemed so happy and relaxed in each other's company. Aggie was inspired by their friendship and struggled a bit to imagine that Sarah had been previously happily married to someone else. Maybe happiness begot happiness.

The conversation naturally moved to Aggie's regression experiences and the facts of her family history she had unravelled. As open-minded as JP was, Aggie could detect a hint of scepticism in some of his questions. Whereas Sarah was wholly within Aggies realm of 'extra sensory perception' and its consequences.

"I have sent off for a DNA test, to the same company you used; JP is so far reluctant. I am intrigued as my

---

[3] https://en.wikipedia.org/wiki/Genetic_memory_(psychology)

mother's side is Jewish and English but, from what I know, totally Italian on my father's side," Sarah said.

The two women were engrossed in the subject and hardly noticed when JP slid off to bed.

As Aggie hugged Sarah goodbye at the door, she felt a deeper sense of connection with this wonderful woman and silently thanked her son for the initial push to make contact. That one action had triggered this whole adventure.

THIRTY-THREE

Leo arrived at Aggie's apartment at precisely 4pm on Friday. He was walking with much less of a limp and had brought a basket of food with him. He was keen to know how the manuscript was going and if Aggie had heard any update from Dr Viner's DNA search into the "Paris man".

Aggie chatted as she made a pot of tea.

"He advised that up to twenty per cent of my family antecedents may be French. He is searching for another more specialised database, which he said normally takes at least one to two weeks for a response. So, we will have to wait for that. As to my writing, I am currently presenting the story in the form of a biography, but until my memory journey is complete I have no idea what the ending will be."

Aggie poured the fragrant tea into the bone China cups as they sat side by side on the velvet sofa.

"I gather I won't be invited to read any of it at this stage?" Leo said as he raised his eyebrows then took a noisy sip of the hot tea.

"You are correct! With all the books I have ever written, I never share a partial draft with anyone, even Jackson or Pushy Penny, my ex-agent. I must complete it to the best I can, then I welcome critique and comments before my first rewrite," Aggie said, took a sip of tea, then added: "But you my Italian stallion shall be mentioned in only the most manly of terms!" She laughed out loud at her own innuendo; Leo beamed, then put down his cup, took her hand and limped, leading her to the bedroom.

After the intense time they had been through with Leo's accident and recovery and Aggie's concentrated memory scan, they both agreed to enjoy a total break from it all through the weekend. On Saturday morning Leo suggested a wander through the old town into the square for a late breakfast, reassuring Aggie he would be fine provided she was happy walking at a snail's pace. They settled down at a café near the carousel, ordered their croissants and coffee, smiling as the little children ran full of excitement to grab the most colourful horse on the ride.

"Hello neighbours!"

Aggie glanced up to see Sarah looking her usual chic self, wearing white jeans and a striped T shirt and large designer sunglasses. JP was in navy chinos, a polo shirt and pristine white sneakers finished off with trendy aviator sunnies. They were each carrying a bag full of food from the morning market.

"We are not interrupting you love birds, are we?" Sarah asked.

"For goodness' sake no, sit down," Aggie responded as JP signalled to the waiter for coffee.

"We were about to text you; we wanted to invite you across the hall for supper tonight if you didn't have plans," JP said.

Both Leo and Aggie nodded in agreement, then Sarah added: "We have something to tell you".

"What?" Aggie asked.

"Not telling until tonight when we have a glass of champagne in our hands!"

That evening Sarah was wearing the biggest smile when she answered the door; a bottle of Champagne sat in a gleaming silver ice bucket.

Little was said as JP popped the cork and poured the chilled elegant elixir into the crystal champagne flutes.

Sarah was the first to speak. She looked directly at Aggie. "Do you look at the updates you receive from Hereditary.com?"

"I haven't opened any since Wednesday last week, why?"

"Well, you know I had my DNA done, and just like you, I ticked the box to allow me to be connected to any relatives, also on the site. I received an email on Friday morning showing several English and Italian family trees as well as a fourth cousin called Agatha Sutcliffe!" Sarah said and raised her glass.

"To cousins!" JP shouted and raised his glass.

Aggie was gob-smacked. She finally said: "But how"?

"It's via a family called Raimondo who have been in the Nervia Valley for generations and married into other families in the five villages of the valley. So, I guess it was inevitable that my father and your grandmother were connected." Sarah's eyes welled with tears of joy.

Aggie put her arms around her. "This is just so wonderful! "

Sarah took a sip of champagne then said. "I have a wonderful adoptive brother and the parents that raised me were the best; my children fulfilled all the hopes I had for them; but when I found my birth father and sister, I felt complete. And now, the icing on the cake is I have a cousin who happens to already be my friend!"

"You omitted someone," JP interjected.

"Oh JP! You are different my darling, as we don't share DNA; ours is a 'carnal' relationship. I especially chose you," Sarah said as she planted a kiss on her husband's lips.

She had printed out a copy of what Hereditary.com had sent her; Leo was studying it. "It will be interesting to see if I am a part of this family as well. I will apply for my kit tomorrow!"

The bottle of champagne was finished and by the time they sat down for dinner the foursome was full of "joie de vivre" at this family revelation. The celebrations continued when JP opened an excellent bottle of Mouton de Rothchild.

It was after midnight when Aggie and Leo returned to their apartment. "What a night!" Leo said, putting his arm around Aggie as they sat down on the sofa. The full moon had cast an impressive shard of golden light onto the mirror-like sea.

"It must be one of my most perfect nights ever! A new cousin, a stunning midnight view from my own window and a perfect lover!" Aggie said, resting her head on Leo's shoulder. Then added: "You know I used to believe things were just a coincidence. But from the moment I looked at the photos of this apartment Sarah sent me, things started happening. I now firmly believe everything happens for a reason!"

"So, I was predestined to meet you?" Leo asked.

Aggie smiled. "Come on it's late, let's go to bed," she said.

Jackson was delighted with the news that in a rather convoluted way he was related to Sarah's son, Nick. Aggie reminded him that there was Sarah's daughter Florence as well. He said he would organise for them all to meet up.

"I am chuffed to have Rebecca as a cousin as well and dear old Mario as an even closer cousin!" Aggie exclaimed and they sat on the terrace enjoying a late leisurely breakfast.

Leo left reluctantly for Dolceacqua the next morning, but Aggie wanted to get on with her writing and agreed to spend the following weekend in Italy with him.

She was impatient to hear back from Dr Viner; she was sure the Paris connection was the key to who seduced her ancestor, Sienna; the man who took her virginity and abandoned her with a baby. Whilst Aggie was realistic enough to know this anger and angst was all in the past and life must move on, she still felt a passionate need to know who the man was and, for her own peace of mind, bring the trauma that Sienna experienced all those years ago, to a conclusion. The DNA thread was strong.

That evening Aggie was going through her accessory drawer trying to locate a pair of earrings she had lost when she came across the small box with the pendant her father had given her. She opened the box, placed the pendant and chain in her hand and gently stroked the unusual shape of the pendant with her forefinger. She sensed her mother's presence. But it was in the realm of her eight-year-old self, the age she was before she understood her mother's illness. At eight she still remembered her parents' happiness together. She savoured the feeling. Still carrying the necklace, Aggie retrieved the file she had collected on everything to do with her dreams and memories and picked out the old black and white photo Lyall had enlarged for her. It was the photo of her grandmother Vera as a child standing with her parents Sofia and Claudio. Aggie located the magnifying glass from her office cupboard and enlarged the photo as big as she could. Then suddenly she spotted it! Sofia was wearing a pendant, and Aggie was pretty sure it was the same one she had here in her hand. So, this pendant was of some significance. She photographed the pendant, then went online to see if she could find anything of a similar type to help source its provenance. Nothing came up and rather than return the pendant to the box, Aggie stood in front of the mirror and placed it around her neck. It was like she'd been wearing it her whole life already.

THIRTY-FOUR

It was Friday morning and Aggie felt her blood pressure rise as she spotted an email from Dr Viner on her laptop. He said they had located a French family name that carried DNA which they could also connect to Aggie. The name was Cauvin. He included the details and added that there was another name, but he was unable to access it as it was in a confidential file. He went on to explain that it was probably related to the provenance of an historic artwork; the Art Repatriation organisation which reunited stolen art with its rightful owners often hid the 'searching' family's DNA from public access until the art had been returned.

As she had promised Leo, she would catch the 10am train and meet him in Ventimiglia; she knew she would have to put her research aside for today and get sorted for her weekend in Dolceacqua.

Aggie had no doubt Leo would be waiting at the train station. He had proven himself to be always punctual and always reliable; both traits Aggie had never previously experienced in a relationship; it was a new notion, and it sat well with her.

At the entrance to the Ventimiglia station her short, slightly rounded, well-dressed lover was waiting, carrying an oversized woven basket; as Aggie approached, he placed the basket on the ground then, with both arms, embraced her and kissed her passionately on the lips. As he released her a loud passing English voice exclaimed in a very unsubtle tone "oversexed Italians!"

Leo and Aggie were still laughing as they reached the food market. They had agreed to buy some pre-made dishes for the weekend and chose some fresh gnocchi from the pasta lady accompanied by a sauce of Leo's choice. By the time they arrived at the car the basket was full of Italian delights.

As they approached Dolceacqua a wave of warmth flickered through Aggie. The sight of the mediaeval village, the towers of the ruins of the castle, then the distinct arch of the bridge that had provoked this unexpected new passage of Aggie's life, now triggered a new feeling of belonging. A belonging with a history speckled with sadness. It was from this village that her maternal ancestors had unintentionally forwarded her their traumatic memories. The DNA journey of these stored memories had caused confusion, stress, and mental illness in the generations before her. In Aggie's case there was a difference; science and education had afforded her a path of understanding, of enlightenment and she was determined to ensure that for her part, life would have a happy ending.

Leo's limp was now minimal, and he insisted on carrying the laden basket up the three flights of stairs to the apartment.

Once they were sitting, eating their fresh pasta, Aggie shared Dr Viner's latest revelation and the French name with Leo.

As soon as the table was clear they pulled up the name Françoise Cauvin on the search engine. She was an established artist that died in 2017 aged 91; they further discovered she was the granddaughter of Léon Monet, Claude Monet's older brother.

"Do you think Léon Monet came here with his brother when he was painting the bridge, or is this a coincidence?" Aggie asked, her voice full of excitement.

"Well, it's possible. Reading through this Wikipedia page, Léon was a great supporter of his brother's work," Leo said, as continued scrolling around the screen of his laptop.

Their conversation and speculation about the Cauvin family continued until the next day but didn't bear much fruit. They couldn't find any evidence that Françoise Cauvin had had any children.

They had settled in alongside what appeared to be most of the village for Sunday lunch at the Ristorante Casa e Bottega, when Leo suggested: "I realise we don't have access to the confidential second name that Dr Viner spoke of, but I thought we could add some enjoyment to the research by taking a trip to Paris and spending a day at Monet's old home, Giverny. I am sure there will be information on other members of the Monet family, including Léon, stored there, as it's now a public museum. We can perhaps request a chat with the curator. I am confident we will learn a lot."

Aggie didn't immediately respond. Leo's face said it all. Intense anticipation.

"So, would this mean we would have to spend a few days in the most romantic city in the world? Would your leg hold up?" Aggie asked, with a mischievous twinkle in her eye.

"I know you are 'winding me up', as you English say! Yes, it is very clear I want to be in Paris with my lover. But I stand by what I said about Giverny; it's a good place to explore the possibility of discovering something about Léon Monet's sex life in 1885," Leo said.

After lunch they looked up the days and times that Giverny was open, discussed travelling by train versus flying, and debated where and for how long they would stay in Paris.

By the time Leo dropped Aggie back in Menton they had agreed to fly in ten days' time, stay at Giverny for one night, and in Paris two nights either side of that visit; Leo would choose, as a surprise, their hotel, and Aggie must allow him to pay for that.

She was pondering the fact that while a new relationship is wonderful, it's always a continued negotiation with compromise. Accepting Leo's offer, she insisted she needed the next full week to herself in Menton to research further possibilities of the name Cauvin and to spend focused time on her manuscript.

Although motivated to get on with her research, Aggie was keen to touch base with Sarah. With the recently discovered new dimension to their relationship both women were enjoying living in such close proximity and being able to step across the hall for a coffee together.

"Well, is this name 'Cauvin' very common in France?" Sarah asked, as they sat at the terrace table with their coffees.

"According to my research, it is a fairly common family name; a large percentage reside in Normandy," Aggie replied.

"So how exactly does that connect to your DNA and or Monet's brother?"

"It's a bit convoluted; Dr Viner's scan of the databases looking for similarities to my DNA resulted in two hits – the Cauvin one and another where details cannot be revealed because of confidentiality issues. I need to find out if Françoise Cauvin has any living descendants as there may be a connection between the confidential person and the Cauvin family. It is a least possible I am more closely related to the mystery person, than the Françoise Cauvin," Aggie explained, then added: "I know it's hard to follow, but if I can find out for sure that I share DNA with Leon Monet's descendants then it's a big start to establishing who may have fathered Sienna's baby."

Sarah laughed. "And Leo gets to have a wonderful romantic time with you in Paris!"

"I am very comfortable with that!" Aggie smiled as she walked Sarah to the door.

Aggie had been slow in updating Jackson on developments, so emailed him and scheduled a Zoom call for after supper.

There were hundreds of Cauvins around the world, and she kept drawing a blank with finding anything about any possible children from Françoise Cauvin. She would need to write to the curator of her last exhibition to see if she would be willing to assist.

Later that evening during her Zoom call with Jackson and Lyall, it was Lyall who appeared most interested in her discovery of the Monet family connection. He made notes and asked diplomatically if Aggie would allow him to do some digging on her behalf. Aggie was delighted.

Then Jackson steered the conversation to her Paris trip. "How would you feel about the possibility of us joining you for a night or two in Paris?" Unusually, Aggie was lost for words; it was tricky attempting to disguise her discomfort on the screen. She rubbed her nose then replied: "Oh, Jackson you know I always adore being with you both, but in this case, I really think it's one of those Paris visits for lovers rather than mothers and sons".

Jackson grimaced. Lyall, who was sitting directly beside him, placed his hand on Jackson's hand. "Come on darling, we three can do Paris another time. Leo is treating your deserving mama to a smart hotel, and it really isn't appropriate for her son and his lover tag along."

"Bloody short, fat Italian!" he blurted out.

The other two roared with laughter, and eventually Jackson forced a smile.

"I am being as possessive as he is, aren't I?"

"Well, you are part-Italian," Aggie said, still laughing, then gave them a wave on the screen and clicked out.

THIRTY-FIVE

Leo was what Aggie would term "over organised", but the upside was, it allowed her to enjoy the journey more. She didn't have to pay attention to the airline tickets, the cab at the airport, or the hotel reservations. He was very secretive about the hotel; she still had no idea where they were staying until the cab pulled up in front of a high double doorway that led into a cobbled, romantic courtyard.

They were greeted by two smartly dressed young men who carried their cases up the single flight of outdoor stairs to the reception area. They were at Relais Christine in the heart of Saint-Germain-des-Prés. Whilst Aggie thought the hotel name sounded slightly suburban in English, the building, the décor, and the ambience oozed with French charm from an earlier age. When they entered the divine two-room suite Leo had arranged, Aggie not only could appreciate the excellent taste and see the comfort, but she could practically smell the money.

"Wow Leo! This is just so wonderful; I am feeling a bit overwhelmed at what it must have cost." Once the words were out, she instantly regretted it. So uncool not to be gracious. But Leo didn't seem too badly affected. He beamed.

"Mi esora, anything for you! And to see how happy your face is now; it was money well spent."

After they had explored the sumptuous bathroom with its large, roll-topped, wrought-iron, claw-footed bath, his-and-her basins and the essential French bidet, Leo guided Aggie into the bedroom and closed the curtains. Then he popped back out the room and hung the "Do not Disturb" sign on the door. He took a bottle of champagne from the fridge, opened it, and poured two glasses.

"Let me undo your dress, and then slide in between these 3,000-thread-count sheets, next to me," Leo said, as he lovingly kissed the back of Aggie's neck.

They were lying on top of the sheet, both naked, sipping the champagne. Aggie held the crisp sheet over her breasts. Leo gently pulled the sheet down. Aggie watched, bemused as Leo dribbled a little champagne from the glass between her breasts; he began to lick it gently which took Aggie from bemused to highly aroused.

They awoke from the kind of nap that senior people need after lovemaking, around 4pm, satiated, and ready to bathe and dress for dinner.

As Aggie applied her makeup her mind wandered to how she would describe this day, this moment, in writers' terms. She would describe it as "all so desperately romantic". Her lover had set the perfect scene in a charming hotel in the most impressive city in the world and she felt hopelessly in love. Then, as she applied her lipstick, she smiled at herself in the mirror; no, she wasn't a 5 feet 10 inch slim 30-year-old; the reality was 52 years old and a chunky 5 feet five tall. But life had a way of giving you just what you need at the right time - this was Aggie's time!

They had discussed in advance that they both wished to eat at restaurants with old world Paris charm. Aggie had made the choice for the first evening and reserved a table at Le Chardenoux in the 11th arrondissement. It still had all the original art nouveau décor. It was impressive. However, when they were handed two menus, Aggie was a little disappointed at the lack of traditional French food choices. Leo commented that he and Aggie were most likely in the minority to desire old fashioned French food.

"Younger people prefer to eat in a lighter fashion with more of a fusion influence" he said.

Before ordering their meal, they decided to experience a "Midnight in Paris" cocktail which contained a new, exotic vodka neither of them had ever heard of. It was infused with hibiscus and there were fresh raspberries, peach, and lemon in it as well, all shaken with great theatrics by the barman.

"I think I am feeling young and modern drinking this concoction!" Aggie said laughing as they clinked glasses.

"Now that I understand how you visualise your surroundings in terms of how you would describe it in writing, would you do me the honour of describing this magnificent room we are sitting in?" Leo asked once they had placed their orders.

Aggie took a long look around the room, followed by a prolonged sip of her cocktail then cleared her throat. "A perfect example of delicious art nouveau architecture; hand-painted, sage-green leaves adorning the mint green walls; sumptuous, deep-red, velvet banquettes offering glamorous seating to tables that are draped in pristine-white linen tablecloths; the tables are arranged on a faded red and black tiled floor where frilled, bejewelled chandeliers hang overhead, enhancing the perfect illumination for a romantic evening."

All this was said in her best BBC voice and Aggie offered Leo a wide smile as their first course arrived.

"I am impressed! The creative, observant part of your brain appears to speedily absorb information, then dissects it incredibly fast. I guess that's also a part of why you have been able to process these stored memories so well," Leo observed, then took a mouthful of food.

"Maybe, who really knows? I believe women do it in a different way to men. It is a fact we only use twenty percent of our brain, and I am discovering the more I learn about this, the more I stretch my thought processes and keep my mind open to theories that aren't mainstream," Aggie said then pushed her fork into the soft-boiled egg, herbs and sautéed mushrooms that constituted her entrée. After a few approving mouthfuls she continued. "The frustrating thing about the memories in my DNA is that they are all related to some sort of trauma, I would love to have a dream that left me feeling happy about my female ancestors!"

"Maybe once you have solved this final riddle, your mind will rest. You may even begin to dream of me!" Leo chuckled at his own rhetoric.

They continued the meal with a mixture of lighthearted humour and speculation about Leon Monet. They both had ordered fillet mignon as a main course served with creamy dauphinoise potatoes. They had ignored the waiter's frown of disapproval when they requested it be cooked medium to well done. It arrived at the table barely medium, but despite this it was delicious; the texture of the beef was so smooth, it was like cutting into butter and melted in the mouth.

They were both too full after their two courses to have dessert and agreed they could walk at least part of the way back to the hotel. Google maps informed them it was a 50-minute walk.

"Paris for me is all about serene evenings like this, and the sights we will see by moonlight, so much better by foot," Aggie mused as they held hands and walked towards the Place de Bastille.

As they reached the edge of the Seine, which was halfway back to the hotel, they realised they may have been a bit ambitious walking this far. But it is almost impossible to hail a cab in Paris, and they hadn't come across any cab ranks. So, they found a bench on a grassy area of the river to sit and catch their breath.

A couple of minutes had passed when Leo leaped up and let out a yelp. "What's wrong?" Aggie asked.

"Bloody rats! Look over there!" he exclaimed, pointing at a spot a couple of metres away, beside a rubbish bin. It was more than one or two rats; the ground appeared to be in motion. Aggie would describe it as a sea of rodents.

They moved as quickly as their short legs and Aggie's heels would carry them over the bridge, then stayed firmly to the pavement as they walked through the Latin quarter.

"Where is that pied piper when you need him?" Aggie quipped as they finally entered the gates of Relais Christine. It was with great relief when they sunk into the luxurious hotel bed and were both asleep within minutes.

They had settled on a plan of visiting the museums which displayed Monet's work, after they had visited Giverny. They had compromised in agreeing to choose a museum to visit; Leo chose the Le Musée de la Chasse et de la Nature à Paris for the morning visit and Aggie chose the Musée Nissim de Camondo for after lunch.

Travelling around Paris on foot and using the Metro was familiar to both. After a leisurely breakfast including a perfect croissant and excellent French coffee, they made their way to the Marais to Leo's Musée. In English it translated to the Museum of Nature and Hunting, which sounded a bit boring to Aggie. However, she made no comment and was pleasantly surprised when they arrived at the building, which was a stunning 17th century construction, originally called L'Hotel De Guenegauad. In 1967 Andre Malraux had converted it into a private museum. Leo had visited many years ago and clearly was delighted to do so again as the exhibitions were regularly updated. The main theme of the displays was the relationship between man and animals through time. It also had an impressive arsenal of vintage guns, armoury and weapons that did nothing for Aggie, but she was most impressed with the array of wonderful taxidermy, including a large polar bear as well as the furniture gallery of such craft and beauty.

After Aggie had yawned a couple of times, Leo sensed that two hours had been enough. Once out in the street they chose a picturesque Parisian style brasserie to eat a light lunch. Aggie listened patiently, feigning interest and checking a message on her phone, while Leo rattled on about prehistoric man and killing animals to live.

"Am I boring you?" he suddenly said abruptly.

Aggie was a little taken aback. "Sorry, no, you weren't really boring me; I am just so distracted. My mind is entrenched in the last four generations of my maternal family and the thought of focusing on prehistoric man triggered the thought that If I was led back any further, my brain would explode, and I would be another casualty of mental illness."

As Aggie spoke, she could instantly see Leo was aggrieved. He went silent, he raised his hand to the waitress to ask for the bill. Aggie believed she hadn't said anything offensive; she had just been honest.

They walked out of the brasserie without speaking.

"Leo, I was just expressing myself, I didn't mean to offend you," Aggie said, somewhat defensively. She should have left it there but when he didn't smile or come back with any reassurance, she felt very annoyed.

"Stop acting so oversensitive and immature!" she blurted out.

This was the first time she had seen him react in this way. He firmly took her arm and steered her beside the building away from the street, then dropped her arm and said: "Aggie I am neither overly sensitive nor immature. I am a patient man. But perhaps you need to look a little closer at your own behaviour and choice of words. It is all very well being on a 'quest' but there happens to be two of us in this relationship and at times you are quite self-centred."

Aggie was aghast. Fuming, she turned and walked briskly away towards the Metro station. She had gone half a block when she realised Leo wasn't following her. This made her even more angry. She stormed down into the station and checked the stop closest to the next planned Museum. The train was crowded; a hot, strong aroma of sweaty humans hung in the air. Aggie couldn't find a seat and was forced to stand; she was cornered in a position with her nose about an inch away from a very sweaty armpit. It was a huge relief when the train finally arrived at Malesherbes station. As Aggie walked up the stairs she burst into tears. By the time she arrived at Musée Nissim de Camondo the tears had stopped, and her anger abated.

The Museum was an immaculately preserved château in the middle of Paris. Aggie walked through the tall gates and sat down on a wooden bench near to the entrance door. She took out her phone. No message from Leo. She needed to sound off to someone, but realised Jackson, given his jealousy, would be the wrong person. She was embarrassed to call Sarah, then as that thought passed through her mind, she was forced to ask herself why she would be uncomfortable telling Sarah? After a few more minutes Aggie had to admit to herself that she had been a bit of a "Princess". Leo was always so accommodating she had clearly taken her position too far. Why did she have this habit of shooting herself in the foot, when things were going well?

She took a deep breath and sent a one-word text to Leo: "Sorry!"

Then, figuring as she had come this far, she decided to do a tour of the Château. The refurbishment of the 18th Century residence was undertaken from 1911 to 1914 by Moïse de Camondo, who spared no expense ensuring the elegance and beauty of this magnificent residence was retained.

Moïse de Camondo was a collector of furniture, paintings, carpets, tapestries, porcelain and gold-smithery.

He expertly showcased these collections in the purpose-built rooms.

Aggie paid for her ticket and the audio guide explained in detail the intricacies of the various rooms and objects of art. The porcelain room really took her fancy, and she felt a keen sense of loss that Leo wasn't there to share the experience with her. She kept checking her phone every few minutes, but he had not responded. By the time she reached the small 'cinema' room to watch the old black and white movie, including shots of a time when the Camondo family were still living in the house, she knew she had probably blown the whole Leo romance. Aggie felt sick to her stomach. At the end of the film, when it was revealed that the entire Camondo family were exterminated in World War Two because they were Jewish, the tears that welled in her eyes were not for them but for herself.

Aggie wasn't sure what to do. She figured she may as well go back to the hotel and take what she figured was coming to her. She handed back her audio headset at the reception desk and momentarily felt a little uncomfortable as someone, who was a little too close, stood behind her. She didn't turn around but stepped sideways and walked out the door. Just as she was about to check her phone for the hundredth time, the message ping sounded. Leo's name flashed. The text read: 'Turn around'. Aggie heard someone clear their voice behind her. She turned around. Leo was standing just past the entrance door. He walked towards her.

"Oh, Leo I really am sorry!" Aggie exclaimed, facing him, but not touching.

"Thank you for saying that" he replied then reached out and took her hand. She burst into tears. He pulled her to him. "I am not that bad; I figured the tears in the 'cinema' room were penance enough."

Aggie stepped back from him. "You were following me?"

"Well, not exactly, had you not been so self-absorbed and looked behind you or gone back on yourself at any point you would have bumped into me. So, I wasn't stalking you, I was just sticking to our plan to visit a museum of our choice," Leo said with a slight smirk.

Aggie embraced the humour and laughed. "So, am I forgiven?"

Leo took her hand as they walked out the gates towards the Metro, then replied: "As long as you will still have dinner with me and tell me how wonderful I am!"

Aggie felt things were still a little chilled between them as they arrived back at the hotel. She didn't wish to push anything with him. She was desperate to have a bath and some space of her own. The bathroom offered a selection of delicious shower and bath treats. Aggie poured the fragrant bath oil into the oversized bath and then ran the water. She closed the door and turned the playlist on her phone on; she had been soaking for about ten minutes with Ed Sheeran on, when Leo appeared wearing the hotel robe.

"I sense we haven't fully reconciled our first serious disagreement, but I would be most grateful if you would accept a back rub with no expectation from me as an act of reconciliation on my part?" Leo said, smiling and raising his eyebrows at the same time. Aggie returned the smile and passed him the facecloth. True to his word, he only soaped and rubbed her back without his hands wandering to any other parts of her body.

They had discussed that they would have a light early supper somewhere casual and close to the hotel as they were catching an early train to Giverny the next morning. There was a wonderful little brasserie along the main street of Saint-Germain; as they walked in, they were offered the last available table. After the first glass of wine, the mood had moved on. Both had managed to push aside the harsh words that were exchanged previously. Leo was making Aggie laugh with tales of his heinous trip to Paris he had had with his then American wife who complained about everything, mostly the food. "It was a real eye-opener to the wide cultural differences between us. We were not compatible. When James finished high school, we both agreed to part company," he said, and then added that he wouldn't talk about his ex-wife anymore.

Once they had finished their main courses and were on their second glass of wine, Leo leant over and took Aggie's hand.

"All couples have differences of opinions; it's more about how they deal with the differences than trying to be in agreement all the time."

Aggie stroked his hand with her finger.

"Do you think we have cultural differences? After all I am mostly British with only a dollop of Italian whereas you are full Italian, albeit with a strong American influence." she said.

"For me, it was fated when I saw you touch the bridge that first day; I believe you and I are meant to be. There will be bumps in any road we choose to travel, but if we are prepared to compromise and exercise patience, 'we' will work," Leo said and squeezed her hand.

"Well, I promise it will be my turn to compromise once I have completed my search or 'quest' as you call it. Besides, without this crazy journey I may have never met you," Aggie said.

They strolled arm in arm back to the hotel and were both happy to end the evening with a prolonged cuddle before falling sound asleep.

THIRTY-SIX

Leo and Aggie caught an Uber to the Gare-Saint-Lazare train station. They had left the bulk of their luggage in the hotel luggage room for their return and just had an overnight bag between them. The train journey to Giverny took less than an hour. The Hotel Le Jardin Des Plumes they had booked for the one night presented an outward ambience of 19th Century charm, but the bedrooms were crisp and modern with chalky white walls and minimal furnishings.

It was a perfect day, so they strolled the ten-minute walk to Claude Monet's house. As they stepped through the little gate into Giverny, Aggie felt as if she was entering a garden paradise. The striking farmhouse with its long pink walls sat comfortably in the impressive gardens, as if it had been painted that way. They had purchased their tickets in advance and decided to do the tour of the garden first. The sun shone, casting rays of honey-coloured light along the path deeper into the garden. It was all just how Monet had planned all those years ago.

Aggie described the colourful fragrant garden to herself – "a visual feast of harmonic blooms of happiness."

The first garden was adorned with irises, chrysanthemums, roses, and hollyhocks; forget-me-nots, violets, and pansies mingled at the feet of the taller flowers.

Leo and Aggie slowly wandered along the paths; they took time to sit down at various points and savour the landscape of floral joy, inhaling the fragrance. Then they moved onto a second garden - the water garden that housed the lily pond and famous bridge that was recognized the world over - Claude Monet's signature, an arched bridge!

As they arrived at the pond, Aggie could not avert her eyes from the vision of the small arched wooden bridge. The shape had been the catalyst, an ever-present nagging distraction in her brain, the shape constantly appearing in her line of vision, transforming everyday objects into a crescent silhouette. The croissant, the clouds she saw from the plane window, fabric patterns, the shape she drew in the sand with her foot when she first visited Menton; the shape that had nearly caused her to doubt her sanity.

"Are you okay?" Leo asked, interrupting her focus.

Aggie drew in a big breath. "I am not quite alright, but I will be. Perhaps Léon Monet spent time here visiting his brother and hanging out in this garden. I seem to be revisiting my 'arch bridge' obsession standing here taking in this incredibly famous scene."

Leo moved up and stood close to her in an act of reassurance, then she added: "I am very keen to see if there is any information on what this brother of Claude was really like"?

They had spotted a tearoom close to the entrance so decided to have a coffee and sandwich there then returned to tour the house.

The first room they entered in the house was the "Yellow Dining Room" as it was officially called. Aggie adored it, she would describe it as "a warm banana" colour. Everything was painted the same colour, which gave a wonderful backdrop for the predominantly blue and white dinnerware that was displayed in the open cabinets. A large oblong table was surrounded with painted wooden chairs and Aggie could just imagine Monet's family and friends gathering in this warm, welcome space.

Leo had wandered off into the next room when Aggie caught up with him. He said it was his kind of space. Officially called "The Blue Salon", the paintings were framed mostly with dark blue frames. This room was where Monet showcased his extensive range of Japanese prints that he had begun collecting in the 1870s.

Then, as they entered Monet's bedroom a momentary shiver passed through Aggie's bones. She quickly shook it off and focused on Leo's comments. What struck them both from the outset was how small Monet's bed was. It was a single bed! He clearly wasn't a tall man, as it was also a short bed. The information card said that aristocrats and wealthy couples often had separate bedrooms and that Monet mostly would rise very early and did not wish to disturb his wife. He loved to paint before sunrise, to capture the river as the mist hovered over it.

The furniture in the room was not at all ostentatious; the wooden bedhead and cupboards were painted a softer hue of lemon and an attractive small 17th century desk sat at the end of the bed.

The room had three windows that offered wonderful views of the garden; the windows had been built to maximise the light coming into the room.

Monet had chosen to hang pictures painted by his friends on his bedroom walls and Leo and Aggie felt privileged to be in the presence of work by such esteemed artists as Cezanne, Renoir and Manet.

As Aggie stood at the window looking out over the garden the shiver returned; it passed from the top of her head down to her feet; she said nothing, but quickly left the room.

Leo followed her into what they agreed was the most beautiful room in the house - the drawing room, studio; was definitely the most important room. It featured floor to ceiling doors that opened into the garden. Monet had hung a selection of his own favourite paintings on all the walls, to mark his progress over each decade of his life as an artist.

Eventually they made their way to the tourist and information shop. Leo chatted to a young lady, enquiring about Léon Monet. She summoned an older colleague who joined them. He said, to his knowledge, Léon Monet didn't spend any time at Giverny; Léon and Claude had fallen out and didn't speak for many years. They were only reunited near the time of Léon's death. Then the custodian cut the conversation short and walked away.

"I think we can safely say we have been dismissed!" Leo said laughing. Aggie was very disappointed. She had seen no mention of Léon Monet anywhere at Giverny. She was looking through the English language books and was studying one that offered wonderful photographs of Monet's work and background information on his family when Leo joined her. "Let me buy this for you as a gift," he said, taking the book from her hands and heading over to the cashier.

Aggie felt she hadn't made any headway in confirming that Léon Monet may have been the father of Sienna's baby.

Once back at the hotel Aggie carefully studied Monet's paintings in the book Leo had bought her.

"Leo, there seem to be more early Monet family portraits at the Musée d'Orsay, so I would be very keen to go there tomorrow when we get back to Paris if that's okay with you?"

"Of-course! I feel frustrated as well; it's as if we are missing an obvious piece in all this; we need another clue," Leo said, as he poured Aggie a sparkling water.

They were very pleased they had reserved a table at the hotel restaurant that night in advance. It was a small but attractive space, and every table was taken. There was an outdoor seating area, but a cool wind was sweeping through and the intimate alcove their table was tucked into was far more appealing. Leo and Aggie both ordered langoustines served with sliced celery and creamy mashed potatoes. They accompanied this with the sommelier's choice of a lovely crisp Chablis - it was divine. This was followed by the baba apricot - a delicate sponge, with lightly sautéed apricots topped with a vanilla creme.

After they were back in their room, Aggie was struggling not to show the frustration she was feeling at not finding anything relevant at Giverny. After the disagreement she had had with Leo in Paris, she did not want to appear self-absorbed.

Leo sensed her unease. "It's okay Mi esora, I am with you on this. Why don't you slip into your robe, and I will give you a relaxing massage," he said and brushed his lips across hers.

Aggie's phone had pinged with a message earlier, but she hadn't checked it, so opened it before she undressed. She was concerned to see a missed call and a text from Lyall. Her immediate thought was something had happened to Jackson. But all was well. Lyall said he had tried to call her to chat, so perhaps she could call him back in the morning - he had found some information on Monet that might be relevant to her search.

Calling back could wait! Right now, she was looking forward to her massage.

Aggie knew exactly what Leo's massage would lead to, and she didn't mind a bit. She adored being stroked, (being rubbed up the right way she called it) and, in the correct hands being seduced. Leo had strong hands and his massage was heavenly. It concluded with a very happy ending, she smiled.

Aggie smelt him before she saw him; she wasn't frightened and within a few moments she understood, she wasn't herself, she was seeing all this through someone else's eyes. As the man stroked her thighs, she was experiencing very enjoyable sensations and not wanting him to stop. The room was very dark, and she couldn't see his face clearly, but he had a scraggly beard, and it was the beard which smelt. He was on top of her, she stayed silent as it felt wonderful. Then he called out "Oh Sienna!" and plunged into the most private part of her body, the pain was excruciating. She cried out.

"Aggie, wake up, it's okay you are dreaming!"

She heard Leo's voice, but it sounded so distant.

"Oh my God I was having sex for the first time; it was definitely Sienna's memory as the man called out her name," Aggie replied, sitting up and reaching for a glass of water.

"Do you feel violated, or physically hurt?" Leo asked.

"Well, it is weird, as now I am awake and can be rational about it, no, I don't feel hurt. Sienna was enjoying the experience, so the trauma must have come later, possibly caused by the desertion and humiliation of finding herself pregnant," Aggie said as she located her small notebook. She needed to jot down what she had experienced in her dream.

Leo made them a cup of chamomile tea; then they both lay back down but were unable to sleep.

The hotel breakfast was served outside in the Garden of Feathers and the tables were watched over by a fabulous large Amazonian parrot called "Mr G".

Once they had placed their order with the waiter, Aggie dialled Lyall's number. He told her he had found an article online about a collection of Monet's paintings of which the wider art world was unaware. The background story was that Claude Monet died before he knew he had a natural granddaughter. His son Michel fathered a daughter before his marriage to his wife. Michel never officially recognised the daughter, but he gave her a number of Monet's paintings, pottery and sculpture. Michel was killed in a car accident in 1966 and his daughter died in 2008. Her heirs, who Lyall said he could not find any details of, put the collection up for sale at Christie's in Hong Kong and that they would have had to prove provenance, beyond doubt, probably by way of a DNA test.

Leo watched as Aggie spoke to Lyall. He noticed her face light up, and her voice rose an octave as she listened intently, then asked questions. He was bursting to hear what Lyall had said.

Aggie recounted it all, then added: "I will email Dr Viner now and ask him directly if the granddaughter's name, which Lyall is texting me, matches the confidential name on the DNA connected to Léon Monet."

As she spoke her phone buzzed with a message; Claude Monet's illegitimate granddaughter was called Rolande Verneiges.

Aggie immediately updated Dr Viner on the developments of the last 24 hours including her latest dream and asked the direct question if Rolande Verneiges, or one of her children, was the party seeking the protection of confidentiality.

"Given the time difference you may have to wait a few hours for a reply," Leo cautioned as they got up from the table.

Aggie was keen to get back to Paris as soon as possible. She needed to look more closely at the family portraits that Monet had painted, which now hung in the D'Orsay.

They were packed and on the train by 10am and arrived back at Relais Christine at lunch time. Leo grabbed a couple of baguettes stuffed with wonderful creamy cheese from the nearby boulangerie and they made coffee in their hotel room while navigating the D'Orsay online ticketing to ensure when they arrived, they had a clear path to Monet's section.

THIRTY-SEVEN

It was a quick Metro ride to the Musée d'Orsay; as they had pre-booked tickets, they didn't have to queue. However, they did have to go through security and Aggie's frustration mounted; she was flushed with angst as they seemed to move at a snail's pace. Leo led the way up to the fifth floor where the impressionist gallery was located. By the time they had arrived at the Monet section, the temperature was cool in keeping with preserving important works of art. Aggie had cooled down and felt a sense of calm as she slowly viewed each portrait. They worked at different paces, Leo seemed to go a bit faster, which was no bother for Aggie; in fact, she was so absorbed in studying the paintings she was totally unaware of anyone around her.

"Aggie," Leo was back at her side, he touched her arm in an act of encouragement for her to follow him. He guided her to a section of paintings called the Femmes au Jardin, a wonderful selection of oil on canvas, scenes of a family in a garden under the trees. Leo steered her to one entitled "Luncheon on the Grass". "Look carefully at the woman wearing the white dress sitting on the grass," he said.

Aggie stood as close as she could to the painting. Hanging from the neck of the woman dressed in white, hung a small pendant. It appeared to be a replica of the one Aggie was wearing. Aggie let out a gasp as she clutched the pendant. "Who is she?"

"Monet's first wife Camille," Leo said.

"My God! Maybe it is the same pendant!" Aggie was transfixed.

Leo allowed a few minutes for all this to sink in, then he said, "Let's take some photos so we can enlarge them, and also, check if they have a book with reproductions of this collection in the museum shop."

Aggie remained for quite some time staring, searching every detail of the painting. So many emotions were swirling through her thoughts. Initially anger, then curiosity, then a sense of relief.

Leo eventually led her to the shop near the museum exit. It offered a great range of books on Monet, but Aggie just purchased the one featuring The Femmes au Jardin collection.

She sat in silence as they travelled on the Metro back to the hotel. Once in their room Aggie removed her pendant and opened the book at the page with the "Luncheon on the Grass' ' scene. The picture wasn't as large as the actual painting, so the pendant shape wasn't as obvious. Leo examined the pendant as best he could and showed the silver hallmark indicating the metal's purity and a second hallmark of which he had no knowledge. "A good antique jewellery will be able to enlighten us on this."

Aggie sighed, put the book down and got up to make a cup of tea for them both. Then sat down on the bed and checked her emails. Dr Viner had replied.

> *Dear Aggie, I am breaking a few rules by telling you this, but I feel confident you won't be making any claims to the estate of Rolande Verneiges, which appears to be the reason for the confidentiality of this DNA. Your DNA is directly connected to that of a child of Rolande Verneiges, so to protect our research facility in this situation I must declare that you draw your own conclusions from this information.*
>
> *Good luck and let us chat on the phone very soon.*
>
> *Warm regards*
> *Dr Viner*

Aggie put down her phone, tears rolled down her cheeks. Then she let out a big sob which brought Leo quickly to her side. He sat down on the bed and held her in his arms.

Once she had worked through the emotions of the discovery, she was able to speak. "I believe without a shadow of a doubt that Claude Monet was my four times great grandfather. It will take me a few days to process the information and analyse the science, but I feel certain I am correct."

They continued to chat through all the possibilities of Claude's behaviour as a married man in 1885, then Leo looked at his watch.

"We have the booking at Le Procope in thirty minutes, do you still want to go, or shall I cancel?"

Aggie's mood had lifted, she had her mojo back. "Let's go and celebrate!"

That evening was Leo's choice of restaurant and he had kept to the agreed theme of "Parisian Old-World Charm". They were back in Saint-GermainDes-Prés. Le Procope was a restaurant steeped in history and hailed as the oldest café in Paris. It was opened in 1686 and was the favoured place for popular writers and intellectuals of the day to gather.

Tonight, the menu did not disappoint, it was proper classic Parisian food. Aggie ordered the large Burgundy-label rouge snails as an entrée and Leo the foie gras with Sarawak pepper and seasonal chutney. Aggie said she would just have the entrée and a dessert as she had spotted something very enticing on the dessert menu. Leo ordered the braised beef cheeks served with parmesan macaroni as a main and said Aggie may have a taste.

"May I be very suburban, forgo the wine and treat us to a bottle of champagne to celebrate?" Aggie asked, smiling.

She invited Leo to select it, making it clear it was her treat. After some deliberation he chose a bottle of Pol Roger.

Once they had clinked their flutes and taken the first sip, Aggie looked directly at Leo: "I couldn't have achieved any of this without your support!"

The Italian was very happy. The food was served.

"Oh my!" Aggie sighed as she savoured the taste, then slid the wine-enriched snail down.

Leo was gastronomically valuing each mouthful of his foie gras. "I think we are having a food orgasm!"

Aggie added, just quiet enough for Leo to hear: "Definitely a perfect way to describe my taste bud sensations," Leo concurred.

He asked the waiter if he could hold off on the main course, as they required a digestive break.

"Now Mi esora, I know we are both celebrating your new status as Claude Monet's four times great granddaughter, but I am keen to point things in my direction, and, as the person who chose this restaurant, my request is, how in the written word, would you describe it all?"

Aggie took a sip of champagne and cleared her throat. "This fine establishment displays a cornucopia of historic, relevant collectables. Its history is reflected on the Pompeian-rich red walls that display impressive mementos of the past, with oval portraits of famous people who dined here and framed impressive documents dating back to the Revolution. A lattice work wrought iron bannister borders the worn marble stairs to the upper floor, which I am yet to explore. However, what makes this occasion most special for me as a humble writer is more than the food and wine, it is the fact that I am sitting right where artists and writing legends of the past sat, including Voltaire, Mosset and George Sand. Maybe even my four-times great grandfather Claude Monet came here to hang out with the lads. "Thank you for bringing me, Leo Molinari," Aggie declared then saluted Leo with her glass.

In this ancient pocket of Paris, on this special night, Aggie was submerged in happiness. Was her DNA revelation fate, or was it predestined? Aggie had listened to science, followed her instinct, and now believed she had put all the ghosts to rest.

*

Two Months Later

It was a fabulous autumn Sunday and still comfortable enough to eat outside on Aggie's Menton terrace.

She had borrowed a trestle table and extra chairs from Sarah.

The extended table was draped in pure white damask. Jackson and Lyall had styled it with pink and white roses, lots of ivy and set it with an array of mismatched vintage silver cutlery.

Seated around the table, there were ten in total. Jackson, Lyall, Nick and Florence, Sarah's adult children, Aggie and Leo, Sarah, and JP as well as old Mario and Rebecca. It was a very relaxed, noisy group enjoying themselves.

As individuals they had heard the conclusion of Aggie's journey back in time through her stored memories. This was her celebration lunch and Jackson tapped his glass with a spoon and called the gathering to order.

"Mama, we are all keen to hear about what you will do next, so please take the floor!"

Aggie blushed, then stood up.

"The science on the theory that memory can be stored in your DNA is still controversial. But, in addition to Dr Viner's research facility in the US, there are several others around the globe coming up with similar conclusions. My mission is not one of convincing people of its validity. I also don't feel a need to tell the world that I am the four times great granddaughter of a famous randy impressionist painter. I have spent a lot of time reading various biographies and considering the man from different perspectives. My conclusion was that he was a real playboy of that era. He was sexually unfaithful to both his wives, who were independently wealthy before he married them. I don't doubt he was captivated by Sienna, my four-times great grandmother, but I am sure he took full advantage of his position. Whilst I believe she was a willing participant in their affair, she was very young and then desperately hurt when he never ever contacted her after he left Dolceacqua. It is hard to imagine, given the way we live and communicate now, that she never contacted him to tell him about the baby. Or maybe she did, and he rejected her, we will never know. I am very satisfied to have worked through this process and kept my sanity and pleased to have resolved my mother's desertion. Discovering we have a new Italian group of cousins adds a whole new dimension to our lives. And best of all, I have met the new love of my life."

Aggie raised her glass and proposed a toast "To love and to family!"

The short Italian beamed…

EPILOGUE

Aggie was thoughtful about the first book she would write under her own name. She'd started a conversation with a new literary agent who had previously approached her to leave Penny. Discovering she was related to Claude Monet was a great angle for PR, the agent noted. But he was keen to act for her whichever way she chose to write.

After much deliberation Aggie decided that her forte was fiction, and she was at her best when she allowed her imagination to take over. She wrote a story that involved a tall, slim, willowy heroine on a journey to Aggie's and facing similar challenges - the recurring dreams, DNA detail, the regression process and of course a wonderful love affair.

Eighteen months later in London, Jackson, Lyall and Leo accompanied Aggie to a Savoy Hotel dinner for the Sunday Times' bestseller with Aggie's name on the cover.

The Bridge at Dolceacqua

The three men stood clapping and shouting "bravo" as their mama and new wife, Aggie Sutcliffe-Molinari stepped onto the stage to receive the prize for the runaway success that was *The Bridge at Dolceacqua*.

ABOUT THE AUTHOR

Merryn Corcoran was born in New Zealand but had lived most of her life in the United Kingdom and Europe. She spends her time divided between her homes in London and the French Riviera with her husband Tim. Merryn is an accomplished entrepreneur and has been writing for the past twelve years. The Bridge at Dolceacqua is her fifth novel. Merryn also works as a production designer and an executive producer for her daughter's film company Cork Films. Merryn is a keen supporter of UNICEF and for over a decade chaired and organised an annual celebrity gala ball which raised around one million pounds for the charity. Merryn was made a UNICEF Honorary Fellow (UK) in 2002.

THE BRIDGE AT DOLCEACQUA

Follow Merryn
www.merryncorcoran.com
facebook.com/merryncorcoran/author
Instagram @merryn_author_creative

Printed in Great Britain
by Amazon